SMOKESCREEN

Recent Titles by Betty Rowlands from Severn House

ALPHA, BETA, GAMMA... DEAD
COPYCAT
DEADLY OBSESSION
DEATH AT DEARLY MANOR
DIRTY WORK
A HIVE OF BEES
AN INCONSIDERATE DEATH
PARTY TO MURDER
TOUCH ME NOT

SMOKESCREEN

Betty Rowlands

This first world edition published 2008
in Great Britain and the USA by
SEVERN HOUSE PUBLISHERS LTD of
9–15 High Street, Sutton, Surrey, England, SM1 1DF.

British Library Cataloguing in Publication Data

Rowlands, Betty
  Smokescreen
  1. Reynolds, Sukey (Fictitious character) - Fiction
  2. Policewomen - Great Britain - Fiction 3. Detective and
  mystery stories
  I. Title
  823.9'14[F]

ISBN-13: 978-0-7278-6669-1   (cased)

All Severn House titles are printed on acid-free paper.

Printed and bound in Great Britain by
MPG Books Ltd., Bodmin, Cornwall.

Prologue

The airport lay to the south-west. Three planes had landed in quick succession, approaching along three separate flight paths. Their vapour trails fanned out from their vanishing points like lines of perspective in a painting. Slowly they began to blur and unfold until they took on feathery shapes against the crisp blue of the winter sky. A writer with a fondness for poetic language might have likened them to quill pens; to a royalist they might have suggested the Prince of Wales' Feathers. But from a vantage point high above the Avon Gorge, one lone observer saw them as arrows, driven deep into the heart of a murderer.

One

'Doing anything at the weekend?' DC Vicky Armstrong looked across her desk in the CID office at her friend and colleague DC Sukey Reynolds. It was Friday afternoon and they were packing up to go home at the end of what had been an unusually quiet week.

'Nothing special,' Sukey replied. 'A bit of early Christmas shopping maybe. How about you?'

'Well, as a matter of fact –' Vicky rummaged in her capacious shoulder bag and pulled out a crumpled A5 sheet of paper, which she passed to Sukey – 'I thought I might go to this.'

Sukey glanced casually at the paper, which was headed 'Western Road Library' and bore the invitation, 'Come and meet best-selling novelist Jennifer Cottrell. Jennifer will talk about her writing, and in particular about her latest book, *A Passion for Life*, which has been shortlisted for the Romantic Novel of the Year Award. Refreshments and an opportunity for questions. 7.00 p.m. on Saturday 12th November.'

'I'm afraid I've never heard of her,' said Sukey as she handed back the flyer. 'I don't read much romantic fiction; I'm more into psychological thrillers just now. Fergus gives me a reading list,' she added, feeling some justification was necessary on seeing Vicky's eyebrows lift. Her twenty-year-old son was studying at the University of Gloucester with the intention of becoming a forensic psychologist, and took a delight in sharing with his mother anything from his newly acquired knowledge that he felt would contribute to her understanding of the criminal mind.

'Been giving you more advice, has he?' said Vicky with

a chuckle. 'I'm surprised you've never heard of Jennifer Cottrell, though. She's hardly ever out of the bestseller lists and several of her books have been filmed for television. You don't know what you're missing,' she went on earnestly. 'She writes the most wonderful family sagas, so true to life, full of human interest and . . . and . . . '

'Passion?' Sukey suggested slyly.

'Well yes, that too,' Vicky said, unabashed.

'I take it you're a fan?'

'Aren't I just? I simply must go and meet her and get her to sign a book for me. Chris won't come with me; he says her stuff is tripe – not that he's actually read any, of course. He doesn't read much anyway except boys' magazines.' Vicky screwed up her nose in mock disgust.

Sukey grinned. 'Racing cars and football?'

'Something like that.'

'And you want me to go with you to hear this woman talk about her latest bonkbuster?'

Vicky shook her head in reproof. 'They're much more serious than that. Anyway, would you? It'd be lovely to have your company.'

'It sounds marginally more interesting than looking for Christmas prezzies. OK, I'll come along.'

Vicky's smile transformed her round, freckled face. 'Great! I'll call in at the library on my way home and pick up a ticket for you.'

When Sukey and Vicky arrived at the library shortly before seven o'clock on Saturday evening they found the reference section had been cleared of movable shelving and the space filled with chairs, arranged in a horseshoe formation facing a table on which stood a jug of water, a glass and a small flower arrangement. In the corner furthest from the door were two more tables, one set with glasses, bottles of wine, cartons of fruit juice and dishes of nuts and crisps, while on the other was a selection of the speaker's novels.

Most of the seats were already occupied, almost exclusively by women whose ages Sukey judged at a quick glance to range between twenty-something and well over sixty, suggesting that Jennifer Cottrell's books appealed mainly to readers of her own sex. The few men present were well past middle age and it would remain to be seen whether they too were fans or had, unlike Chris, been persuaded to accompany their wives or partners.

There were still a few empty seats in the back row and the two off-duty police officers sat down near the end. The remaining seats were quickly filled and one of the library staff had to hunt around for more to accommodate some last-minute arrivals. Promptly at seven o'clock a door behind the reception desk opened and the head librarian appeared, escorting a small woman with sharp features and bright dark eyes. Her black hair was piled on her head and fastened with a jewelled comb; over her calf-length cherry-coloured dress was thrown a loosely crocheted black shawl, and a considerable quantity of gold chains and bracelets, which appeared almost too heavy for her slight frame, dangled from her neck and wrists.

'She reminds me of a Romany gipsy who once called at my house selling bunches of lucky heather and offering to tell my fortune,' Vicky whispered under cover of the applause – in which she enthusiastically joined – that greeted the novelist's entrance. 'I never realized she was so tiny,' she added.

'I think she looks more like a cat on the lookout for a nice juicy mouse,' Sukey whispered back mischievously and received a reproachful frown in return.

Jennifer Cottrell walked daintily to the table, smiled graciously in response to the librarian's glowing introduction, pushed the flower arrangement aside and replaced it with a copy of *A Passion for Life*. This she carefully propped upright to display the jacket which bore, in gold-embossed letters, her name and the title – the latter in smaller characters – emblazoned across the top. Below was an artist's impression of a young woman gazing up at the sky with an ecstatic expression on her face and her arms flung wide as if about to embrace the entire world.

'My latest oeuvre, hot off the press!' she announced in

evident anticipation of further applause, and without hesitation her audience complied.

'I just *love* that design, don't you?' said Vicky.

'A bit gaudy with all that gold, don't you think?' said
Sukey.

'I meant the illustration.'

Sukey shrugged. 'Too sentimental for my taste.'

'But it conveys the spirit of the book,' Vicky insisted.

With some difficulty, Sukey kept a straight face. 'If you
say so.'

'Shh!' hissed a neighbouring voice and the two obediently settled down to listen.

'I shall begin,' the speaker announced in a flute-like voice
that Sukey later described to Fergus as 'unnaturally refined',
'by dealing with some of the questions that are put to me
most frequently on these occasions. The first – and this is
a question that almost all writers of fiction are constantly
being asked – is, "Where do you get your ideas?" I dare
say that's something you would all like to know.' She paused
for a moment while her audience responded with nods and
murmurs of agreement. 'And the most interesting, indeed,
the most *fascinating* yet at the same time almost *obvious*
answer is –' at this point she lifted both hands and spread
them apart, rather in the manner of the woman on the book
jacket and with much jangling of bracelets – 'ideas are *everywhere*! It's not *searching* for them, it's the bewildering *choice*
that I find almost overwhelming. I have to wait until one
particular plot, or character, or situation takes such a strong
hold over my imagination that I can think of *nothing else*!'

More nodding heads and admiring murmurs greeted this
statement. Evidently satisfied that she had struck the right
note with this particular audience, she broke off to take a
sip of water. Vicky took the opportunity of whispering to
Sukey, 'I'm not surprised she gets asked that question so
often. Her plots are so true to life, yet so gripping – real
page-turners!' she enthused.

'I'll take your word for it,' whispered Sukey, whose
hackles had already begun to rise in response to the woman's
condescending manner and theatrical gestures.

'And of course,' Jennifer Cottrell resumed, 'I am extremely fortunate in that I have been endowed with an unusual insight into human nature. I know what makes people *tick*, and that is *so* important when creating believable characters. That's something reviewers are constantly saying about my work.' She picked up the book and quoted from the back of the jacket. ' "As always, Cottrell's characters step off the page and into the hearts and minds of her readers" – that one's from the *Guardian*. And there are several more in the same vein.'

She carefully replaced the book, referred briefly to some notes and resumed her talk, which was almost exclusively devoted to an analysis of various incidents, encounters with individuals (whom she was careful not to identify) or situations that had triggered ideas for a selection of her titles, ranging from some of the earliest to the most recent. After speaking for forty-five minutes or so she said, 'Well, I think that's enough from me at the moment; now it's your turn. You may recall that I began by referring to my knack of creating believable characters – in fact, I think it's safe to say that my books are without exception *character-driven*.' Her eyes swept round the room as if engaging each one of her audience in turn. 'I should like to know if anyone here has developed a particular interest in – or perhaps an affinity with – any particular character in my books?'

There was a faint gasp from a woman who had slipped in at the last moment and taken the only empty seat, which happened to be next to Sukey. She wore a padded anorak that accentuated her dumpy frame, a woollen cap pulled down over her brow and a voluminous woollen scarf round her neck. Throughout the first part of the event Sukey had been aware of an occasional, almost convulsive movement, as if every so often something the speaker said had struck a particular chord. The invitation for questions seemed to have had an even stronger effect on her and she sat listening intently as several women stood up in response to the invitation and made ingratiating remarks about characters from their favourite books. These were received with an almost regal complacency, which induced a faint hiss from Sukey's neighbour, who began nervously twisting the handles of a shabby leather handbag between her fingers as if trying to screw up her courage to put a question of her own.

'I don't think the lady next to me is exactly a fan,' Sukey whispered in Vicky's ear. 'I must say I find Madame Cottrell's manner rather off-putting, don't you?'

'Well . . . ' Vicky hesitated and Sukey sensed that she was less impressed by the writer than by her work, but at that moment someone else put up a hand to ask a question and her reply remained unspoken.

Jennifer Cottrell gave her customary gracious response to the question, after which the librarian stood up and said, with a glance at the clock on the wall, 'I think we have time for just one more question.' There was a moment's silence before Sukey's neighbour suddenly leapt to her feet and shouted in a hoarse voice that shook with emotion, 'I have a question!'

The writer directed her glittering eyes towards the speaker. 'Yes?' The monosyllable was accompanied by a faintly supercilious smile, as if something about the questioner's appearance amused her.

'Why did you kill my lover?' the woman demanded in the same unsteady voice.

Heads swivelled in the speaker's direction. Reaction among the audience varied from shock to bewilderment, but Jennifer Cottrell merely raised her eyebrows and said calmly, 'I have absolutely no idea what you're talking about.'

'You know exactly what I'm talking about. Why didn't you return my calls . . . or reply to my letters?' The woman was plainly on the verge of breaking down and her next words were uttered in short, staccato bursts, punctuated by intervals during which she fought to control her emotion. 'Why did you kill him? We were to be married . . . and now he's dead . . . and I've got nothing to live for!' Her voice rose to an hysterical scream. 'I hate you . . . and I wish *you* were dead too!'

In the stunned silence that followed this outburst she ran to the door, flung it open and rushed out into the night.

Several people jumped up from their seats and peered out

of the window. One woman said, 'She's running across the car park . . . she's getting into a car . . . she shouldn't be driving in that state . . . go after her, Ted!' Obediently the man at her side set off in pursuit of the fleeing woman, but before he had gone a dozen paces he had to stop and leap clear as a car, headlights blazing, tore past him towards the exit and out through the gates without slowing down. There was a squeal of tyres as an approaching car made an emergency stop and the onlookers braced themselves in anticipation of a crash, but none came. Everyone returned to their seats while remarks like, 'Must be schizophrenic!' and 'Shouldn't be allowed out on her own!' drifted around the room.

'Poor soul!' said Jennifer Cottrell with a sorrowful shake of her head. 'Of course,' she added with a touch of complacency that made Sukey grit her teeth, 'people in my position have to be prepared for that sort of eccentricity from time to time. It's just the penalty of fame.'

The librarian said hastily, 'That was a most unfortunate interruption, for which I apologize, although I hasten to add that to my knowledge I have never set eyes on that person before. I think perhaps this would be a good moment to thank our speaker and then we'll serve the refreshments.' A lady in the front row stood up and gave a vote of thanks, even more fulsome than the introduction; the audience responded with hearty applause, which the speaker acknowledged with many a gracious smile as she told them what a *lovely* and *responsive* audience they had been, how much she had enjoyed answering their *very intelligent* questions and added that she would be *absolutely delighted* to sign copies of her books.

The librarian and an assistant began removing corks and pouring out wine and fruit juice. After collecting their drinks and a selection of crisps and nuts from the table, a few members of the audience formed small groups and speculated about the reasons behind the unexpected end to the meeting, but the majority seemed to have dismissed the episode and were exchanging enthusiastic comments about the speaker and her novels while waiting in line clutching books for signature.

'Shall we go?' said Vicky, who had shown no sign of wanting to join the queue for refreshments or to approach her favourite author.

'Don't you want your book signed?' said Sukey in surprise.

'No thanks.'

'But why? I thought —'

'Love the books, think the writer's a smug, self-opinionated cow,' was the muttered response as a stony-faced Vicky led the way to the door.

'You don't think there's anything in what that woman said?' said Sukey as they made their way to their respective cars.

Vicky shrugged. 'Shouldn't think so. She's probably some lonely soul who fantasized about a character in one of the books and got upset when he died. Not all the books have happy-ever-after endings – that's why they're so true to life.'

'Just the same, it was a bit odd the way she sat there all muffled up in that warm room,' Sukey said thoughtfully. 'It was almost as if she didn't want to be recognized. Do you think Jennifer Cottrell knew her? Maybe there's an unsolved murder that both of them are connected to in some way. We could do with something to brighten things up a bit!' she added with a chuckle.

Vicky grinned and shook her head. 'Not on our patch, there isn't. I know we've had a dull week, but I don't think there's any hope in that direction. The poor thing is off her rocker, that's all. Bye, see you on Monday.'

On Monday they took the precaution of checking on cold cases but found nothing of any possible relevance to the woman's allegations. The episode slipped from their minds until, the following morning, Jennifer Cottrell's companion found her dead in her bath.

Two

'Why the hell didn't you report this right away?' DS Rathbone's furious glare switched from Vicky to Sukey and back again.

'We checked on cold cases first thing yesterday, Sarge,' said Vicky, 'and we found absolutely nothing on the file that could possibly have matched that woman's allegations. And Jennifer Cottrell was totally laid back about the whole episode; she even hinted that it wasn't unusual for writers to get abusive letters from fans who were upset by something in their books – she called it "the penalty of fame".'

'She seemed quite chuffed about it,' Sukey ventured. 'It happens with programmes on the TV and radio when someone dies or is ill,' she went on. 'People get terribly involved; they begin to look on characters as personal friends.'

'That's right,' Vicky added eagerly, 'I remember once, when someone's grandma in a radio soap was ill in hospital, loads of listeners sent get-well cards and when she died they even sent sympathy cards and flowers.'

'People get so involved with these characters they seem real,' pleaded Sukey. 'We honestly thought this woman—'

'Never mind what you thought, your duty was to put in a report and leave the decision to your superior officers,' Rathbone broke in sternly. 'And now Jennifer Cottrell is dead and it looks suspicious; time will tell whether the death could have been prevented and we'll hope for both your sakes that it couldn't. You, Vicky, will stay here and write out a detailed account of the entire episode, a full description of the woman, what she was wearing, every word she said, how Cottrell reacted, what car she was

driving . . . every scrap of information about her that you
can dredge out of your tiny mind. The two of you can go
over it together later to make sure you've remembered every
last detail.'

'Yes, Sarge,' Vicky said meekly.

'Sukey, you come with me to the Cottrell house and tell
me everything you can remember on the way. I've booked
a car.' He tossed a key at Sukey, swung on his heel and
marched to the door. The two women exchanged rueful
grimaces behind his back before Sukey hurried after him.

During the drive, Rathbone listened in silence while Sukey
recounted, in as much detail as she could, the incident at
the Western Road library on the Saturday evening. When
she had finished he said, 'Right, find time later on to check
Vicky's account; make sure you've remembered everything
between you – and see if the library has a note of the people
who bought tickets.' He then sat back, closed his eyes and
said nothing more until they arrived at their destination.

Woodlands, the house where Jennifer Cottrell lived, was
tucked away in what had once been an extensive private
estate that included the north Somerset hamlet of Hixton.
It was approached by a long drive that wound through a
dense shrubbery, overshadowed with trees. On this dull,
damp November day the first sight of the house did little
to relieve the gloomy atmosphere. It was a substantial but
ill-proportioned building in the style of the 1930s – dark-
red brick, a tiled roof encrusted with lichen and the type
of metal window frames that were popular with the affluent
middle classes during the period.

'You'd have thought with all her money she could have
run to something a bit more attractive than this,' observed
DS Greg Rathbone as he and Sukey got out of the car. 'This
driveway could do with a bit of maintenance for a start,'
he added with a disdainful glance down at the loose gravel
that crunched under their feet as they crossed the courtyard
to the solid oak front door, which bore a massive iron
knocker in the shape of a lion's head.

'Morning, Sarge,' said the uniformed officer who stood

guard. 'The body's in one of the upstairs bathrooms. The victim's GP has some concerns about its condition, which is why we called you in. Sergeant Brookes is waiting up there and she'll fill you in. The housekeeper will direct you – just knock and she'll pop out like a lady in a weather house. You'd need a compass to find your way round the place on your own,' he added, 'it's like a bloomin' rabbit warren. Seems the original owner kept adding bits on.'

'Who found the body?' asked Rathbone.

'The companion. She's waiting downstairs with the house-keeper and PC MacCall is looking after the two of them.' He lowered his voice. 'Bit of a battleaxe, the companion, watches you like a hawk as if she's afraid you'll pinch the spoons.'

'Any sign of the pathologist?'

'Got stuck in traffic but he's on his way, Sarge. Ah, that'll be him.' The man indicated a car that had just appeared and was pulling up alongside the police vehicles.

'Good morning, folks,' said Dr Hanley as he joined them. 'A drowning this time, is it?'

'We're waiting for you to tell us the cause of death,' replied Rathbone. 'All we know is a woman died either in her bath or shortly after being dragged out, and the doctor who attended raised some doubts that he passed on to us.' He gave a double knock on the door, which was opened almost immediately by a middle-aged woman with short, slightly faded blonde hair cut in a neat bob, and wearing a plain but well-cut olive-green dress. She gave a slight nod as Rathbone identified himself, Sukey and Dr Hanley and glanced over her shoulder as if seeking a response from someone out of sight behind her. A woman's voice said impatiently, 'Let them in, Norris,' and she stood aside to obey.

'I believe you're Mrs Norris, Ms Cottrell's housekeeper,' said Rathbone politely.

'That's right, Sergeant,' she said in a low but well-modulated voice.

The three stepped inside; she closed the door behind them and they found themselves in a square entrance hall. On the immediate left a massive, thickly carpeted staircase led to the upper floor; ahead was a wide corridor with doors at intervals on either side. Various items of heavy, apparently antique furniture were ranged against the walls, which were hung with numerous pictures in heavy gilt frames, ranging from landscapes and flower paintings to portraits of men and women in costumes of previous centuries. The dark oak floor was covered with a series of oriental rugs that to Sukey appeared old and probably valuable. As she later described it to Vicky, the effect was that of a scale model of the long gallery of a stately home.

As they entered, a young woman constable came forward and indicated a woman with short mid-brown hair flecked with grey and strong, regular features, who was seated on a carved oak settle opposite the staircase.

'Sarge, this lady is—' she began, but the woman interrupted by saying, 'Lillian Brand, companion and personal assistant to Jennifer Cottrell.' Her voice and manner were crisp and businesslike, an impression accentuated by keen grey eyes behind designer glasses with thin black frames. She wore a well-cut navy blue trouser suit over a white tailored shirt, a pearl choker and pearl earrings. Her hands were ringless; she wore very little make-up and despite being well manicured her nails were unvarnished.

'I understand it was you who found her, Ms Brand,' said Rathbone.

'That's right. No doubt you want to ask me some questions. Perhaps you could make some coffee for the officers, Norris!' she added.

'Thank you, not for the moment. Perhaps later. We do understand how upsetting this must be for you ladies,' he went on, 'but certain procedures have to be followed in the case of an unexpected death before the body can be removed. That gentleman,' he gestured in the direction taken by Hanley, who, following directions from PC MacCall, had just disappeared at the end of the corridor, 'is the forensic pathologist and he has to examine the body and if possible determine the cause of death. While he's doing that I'll be asking you both a few preliminary questions; then DC

Reynolds and I have to visit the scene and try to establish exactly what happened. Then I'm afraid we shall have to ask you some more detailed questions, but I promise we'll do our best not to cause you unnecessary distress.'

'Surely it's obvious what happened,' said Lillian Brand sharply. 'For some reason or other Jen slipped under the water in her bath and was unable to get out before losing consciousness. Norris and I managed to drag her out and we tried to revive her but when she didn't come round I told Norris to call an ambulance. When it got here the para-medics said she was dead and we had to send for a doctor before she could be moved. What no one has had the courtesy to tell us is why the police should be involved.'

'She was still alive when you got her out of the bath, then?'

'Why do you suppose we tried to revive her?' Lillian Brand spoke with a touch of scorn, as if she considered the question superfluous. 'We put her in the recovery position first, and then I tried artificial respiration.'

Rathbone turned to the housekeeper. 'Mrs Norris, I understand that when Ms Brand found your employer unconscious she immediately called for you?'

The housekeeper nodded. 'That's right, Sergeant. I was in the kitchen and I heard her screaming down the back stairs. I hurried up immediately and between us we dragged Miss Cottrell out of the bath.'

'What time was this?'

'I suppose it must have been about half-past nine.'

'Did Ms Cottrell normally take her bath about this time?'

'She enjoyed a good long soak after breakfast every morning before beginning her day's work,' Lillian Brand explained. 'I can't say exactly what time she went to run her bath, but she would usually be finished and dressed by nine. First she'd come straight to my office to discuss any business matters and then she'd retire to her study and write for four or five hours before taking a late lunch.'

'And during this time, what would you be doing?'

'Working in my office. She left most of her business affairs for me to handle, and Norris and I ran the household. Jen just wanted to be left to get on with her writing – her books were like her children to her.' For the first time, Lillian Brand showed a glimmer of emotion and it was several seconds before she continued. 'Jen usually appeared around a few minutes after nine and we'd discuss anything that needed her attention before she began work.'

'She didn't normally require your services before then?'

'No.'

'And you breakfasted separately?'

'Yes.'

'So what made you go to her bathroom on this occasion?' asked Sukey in response to Rathbone's glance in her direction.

'It occurred to me that she was taking longer than usual and there were several things I wanted to speak to her about, so I went along and tapped on her door. When she didn't answer my second knock, and I couldn't hear her moving about, I went in and found her.'

At this point Hanley reappeared and took Rathbone aside. 'There are signs of bruising on the body, which must have occurred while she was still alive,' he said in a low voice. 'Death was definitely from drowning; I'd say she's been dead about three hours and was immersed in the water no more than an hour.'

'Any idea how the bruising occurred?'

Hanley shrugged. 'You're the detective. See you at the PM.'

After he left, Rathbone spoke briefly on his mobile phone before going back to where the women were waiting. 'The coroner will have to be informed and—' he began, but Lillian Brand cut in.

'Of course, that's understood,' she said sharply, 'but as I said just now, I fail to see why the police should be involved. You surely aren't suggesting there's anything suspicious about her death?'

'All I can tell you at the moment, Ms Brand, is that we are here as a result of certain features of the case brought to our attention by the doctor who pronounced Ms Cottrell dead and confirmed by the pathologist.'

'What "features", as you call them?' she demanded.

'I'm not in a position to answer that at the moment,' said Rathbone and added swiftly as she appeared to be about to ask a further question, 'DC Reynolds and I will go up to view the body now, and meanwhile I'm afraid I've had to arrange for . . . some of our operatives to record the scene.' From his momentary hesitation Sukey guessed he had deliberately avoided using the term 'crime scene investigators', sensing that a reference to the possibility of a crime would provoke more argument. 'It's standard practice in the case of an unexpected death,' he went on. 'They should be here quite shortly and when they've completed their work we'll arrange for the body to be removed. Please remain in the house for the time being. I'll need to speak to you both again presently. Now, if you will kindly show us where to go . . . ?'

She pointed along the corridor and said curtly, 'Along here and turn left. It's the room at the end of the passage.'

'Thank you. We'll leave you with PC MacCall for now.'

Following her directions, the detectives found themselves in another, narrower passage that appeared to lead along the back of the house. On their left they passed a short staircase leading down and another, adjacent to it, leading to the floor above. 'I suppose the one down leads to the kitchen,' Rathbone observed. 'The house must be built on a split level. I wonder how many other staff she employed,' he added.

'At least a housemaid and a gardener, I imagine,' said Sukey. 'According to Lillian Brand she ran her own bath, so she doesn't seem to have a personal maid,' she added as an afterthought.

'Unless Ms Brand included that in her duties?' She gave him a questioning glance, but he did not offer to develop the notion.

A uniformed sergeant stood outside a door at the far end of the passage. 'Morning, Sarge.' The officer held out her hand. 'Sergeant Rosy Brookes.'

'DS Greg Rathbone.' He took the proffered hand and said, 'This is DC Sukey Reynolds. Still a rookie but she shows promise.'

Sergeant Brookes' pink cheeks, which made Sukey wonder whether Rosy was her real name or a nickname given by her colleagues, creased in a smile. 'Is he always this patronizing?' she asked.

Sukey grinned back. 'I can live with it.'

'Right, now lead us to the body,' said Rathbone, a trifle impatiently.

'There's something I overheard just now that I think you should know,' said Rosy. 'Some scraps of conversation – I think it was coming from the servants' quarters. It sounded like a man and a young woman talking; she sounded as if she was crying and I couldn't make out what she said at first, but I made a note.' She pulled out her notebook and read aloud, 'The man said, "You'd best forget you heard that, Maggie. It's none of your business." Then she said, "But what d'you suppose it was about?" and "Is it anything to do with why the police are here?" And he said, "I've no idea. Just keep out of it. Like I said, it's none of your business – or mine." '

'Is that it?' said Rathbone when she had finished.

'That's it.'

'Interesting. Let me have a copy of your notes and we'll follow it up later. Now let's get to the scene of the crime.'

'She's in the en-suite bathroom. This way.'

Recalling Jennifer Cottrell's colourful clothes and generally flamboyant appearance, Sukey was surprised at the essentially feminine quality of the decor in her bedroom. The curtains were a pale, creamy pink patterned with sprigs of roses, and the duvet cover, pillowcases and frilled valance round the bed were of the same material. The dressing table and a series of storage fitments were painted white, and several fluffy rugs in pastel colours were strewn around on the floor. A lilac sweatshirt and matching trousers and socks were laid out on a chair beside the bed, together with a set of underwear.

'We assume that was the stuff she was planning to wear after her bath,' Rosy commented. 'The companion told us she didn't have a personal maid, so she must have put it all out herself. She's in there,' she added, pointing to an open door in the far corner of the room.

Like the bedroom, the bathroom was decorated in an almost aggressively feminine style, with a pink suite, rose-patterned tiles and curtains and a pale pink carpet. There were neatly folded towels in graduated shades of pink on the towel rail and another on the floor beside Jennifer Cottrell's body, which was lying face upwards alongside the bath. Her arms were stretched out at an angle on either side, the hands open as if in a mute appeal for help. Her black hair, still damp from immersion, was spread untidily round her face which, devoid of make-up and with none of the lavish gold jewellery at throat and ears that she wore in public, appeared small and somehow vulnerable. 'It's almost as if she had a different persona in her private life,' said Sukey, half to herself.

'You can enlarge on that later,' said Rathbone. 'She drowned all right. See that?' He pointed to the froth of bubbles that had erupted around the half-open mouth. 'I learned long ago that's a sure indication.' He turned to Sergeant Brookes. 'Is this how she was when you arrived, Rosy?'

'Yes, but we understand the ambulance crew found her face down. It seems the women put her in the recovery position first – or something approximating to it, we don't think they know a lot about first aid – when they got her out of the bath, and then one of them said she tried artificial respiration. When that failed they called an ambulance; the paramedics couldn't find a pulse so the doctor was called, and he must have put her on her back. After he'd carried out his examination and pronounced her dead he spotted those marks on the body and reported to us.' She pointed to the victim's wrists and ankles, which bore signs of discoloration.

Rathbone glanced at Sukey and said quietly, 'Are you thinking what I'm thinking?'

'If she drowned, she was already dead when Lillian Brand found her,' Sukey said slowly, 'and from what Doc Hanley said, that bruising must have occurred before death. So if she slipped, it wasn't an accident – someone grabbed her hard by the ankles and pulled her under the water.'

'And then held her arms so she couldn't pull herself up by the grab handles,' said Rathbone. 'There doesn't seem much doubt about it – we've got a murder on our hands. On the face of it, that nutcase who screamed at her at that meeting you and Vicky attended on Saturday has to be a prime suspect. Your first job is to track her down and bring her in for questioning.'

Three

On their way back, the detectives met a couple of CSIs, clad in their protective clothing and carrying their cases of equipment. Rathbone had a brief consultation with them before he and Sukey returned to the hall. They found Lillian Brand and the housekeeper waiting on the settle where they had left them. It was noticeable that they sat some distance apart and although they looked up simultaneously and with similar expectant expressions on their faces, they gave the impression that until then each had been absorbed in her own thoughts.

PC MacCall was leaning against the newel post at the bottom of the staircase. Rathbone took her to one side and said in a low voice, 'Did they have much to say while we were gone?'

She shook her head. 'Hardly a word, Sarge, and they haven't moved. The housekeeper's been a bit twitchy, but Ms Brand has been sitting there like a stone statue. By the way, the press have arrived. Apparently a reporter from the local radio station saw our people go through the village as he was getting into his car to go to work and alerted the news editor.'

'OK, thanks.'

As he approached the two seated women, Lillian Brand demanded, 'Sergeant, I think it's time you told us what is going on. Those people in their extraordinary clothing – exactly who are they and what is the precise reason for their being here?'

'As I mentioned earlier, they are here to make a record of the scene and collect any evidence they may find. Their official title is crime scene investigators.'

At the word 'crime', both women started. The housekeeper covered her face with her hands and every vestige
of colour drained from Lillian's face. 'I don't understand.
Evidence of what, Sergeant?' she said in a voice that shook.

'Ms Brand,' Rathbone replied, 'it's my unfortunate duty
to have to tell you that we are treating your employer's
death as suspicious.'

'Suspicious? You mean you think she was . . . murdered?'
Lillian's voice trailed away to a horrified whisper on the
final word. 'I don't believe it! Jen didn't have an enemy in
the world – why would anyone want to kill her?'

'That is what we intend to find out. We'll begin our
enquiries by asking both you ladies to answer some more
detailed questions. Perhaps, Ms Brand, you could suggest
somewhere a little more private?'

She appeared taken aback by the request and hesitated
for a moment before saying, 'I suppose we could use my
office. It's this way.'

Almost reluctantly, she got to her feet; the housekeeper
prepared to follow, but Rathbone put out a hand and said,
'We have to see you separately this time, Mrs Norris. While
we're speaking to Ms Brand, perhaps you would be kind
enough to make some tea or coffee for this officer?'

'Yes, of course,' she said, evidently relieved at having
something practical to do. 'Come with me, Constable.' She
pushed open a door tucked away behind the staircase, and
the two of them disappeared. Lillian led the detectives back
along the corridor and turned left. Sukey noticed that she
glanced along the passage, where a uniformed officer was
on guard outside Jennifer Cottrell's room, before opening
the second door on the right and indicating with a tilt of
the head that they should follow.

Lillian's office was furnished with plain but good-
quality wooden furniture: a desk, two filing cabinets and
two bookcases, one containing various reference books
and dictionaries and the other – considerably larger – packed
with Jennifer Cottrell's own titles. On a separate table against
the right-hand wall was a computer. The carpet was a
serviceable but undistinguished shade of fawn and the pale

buff walls were decorated with a few colourful prints of Mediterranean scenes. Behind the desk a window looked out over a lawn surrounded by trees and bordered with flower beds, where clumps of chrysanthemums and Michaelmas daisies and a few late-flowering shrubs brightened an otherwise dormant selection of herbaceous plants.

Lillian sat down behind the desk and waited while Rathbone and Sukey pulled up a couple of chairs and sat down facing her. Sukey detected a subtle change in her manner; at first she had been visibly shaken by the mention of murder, but here in her own domain she appeared more composed, almost as if she and not the detectives was in command of the situation.

'So,' she said when they were settled, 'what is it you want from me? Or do you begin by cautioning me?' she added with more than a hint of sarcasm. 'If I'm a suspect, perhaps I should call my solicitor?'

For a moment, Sukey thought Rathbone was about to explode, but he restrained himself and said evenly, 'Ms Brand, to be frank, everyone known to be on the premises when a murder takes place is a potential suspect. What we have to do for a start is to eliminate as many of them as possible. I have to begin by asking you, and later everyone else in the house, to account for their movements during the critical period. Is that clear?'

'Perfectly. So, Sergeant, what is your first question?'

'Just one more thing: DC Reynolds will be taking some notes. I take it you have no objection?'

'Why should I? I have nothing to hide.'

'No one is suggesting that you have. Now, would you kindly tell me what you did from the last time you saw Ms Cottrell alive until the moment when you discovered her in her bath, apparently unconscious.'

'I immediately shouted for Norris and—' She broke off in some surprise and said, 'Why do you say "apparently", Sergeant? Obviously she was unconscious, or why else would we have tried to bring her round?'

'But in your opinion, still alive?'

'How many times do I have to tell you? When Norris

and I pulled her out of the water and put her down on the floor she was definitely trying to breathe.'

'What gave you that impression?'

'Water and air bubbles were coming out of her mouth and nose and I wiped them away to clear her air passages. We turned her over and I began giving her artificial respiration using the old-fashioned method, not this mouth-to-mouth system they use nowadays. I tried for several minutes and more water came bubbling out, but she still didn't start breathing properly so I told Norris to call an ambulance.'

'And this was about nine thirty?'

'About that, yes.'

'What was your reason for not using the mouth-to-mouth system of resuscitation?'

'It seemed important to clear the water from her mouth and lungs, but in any case I simply didn't know how to do it. My mother was a Girl Guide and she taught me the method she had learned when I began taking my younger sister to the swimming baths.'

'I see. Let's go back a bit. Did you and Ms Cottrell spend yesterday evening together?'

'Yes. We had dinner and then watched a film on the television. It ended a little after half-past ten and a few minutes later I went to the kitchen to make our bedtime cocoa. We sat and drank it together and chatted about the film and then we said goodnight and went to our rooms.'

'This would be about eleven o'clock?' said Sukey.

'That's right. I undressed and got ready for bed and then read for a while before putting out my light.'

'About what time was that?'

'About midnight. I slept soundly until seven o'clock this morning when I made myself a cup of tea, had a shower and got dressed. Norris brought me my breakfast as usual at eight o'clock in my sitting room and I was here at my desk by nine.'

'Where did Ms Cottrell take her breakfast?'

'In her sitting room. She has a small refrigerator in there and a stock of milk, fruit and provisions that Norris keeps topped up for her. It was always something light that she prepared for herself – some cereal and a banana or maybe a yoghurt, and a cup of coffee.'

'And then she would take her bath, get dressed and come to your office soon after nine?'

'That's right.'

'Exactly where are your quarters in relation to Ms Cottrell's?' asked Rathbone.

'Immediately above. We each have a bedroom, sitting room and bathroom. The individual rooms vary slightly in size and layout, but in total they occupy the same amount of space.'

'So if there was any movement in her room, you would probably hear it?'

'I might hear her go to the bathroom, if that's what you mean, but normally she moves . . . moved around very quietly.'

'So eleven o'clock last night was the last time you saw her alive?'

'If what you say is true I suppose it must have been.' For the second time, Lillian's mouth distorted with her efforts to control her emotion. 'Sergeant Rathbone, what makes you so sure Jen was murdered? Surely it was an accident?'

He shook his head. 'I'm afraid not. There are bruises on the legs and wrists that must have occurred before death.'

'But surely that must have happened when we grabbed her arms and legs to pull her out of the bath?'

'Only if she was still alive. And the details you have described confirm what the pathologist told me before he left. She was already dead.'

'I can't believe it,' she whispered. She bowed her head and Sukey saw her lips move as if she was praying. Then she said, 'Is there anything else you want to know?'

'I need some background information. If you don't feel up to answering any more questions now, I dare say Mrs Norris will be able to provide most of it and we can fill in the gaps later.'

At the mention of the housekeeper's name, Lillian straightened her back and gave a sniff that held a hint of disdain. 'You can ask me, Sergeant, I'm perfectly all right.'

'You wouldn't like to take a rest and have a cup of tea or coffee perhaps?'

Lillian's mouth twitched in a hint of a smile. 'I'll have something later on, thank you. Go ahead, please.'

It quickly emerged that in addition to the housekeeper, who had worked for Jennifer Cottrell for over thirty years and was also her cook, there were two other full-time domestic staff, a housemaid and a gardener/handyman. Lillian Brand had begun work as her PA about twenty years ago, when Jennifer was living in London, and had moved in as her companion when, five years later, she decided to sell her London home and buy a property in the West Country.

It was at this point that Lillian's manner changed. Hitherto she had answered Rathbone's questions with brisk but entirely non-committal efficiency, but at the mention of the move to Woodlands she said, with some feeling, 'It always amazed me what she saw in the place. I thought it was a dump, and I said so the day we came to view it, but she was crazy about it from the start. "It's got such incredible vibes," she kept saying, "and all that wonderful old furniture and stuff – I just know it will inspire me!" I can hear her saying it now.' Her voice wavered yet again and she put a handkerchief to her eyes. 'Forgive me, Sergeant . . . this has been such a terrible shock—'

'Of course – we quite understand,' said Rathbone gently. He waited until she had steadied herself before saying, 'Do I understand she bought the property complete with contents?'

'Oh yes. The previous owner had died and his only relative was a brother who simply wanted to dispose of it lock, stock and barrel with as little fuss as possible.'

A thought occurred to Sukey and after a quick glance at Rathbone she asked, 'What exactly were your reasons for disliking the place?'

'I didn't like the gloomy surroundings and it's miles from anywhere. I thought it might have all sorts of defects like dry rot and I managed to persuade Jen to have it surveyed before she signed on the dotted line. I was hoping the surveyor's report would be bad enough to put her off but all he said was that in his opinion it was an architectural nightmare on account of all the alterations the previous owner had carried out over the years, but otherwise it was structurally sound.'

'Were any changes made after you moved in?'

'Some, not many. Jen had her rooms completely made over beforehand and at the same time she said I could have mine done out the way I wanted them. She used the original owner's library as her study and I had this room redecorated and furnished as my office. Otherwise things are more or less as they were.'

'The whole package must have cost a fortune,' Rathbone commented.

'Jen never told me what she paid for it,' Lillian said, with what sounded like a touch of resentment.

'But I understood you handled her business affairs?'

'Only those connected with her writing. Her solicitor and her financial adviser took care of everything else.'

'I see. Perhaps you'll give me a note of their addresses when we've finished this talk.'

'I'll give them to you now.' She wrote two addresses on a notepad, tore off the sheet and gave it to him. 'She uses the same financial adviser as when she lived in London, but changed her solicitor when we moved down here. By the way, there's one thing I feel you should know. Obviously the house and grounds are worth a lot of money, but most of the furniture and stuff that appears to be antique is reproduction, so it wouldn't have fetched much at auction.'

Rathbone raised an eyebrow. 'Interesting. Now, although you took a dislike to the house your objections weren't strong enough to stop you moving in here with Ms Cottrell.'

Lillian hesitated for a moment before saying, 'When I told her I was thinking of giving in my notice, she was very upset . . . she offered me a substantial increase in salary to stay with her. I had no family ties and I certainly didn't want to lose a very comfortable job, so in the end I agreed to give it a try.'

'No family ties? What about your mother and sister?'

'My mother died twenty years ago. My sister is married and lives in Australia. We haven't seen one another for years.'

'You said you hated the place at first. How do you feel about it now?'

The question seemed to surprise her, but she answered readily enough. 'It's been my home for fifteen years and I suppose I've got used to it.'

'Ms Brand,' said Sukey, 'Ms Cottrell gave a talk at Western Road Library in Bristol last Saturday.'

'I know that. I arranged it for her.'

'Did you go with her?'

'No, I never went to hear her talk. She didn't expect it – she admitted it was what she called "the same old waffle" every time, but the fans lapped it up.'

'Did she happen to mention anything unusual about this particular event?'

'She said some woman made a great fuss because a favourite character had died, but that was nothing unusual. Many of her books are part of a series and some readers become very involved in the development of the characters, rather like they do with television soaps.'

'Did she ever receive abusive or threatening letters or phone calls?'

'Critical letters from time to time, yes, mostly complaining about her sex scenes, which I have to admit are pretty explicit at times, especially in her more recent titles.'

'Did any of the letters contain any kind of abuse, or explicit or implied threats?'

'None that I ever saw, but I should explain that her editor is very protective of her writers and would never forward a letter likely to cause distress.'

'You mean she screens all the so-called fan letters before passing them on to the authors?' said Sukey.

'I'm afraid it's become necessary for their protection,' said Lillian. 'There was a time when fans only wrote to favourite authors to sing their praises. Unfortunately, times have changed and certain people seem to take a delight in expressing their disapproval in the most unpleasant terms.'

'So if such a letter or letters were addressed to Jennifer Cottrell, neither you nor she would see it?'

'That is correct.'

'Did she reply to the letters she did receive?'

'Oh yes, she was very conscientious about that, even the ones that were critical. She dictated her replies, I printed them and she signed every one herself. They're all on the computer if you wish to see them.'

'Thank you, maybe later. Were this address and phone number on the letters?'

'Definitely not. And the phone number here is ex-directory so there's no question of any crank callers reaching her.'

'One other thing,' said Rathbone, 'apart from public appearances, did she lead much of a social life?'

Lillian shook her head. 'While she was working on a book it absorbed all her thoughts and she wouldn't tolerate unnecessary distractions, although occasionally we go . . . that is, used to go . . . to the theatre or a concert in Bristol or Bath, but only at weekends. And between books we went on holidays to France or Italy, although she often used these trips to research the next book.'

'What about entertaining?'

'She gave small dinner parties from time to time, especially when she'd just finished a book or to celebrate some particular success such as an award or being at the top of the bestseller list.'

'When was the last one?'

Lillian reached for her desk diary and began searching through its pages. 'On the tenth of October,' she said, having eventually found the entry.

'Perhaps you could let me have the names of the guests, and we'll also need details of her editor and any business associates – her agent, for example.'

'I'll prepare a list for you.' She was plainly becoming restless and her eyes went to the clock on her desk. 'Is that all?'

'Just a couple more questions. First, did Ms Cottrell have any living relatives?'

'No, she was alone in the world.'

'So who stands to benefit from her death?'

Lillian Brand stiffened and assumed what struck Sukey as a distinctly haughty expression. 'I thought I had already made it clear that Jen's legal and financial affairs were dealt with by her professional advisers,' she said curtly. 'In the case of her will, that would have been her solicitor – you already have his address.'

'Thank you, Ms Brand,' said Rathbone. 'You've been very helpful and I apologize for taking up so much of your time. DC Reynolds will prepare a statement for you to sign in due course. And I'm afraid we have to take everyone's fingerprints. Not that we suspect anyone in particular,' he hastened to assure her, 'it's for elimination purposes.'

She gave a slight nod. 'I understand.'

'Perhaps we can see Mrs Norris next? By the way, I see she wears a wedding ring. Is she a widow?'

Lillian shrugged. 'I presume so. I know nothing about her private life.' She stood up. 'I'll send her to you. You can use this office for the rest of your interviews.'

She left the room leaving the door open. Rathbone stood up and watched her walk back along the corridor before closing it and saying quietly, 'What did you make of that?'

'I think she's holding something back,' said Sukey.

'I agree,' he replied, 'and I have a shrewd idea that she knows very well who will inherit Cottrell's property.'

Sukey nodded. 'I noticed she avoided giving a direct answer to your question.'

'And I have a feeling she was uncomfortable when I asked about the dinner parties. By the way, what did you mean by your reference to "a different persona" while we were in Cottrell's bedroom?'

'The woman I saw giving that talk last Saturday had a strong, vibrant, almost flamboyant personality,' said Sukey. 'She wore brightly coloured clothes and a lot of flashy jewellery and made extravagant gestures with her hands. It was more than a talk, it was a performance; she was like a drama queen, yet much of her home and working life speaks of an intensely feminine and at the same time a very private woman.'

'But we got a hint of drama from the comment about vibes and how inspirational she found the house,' he reminded her.

'That's true, but she was obviously thinking of the effect on her writing. I can imagine her stepping into that old man's library and entering another world, rather like the children going into the enchanted wardrobe . . . and finding the land of Narnia on the other side,' she added in response to his slightly puzzled look.

At the mention of Narnia he nodded and gave an unexpected smile. 'I get your point. That was a brilliant film,' he added. 'I took my kid and his mate to see it and I enjoyed it as much as they did.'

Sukey recalled that soon after she joined the team Vicky had hinted at a failed marriage, but it was the first time he had openly referred to his family life. She made no comment other than, 'It will be interesting to have a look at that room.'

'Yes, make a note to do that some time,' he said. 'I'll have a chat with the solicitor and the financial adviser at the earliest opportunity. I'm really curious to know who inherits this lot.'

A tap on the door put an end to the conversation. Rathbone sat down in Lillian Brand's chair, signalled to Sukey to bring one of the others round the desk and sit next to him and then called, 'Come in.' Mrs Norris entered, a trifle hesitantly. To the detectives' surprise she was accompanied by a small Jack Russell terrier.

'I hope it's all right to bring Piper with me,' she said. 'He's been a bit upset by all the disturbance.'

'This is your dog?' Sukey bent down and held out a hand; the dog licked it and wagged its stump of a tail.

Mrs Norris gave a faint smile and nodded. At Rathbone's invitation she took the remaining chair facing them. She sat quietly waiting for him to speak; she appeared outwardly composed but Sukey noticed she kept her hands tightly clasped in her lap as if to prevent them from trembling.

'Mrs Norris, we appreciate that this must be very distressing for you,' Rathbone began kindly, 'especially as I understand from Ms Brand that you have been in Ms Cottrell's service for many years.'

At the mention of Lillian's name the housekeeper appeared to stiffen slightly; she raised her head and answered, with a hint of pride, 'Thirty years next January, Sergeant. I came straight from college, first as her cook and later, when her old housekeeper retired, I took over that job as well.'

'At that time, did she employ a full-time personal assistant?'

The expression 'personal assistant' evoked a slight sniff of disdain. 'She had a lady – a Miss Meade – to type her books and letters. She wasn't so famous in those days and she looked after her business affairs herself. Then the work began to increase and Miss Meade couldn't cope and gave her notice.'

'And that was when Ms Brand began working for her?'

'That's right. That would be about twenty years ago.'

'And five years later she sold her London house and moved down here?'

'That's right.'

'How did you feel about that?'

'It was her decision.'

'Did you approve?'

'That's not for me to say, Sergeant.'

'It must have meant a great change in your lifestyle,' said Sukey.

'It was either that or lose my position.' There was a hint of finality in her tone that discouraged further questioning on that subject.

'What I would like you to do,' Rathbone began, but before he could go any further his mobile phone rang. He got up and went out of the room. When he came back he said, 'I'm sorry, Mrs Norris, but we have to suspend this inter-view. Something has come up and DC Reynolds and I have to return to the station at once. We'll either come back later or I'll send another member of our team to take the rest of your statement. In the meantime I must ask you and the rest of the staff to remain in the house.'

Looking somewhat affronted, Mrs Norris withdrew. 'That was a message from the office,' he told Sukey as the door closed behind her. 'A woman has called in wanting to speak to whoever's in charge of the inquiry into Jennifer Cottrell's murder. She says her name's Jennifer Cottrell.'

Four

'Did this woman give any details about herself?' asked Sukey as they drove back to the city.

'Apparently not. Just said she had information that she thought would help with the enquiries.'

'And the victim is her namesake,' Sukey said thoughtfully. 'Are we looking at a case of mistaken identity, do you think?'

Rathbone shrugged. 'It's possible, I suppose. We'll have to wait and see what she says. By the way, what are your first impressions of Brand and Norris?'

'I still think Brand is hiding something,' said Sukey, 'but I don't think the reality of the situation has really hit either of them yet. Brand revealed more signs of emotion and it's obvious that she had a close personal relationship with Cottrell. Norris is evidently in shock but I didn't get the impression of someone feeling a strong sense of personal loss. And there doesn't seem to be a lot of love lost between the two of them,' she added as an afterthought.

'That was broadly my feeling as well,' he agreed.

When they got back to the station they went first to the CID office, where DC Vicky Armstrong was waiting for them. 'She's in interview room one,' she informed them, 'and she's a very different kettle of fish from the woman Sukey and I heard speak last Saturday. Incidentally, I've been checking in the phone book; first I looked under Cottrell but there's no Jennifer or even a J listed under that name. Then I tried under "J" and I found this.' She held out the open directory she was holding and pointed to where 'Jennifer Cottrell' appeared in heavy type immediately before a list of subscribers with the surname Jennings. There was no address, only a phone number.

'Unusual,' said Rathbone. He glanced first at Vicky and then at Sukey. 'Any ideas, either of you?'

'At a guess, she's in some kind of business,' said Sukey.

'Such as?'

'Something exclusive that she wants people to be able to contact but doesn't want to publicize its nature,' said Vicky, 'and it's not too hard to guess what that is.'

'Well, we'll see. Good work, Vicky. I've got another job for you now. Sukey and I had just begun to interview the housekeeper at Woodlands when we were called back here. I want you to go there and continue with her statement – the usual stuff about her movements and so on – and at the same time find out how many people Cottrell employed and how the household is organized. Mrs Norris has been in the dead woman's employ for thirty years, by the way – ten years longer than Lillian Brand, the PA cum companion, as she was at pains to point out – so she should be able to give us some useful background. There's a female officer looking after her – you'd better have her sit in with you while you're talking to her. Right, Sukey, give Vicky the notes you've taken so far and you and I will go and have a chat with Jennifer Cottrell Mark Two.'

The woman awaiting them was slim and elegantly dressed. 'Well-groomed' was the adjective that sprang instantly to Sukey's mind as she took in the discreet but expertly applied make-up, the softly cut blonde hair that flattered her oval face and the stylish and obviously expensive brown leather jacket and skirt teamed with fashionable high-heeled boots.

'Ms Cottrell?' said Rathbone. She acknowledged his introductions with a cool nod. 'I understand,' he went on as he and Sukey sat down opposite her at the table, on which stood an apparently untouched cup of tea, 'that you have some information you feel may assist us with our enquiries into the murder of your namesake, the writer Jennifer Cottrell.'

'That's right. When I heard that news flash on the radio at midday I could hardly believe what I was hearing.'

'It must have given you a bit of a shock,' Rathbone agreed, 'but I imagine there is something more than a simple co-incidence about names that brings you here.'

'Of course. To begin with, I want to make it clear that until now I had never heard of a writer called Jennifer Cottrell. If I had, I'd have done something about the phone calls days ago.'

'Phone calls?'

'From some crazy woman. She rang me up two or three times screaming abuse and accusing me of killing her boyfriend. At first I just put the phone down, but the last time she warned me the same thing might happen to me and I threatened her with the police if she rang again.'

'You didn't think to report it to us at the time?'

'I suppose I should have done, but . . . ' She frowned and bit her lip. 'Maybe if I had, this terrible murder wouldn't have happened.'

'When was the last time you heard from her?'

'About a week ago. If I had heard from her once more I would certainly have reported it to you.'

'How frequent were the calls?'

'They came within a couple of days of each other. When a week passed after the last one and I hadn't heard again I assumed she'd been frightened off when I mentioned the police.'

'Ms Cottrell,' said Sukey, 'we know that the phone number of the writer who shares your name is ex-directory. We also know you are listed in the phone book under your full name of Jennifer Cottrell, with a number but no address – and among the "Js" rather than under "Cottrell, Jennifer" or simply "Cottrell, J".'

'That is correct.'

'It's somewhat unusual for a private subscriber to be listed in that way,' said Rathbone. He leaned across the table and looked her full in the eye, and for the first time she appeared slightly ill at ease. 'Is there any particular reason for having your entry in this form?'

'I'm not, strictly speaking, a private subscriber,' she said slowly and with a hint of diffidence added, 'I run an escort agency. Oh, I can guess what you're thinking,' she hurried on, 'but I assure you that every client signs an agreement that sets out in detail the nature of the escort's duties. These may vary from one case to another, but sex is definitely not among them.'

'So what do these duties comprise?' Rathbone asked bluntly.

'In the majority of cases to accompany the client to some kind of function where to attend unescorted would be impractical or even embarrassing. It can be either a business or a private function, although usually the former, and may involve overseas travel. Quite often a client needs someone who can act as an interpreter and I have several people on my books who speak foreign languages.'

'Do you ask your clients for references?'

'Most of them come through personal introductions. New clients are asked to give the names of two referees as I naturally like to be satisfied that they are genuine.'

'In other words, not using your service as a covert way of finding sex.'

'Exactly.'

'So sex is specifically excluded from the arrangement . . . or maybe implicitly would be a better word?' Rathbone continued, his eyes searching her face.

'What exactly are you suggesting, Sergeant?'

'Simply that in some cases a sexual attraction can arise unexpectedly between two people in the situations you have outlined.'

'It's possible, I suppose,' she admitted after a brief hesitation, 'but that would be a private matter between them and I certainly wouldn't expect to be told about it.'

'Ms Cottrell,' said Sukey, 'have you personally acted as an escort at any time?'

'Of course.' She showed no surprise or resentment at the question. 'I once worked for a so-called escort agency myself, but I quickly realized that it was nothing more than a cover for a high-class pimp so I left and set up on my own.'

'How long ago was that?'

'About five years.'

'So although you have several people on your books, perhaps you occasionally escort clients yourself?'

She nodded. 'If there's no one else suitable at the time.'

'And to your knowledge has there ever been any kind of unpleasantness as a result – for example, a wife or partner jumping to the wrong conclusion about the arrangement?'

She shook her head. 'Not that I'm aware of. It's possible, of course, that something of the sort may have happened, but if so it never got back to me.'

'So you can think of nothing to account for this woman's accusations?'

'Absolutely nothing.'

'Did you ever receive a letter from her?' asked Rathbone.

'It's funny you should mention that. During her ravings she accused me of not answering her letters, but I never had one. I don't know where she would have got hold of my address anyway as it's not in the book. I did, however, take the precaution of checking her number after the last call.' She took a leather wallet from her handbag and extracted a card, which she handed to Rathbone. He glanced at it and then passed it to Sukey. It read simply 'Jennifer Cottrell, Introductions', with a telephone number and an address in Clifton. On the back was written a second number.

'This is a mobile number,' Sukey commented.

Jennifer Cottrell nodded. 'Yes. I imagine you can trace the subscriber.' She replaced the wallet in her handbag and stood up. 'Please let me know if I can be of any further help.'

'Do sit down, Mrs Norris,' said Vicky with an encouraging smile. 'And what a dear little dog,' she added.

'Thank you. Yes, he's good company for me,' the house-keeper replied. 'We have good w.a.l.k.s. together, don't we, Piper?' She bent and patted the dog as she spoke, adding, 'I have to spell it or he gets all excited.'

'Of course. Well, this shouldn't take too long and then you can take him. I think DS Rathbone explained why he had to leave in such a hurry,' Vicky went on. 'I'm sorry if it was inconvenient but it was something really important and—'

'Oh, that's quite all right,' Mrs Norris broke in. 'As a matter of fact, I feel more comfortable talking to you two ladies.' Her nod took in both Vicky and PC Sue MacCall, seated beside her behind the desk. 'Not that I've any complaint about the sergeant,' she hurried on, 'it's just—'

'There's no need to apologize,' Vicky assured her, 'lots of ladies prefer to talk to female officers. Now, perhaps you'd be kind enough to tell us about Ms Cottrell's household, that's to say, how it's organized and how many people are employed to run it.'

From the surprisingly concise nature of her reply, it was plain the housekeeper had anticipated the question. She explained that she had overall responsibility for the smooth running of the household, including the supervision of Maggie Pearce, a young woman from the village who did the housework. Maggie was the latest of a succession of girls to work at Woodlands during the fifteen years since Jennifer Cottrell took up residence; it was at this point that Mrs Norris became a little more guarded in her replies and despite Vicky's attempts to discover why none of them stayed more than a few months she made only vague suggestions on the lines of, 'it's a bit out in the wilds and there's nothing to do in the lunch hour'. Giles Hickson, who looked after the grounds and acted as general odd-job man, was the only other full-time employee. He was the son of the man employed in the same capacity by the previous owner and was, as the housekeeper put it, 'part of the furniture'.

'Well, thank you, Mrs Norris,' said Vicky when she had finished, 'you've given us a very clear picture of life at Woodlands. Now the next question will I know be a little painful for you, but I have to put it to you. What were your movements between the last time you saw Ms Cottrell alive and the time you heard Ms Brand shouting for help?'

Once again, the replies came without hesitation. 'They were on their own as usual last night; I served their dinner at seven o'clock and then went to my room. I read for a while, watched the news on television and was in bed and asleep soon after eleven o'clock. I was up and dressed a little before seven, took Piper for a run and came back in time to prepare Ms Brand's breakfast at eight o'clock. After that I had my own breakfast and began to plan the meals for the day and draw up a shopping list. I'd just finished that and was talking to Giles about some things he needed for the garden when I heard Ms Brand screaming and I ran straight upstairs and . . . we found her.'

In response to a few more questions she confirmed Lillian's account of the action they took in their efforts to revive Jennifer Cottrell. Maggie, the housemaid, had arrived as usual around half-past eight. Her first task was to clear away the remains of last night's dinner and fill the dishwasher; she had then been set to work vacuuming the ground-floor rooms. She was unaware of anything untoward happening until the police arrived; when she learned why they were there she promptly had a fit of hysterics and had to be given brandy to calm her down. Eventually she recovered sufficiently to make Lillian's bed and tidy her room, but only on condition that she was allowed to take Piper with her for protection. Mrs Norris ended her account by saying, 'Nothing could have persuaded her to go to Miss Cottrell's room, even if the police had allowed it,'

'Quite understandable,' said Vicky. 'What about Hickson? I think you said he was in the house at the time Ms Cottrell's body was discovered?'

'That's right; he was in the kitchen with me when Miss Brand called.'

'Did he follow you upstairs?'

Mrs Norris shook her head. 'He said something like "What's her ladyship want now?" and as far as I know he went back to work.'

'Neither you nor Ms Brand called for him to help when you found Ms Cottrell?'

Mrs Norris looked slightly shocked. 'It wouldn't have been proper, would it? I mean, she was in her . . .'

'Yes of course,' said Vicky, 'I just wanted to be sure. Was he still in the kitchen when you went back?'

'No. As I said, he probably went outside to get on with his work.'

'So it was some time later that he heard what had happened?'

'I suppose so. It wasn't I who told him. If he was at the other end of the estate he might not have known till he came back to the house for his coffee. That would be some time after half-past ten.'

'I see.' Vicky added another comment in her notebook. 'Just one more thing. Who has the responsibility for security here?'

The question appeared to surprise the housekeeper, but she answered readily enough. 'There's a burglar-alarm system that was installed by the previous owner. He seems to have been a very nervous gentleman, but Miss Cottrell never took the idea of being burgled seriously. She told me to keep it switched off during the day because a buzzer used to sound every time anyone approached the house and it disturbed her. I always reset it when I lock up at the end of the day, although left to herself I doubt if she'd have bothered. In any case, Piper barks if he hears a strange footstep.'

'Thank you, Mrs Norris, you've been very helpful.' Vicky stood up and went to the door. 'Please feel free now to take Piper for his w.a.l.k., he's been waiting so patiently. And if you could ask Maggie to spare us a minute?'

'Oh, Maggie went home. She was still very upset and the other officer said he'd send someone to talk to her in the morning. Would you like to see Giles now?'

Vicky closed her notebook and stood up. 'Not for the moment, thank you – my sergeant may prefer to interview Hickson himself. I'll have a word with him and let you know.'

Five

'I don't know about you, but I'm ravenous,' said Rathbone after he returned from escorting Jennifer Cottrell from the building. 'Let's grab a bite in the canteen while we talk this over.'

Sukey was thankful to comply. For some while past she had been increasingly conscious of her empty stomach and was relieved that Rathbone had mentioned it first. Having worked with him for several months she was becoming more at ease with him, but occasionally found his reactions unpredictable. They bought tea and sandwiches and took them to a vacant table in a corner.

'What do you make of the second Ms Cottrell, then?' he said when they had eaten a few mouthfuls.

'I don't think she was keeping anything back,' said Sukey.

'She might not have mentioned the woman's reference to letters if I hadn't,' he reminded her.

'That could have been an oversight. She was quite definite she hadn't received any, and in any case, how could the woman have known the address?'

'Supposing she'd found Jennifer's business card in her lover's pocket and jumped to the wrong conclusion?'

'In which case she'd have known she wasn't Jennifer Cottrell the writer and she wouldn't have come to that meeting and made a scene,' Sukey pointed out.

Rathbone shook his head. 'I think it's more likely that her lover's death was such a shock that she became so unbalanced and confused that it wouldn't have entered her head that there could be two women with the same name.'

'You still see her as prime suspect?'

'Don't you?'

Sukey ate the remaining crumbs from her sandwiches and finished her tea before replying. 'It doesn't ring true somehow,' she said slowly. 'The woman was obviously beside herself at the time, but she didn't strike me as being capable of physical violence. It was more like an hysterical outburst.'

'So what's your theory?'

'I'm afraid I don't have one,' she admitted.

'Then we'll stick with mine for the time being.' He glanced at his watch. 'Vicky should be back from Woodlands by now. Let's see what she has to tell us.'

Vicky was just completing her report when they returned to the CID office. 'It's pretty straightforward,' she said. 'Mrs Norris confirms Lillian Brand's account of how they found Jennifer Cottrell in her bath and tried to revive her. As far as the rest of the household is concerned, there are just two other regular employees, a man called Giles Hickson who looks after the estate – incidentally he took over the job from his father, who has since died – and a girl from the village who comes in every day to do the housework. She's one of a succession; apparently none of them stay long. The place is too quiet, there's nothing to do during the lunch break and so on, according to Mrs Norris, but I have a feeling there may be another reason.'

'Does Hickson live on the estate?'

'No, he comes from a neighbouring village. He was on the staff of the previous owner of Woodlands and Jennifer simply kept him on.'

'Did you interview him?'

'No, Sarge, I thought you might prefer to see him yourself.'

'Quite right.' Rathbone gave an approving nod. He picked up the phone and called Sergeant Rosy Brookes at Woodlands. 'I'm coming now to interview Hickson. What? Well, tough; tell him he can just hang on a bit longer. I'll be with you shortly.' He put down the phone and turned to the two DCs. 'Right, Sukey, you come with me. Vicky, you set about tracking down the holder of that mobile number.'

* * *

On the way back to Woodlands, Rathbone commented, 'Hickson sounds as if he might be a bit stroppy. Rosy Brookes says he's been moaning about not being allowed to go home for his tea.'

'He should have our job,' said Sukey with a grin.

'Too right.'

When they arrived, the house door was flung open and a muscular, good-looking man of about thirty-five emerged and marched up to their car. 'Are you Detective Sergeant Rathbone?' he demanded as the two detectives got out.

'I am,' said Rathbone calmly, 'and this lady is Detective Constable Reynolds. I take it you are Giles—'

'Hickson,' the man interrupted rudely. 'What I want to know is why I've been kept here like a criminal.'

'I'm sorry you've been inconvenienced, Mr Hickson,' said Rathbone. 'Shall we go indoors and have a chat?' There was a disarmingly conciliatory note in his voice that took Sukey by surprise, but it had the effect of taking some of the wind out of Hickson's sails; his expression became sullen rather than belligerent and without further argument he turned and followed them into the house and along the passage to Lillian Brand's office. 'Sit down, Mr Hickson.' Rathbone indicated a chair and the man obeyed, glowering at them across the desk. 'You have been asked to stay because we are investigating a suspicious death and you may be an important witness in our enquiry,' he continued. Hickson's lip lifted in a sneer at the words 'asked to stay' but he made no comment. 'We want to know exactly what your movements were between the last time you saw your employer alive and the time her body was discovered.'

'I last saw her just before I went home yesterday after-noon,' Hickson began. 'That would be about four o'clock – I start and finish early when the clocks go back. She was standing at the window of her study as I walked past and we exchanged a wave.' He shook his head with a sorrowful expression. 'I never saw the poor lady again,' he said sadly.

'And when did you become aware that something unto-ward had happened?'

'I can't be sure of the exact time. I was in the kitchen

talking to Mrs Norris about some stuff I need for the garden – we have an account with a local supplier and she handles the orders – when I heard Brand screaming for her and she rushed out. There was no point in hanging around; I was working at the bottom of Ash Piece – that's a stand of trees between the house and the river – so I never heard the ambulance or the police arrive. It was only when I went up to the kitchen later on to have my cup of tea and found Maggie in a state and Mrs Norris nowhere around that I realized something had happened, but Maggie didn't seem to know what. I couldn't get any sense out of the silly little cow, so I drank my tea and left her to it.'

'Having warned her not to repeat something she had said to you – something that obviously did make sense to you?'

Rathbone put his question so sharply and bluntly that Hickson sat up, consternation on his face. 'Where d'you get that idea?' he demanded truculently.

'Do you deny it?'

Hickson looked uncomfortable. 'I may have said something of the sort,' he muttered. 'It was because she was carrying on about how something terrible must have happened because the police were here, which I told her was a load of rubbish because neither of us knew then that Miss Jennifer was dead. I may have been a bit sharp with her for making such a fuss, but that was all it was.'

'So then you went straight back to work?'

'I was going to, but a policewoman cut me off as I was heading back to Ash Piece and told me my employer had been found dead and the CID had been called in and a detective was going to ask us all some questions. When it came to me this policewoman said he'd been called away in a hurry and she didn't know when he'd be back but in the meantime I could get on with my work. By the time I'd finished that job it was too late to start another so I asked if I could go home, but they said I had to hang on. And I've been sitting in that bloody kitchen for half an hour at least,' he ended resentfully. 'They let Maggie go home, so why not me?'

'And that was the first indication you had that Ms Cottrell was dead?' Rathbone continued.

'That's right. I still don't see why I couldn't just leave my name and address and go home. Of course,' he added with a sidelong glance in Sukey's direction, 'it's always a pleasure to meet a charming lady.'

'Well, murder has a way of causing inconvenience,' said Rathbone dryly.

'Murder?' The cocky expression Hickson had assumed when making the last remark faded abruptly. 'You saying she was murdered?'

'You appear surprised.'

'Course I'm surprised. Nobody said anything about murder. Nobody tells me anything,' he went on resentfully. 'Mrs Norris put her head round the door a while ago and then went off somewhere without saying a word.'

'So you last saw your employer alive and well at four o'clock yesterday afternoon?'

'That's what I said.'

'And you "exchanged a wave". Do I take it you were on friendly terms with her?'

'Friendly?' Hickson's expression became guarded. 'I was just being polite and it seemed the proper thing to do as she was standing there looking out as I passed. She was a nice old girl and I'd been working for her since she bought this place. My dad was in charge here then of course but he was getting on and couldn't manage on his own any more.'

'Do you have any help?'

'Now and again if there's a big job needs doing, like a tree that has to be trimmed or felled. Then I have to get some extra help, but otherwise I can cope.'

At this point Rathbone indicated with a nod that Sukey should take up the questioning. 'What about your relations with the other employees?' she asked. 'Ms Brand, for example?'

The winning smile that Hickson put on at being addressed by the 'charming lady' faded at her mention of the name. 'Oh, her!' He gave a snort of disdain. 'Stuck-up cow – reckons she's in charge of the staff. I made it clear to her on day one that I take my instructions from my employer.'

'And how did she react to that?'

'She huffed and puffed a bit, went on about how Miss Cottrell left everything to her so she could get on with her writing in peace, but I stood my ground and in the end Miss Cottrell agreed to see me and we got on fine.'

'You saw her regularly?'

'Every so often she'd come out if I was working near the house and ask me how things were going on the estate. She was very interested in its history and especially about the former owner because of all the books and old stuff he collected, but I couldn't be much help there. My dad would have known but he was a sick man when she took the place and he died not long after.'

'What about the other employees – Mrs Norris and Maggie?'

'Mrs Norris is OK; she doesn't interfere with me, she's always pleasant and gives us home-made cake. Maggie?' He shrugged his shoulders. 'Never had much to do with her – not my type.'

'I see.' Sukey glanced at Rathbone and he nodded and took over the interview.

'Thank you, Mr Hickson, that will be all for now. I take it you will continue with your work here every day as usual?'

'Unless you tell me to stay away,' said Hickson sarcastically.

'That's up to you, so long as you don't leave the district for the time being.'

'You mean I'm a suspect?' Hickson looked startled. 'For God's sake, why should I—?'

'For the time being, everyone known to be present at the time of a murder is a potential suspect until we can eliminate them,' said Rathbone.

'Then I am a suspect – you haven't eliminated me?'

'Let's simply say we may want to speak to you again, but I assure you at the moment we have a completely open mind.'

Hickson looked far from reassured, but at a gesture from Rathbone he got up and left the room.

'Well, I guess that's it for now,' said Rathbone. 'I'll tell

Rosy we're leaving her in charge of the place.' He spoke briefly on his mobile phone and he and Sukey went back to the car. When they were on the way to the station he said, 'What do you think of Giles Hickson? Bit of a Jack the Lad, I thought. He was certainly giving you the eye.'

'I'm sure he thinks he's God's gift to women,' she agreed. 'He is very good-looking and of course working in the open air has given him a very fetching tan. Intelligent, though, and quite well spoken; maybe he cut short his education to help his dad. Some women would probably find him quite sexy,' she added as an afterthought.

'Don't tell me you fancy him?'

She chuckled. 'Not my type at all.'

'That's what he said about Maggie, remember?'

'So he did. Who's going to question her tomorrow?'

'You go, and get PC MacCall to sit in with you. It shouldn't take long; I don't suppose she'll have anything useful to say.' He fell silent for the rest of the journey; as they got out of the car he remarked, 'I wonder what Vicky's got to tell us.'

Vicky's report was short but highly significant. 'The woman's name is Wendy Downie and she lives in Cotham,' she reported. 'There was no response to my knock and I was about to leave when a neighbour popped her head out of the window and said, "I think she's gone away, I haven't seen her lately." When I asked her what she meant by "lately" I gathered it could mean anything from yesterday to a couple of days or a week ago. She said Downie goes to the shops every day and waves to her as she goes by. I tried to pin her down as to the exact day she last saw her, but to be honest she doesn't seem quite with it – kept contradicting herself, "It might have been yesterday, or maybe the day before – or maybe last Tuesday." The one thing she was sure of was that it definitely wasn't today.'

'What about the mobile? Did you call that?'

'Yes, but it was switched off. But I did get hold of a list of recent calls, and Jennifer Cottrell's agency number was there.'

Rathbone turned to Sukey. 'What did I tell you?' he said

with a slightly self-satisfied smirk. 'Obviously she didn't realize there were two Jennifer Cottrells. She went to the talk given by Cottrell the writer and shouted her accusations before rushing away. Then, somehow, she found out where she lived, killed her and then panicked and did a runner. Now all we have to do is find her. That's your first assignment for tomorrow and I think you'd better both go.'

'What about Maggie?'

'You can see her later.'

Six

'So, where do we begin?' said Vicky when she and Sukey reported for duty the following morning. 'House-to-house enquiries, I suppose. Trouble is, we haven't even got a description, let alone a photo, and I don't suppose that dotty old dear I spoke to will be much help.'

'She said she saw Wendy Downie pass on her way to the shops,' Sukey pointed out. 'They're obviously within walking distance so let's see if anyone there happens to know her by name.'

They got a pool car and drove to the address in Cotham. When they approached the house where Wendy Downie lived, the neighbour immediately opened her window, popped out her head and called, 'Are you looking for someone?'

'Wendy Downie,' said Vicky. 'Have you seen her by any chance?'

The woman gave them a vacant stare. 'Wendy who?' she asked.

'Wendy Downie, the lady I was asking about yesterday.'

The woman frowned and shook her head. 'Oh, her. Were you asking about her?'

'Yes, I was here yesterday. She lives next door to you and waves when she goes to the shops.'

A glimmer of light dawned in the dull eyes. 'Oh yes, I know her.'

'Have you seen her lately?'

'Not for a long time. Who shall I say if she asks?'

'Never mind,' said Vicky, trying to conceal her exasperation.

'Which way are the shops?' asked Sukey.

'That way.' For once the woman seemed confident as she pointed down the street.

'Thank you.' The two detectives waved and smiled and went on their way.

A short distance further on they came to a row of shops. 'So which one shall we try first?' said Vicky as they ran their eyes past a hairdresser, a bakery, a dress shop, a newspaper shop, a greengrocer and a pharmacy. 'How about the paper shop? If she has a standing order for one they might know her.'

Sukey agreed it was worth a try, but they drew a blank. The proprietor of the paper shop was anxious to please and checked his order book but regretfully shook his head as he drew a blank. 'So what now?' said Vicky helplessly. 'Greengrocer's and baker's shops aren't likely to know their customers by name. How about the dress shop?' she added in a flash of inspiration. 'If she buys clothes there she may pay with a credit card, in which case—' But there was no joy there either.

Then Sukey had what turned out to be a brainwave. 'The pharmacy!' she exclaimed. 'She's obviously got mental or nervous trouble, in which case she's probably on some form of medication.'

The pharmacist recognized the name immediately, but although they waved their ID cards under her nose she hesitated to give them any confidential information until they told her that Wendy Downie had not been seen for several days and there were fears for her safety. She then revealed that Wendy was being treated for depression and her last prescription had been dispensed just over a week ago.

'Can you let us have the name of her doctor, please?' asked Vicky.

'I suppose it will be all right.' The pharmacist wrote a name and the address of a local medical practice and gave it to them. 'I do hope you find her,' she said. 'Her doctor changed her medication recently as she was obviously not responding to the earlier one.'

They thanked her and left the shop. 'Right, we seem to be getting somewhere,' said Sukey. 'Let's find that practice and see if we can have a word with the doctor.'

Fortunately the doctor had a surgery that morning, but they had to wait some time before he was free to see them. What he had to tell them was, to say the least, disturbing. Wendy had told him of her grief at the death of her fiancé and hinted that she held another woman responsible, but he had serious doubts. 'She'd had other fantasies and to be honest, I've been wondering whether I should arrange for her to have some counselling,' he said gravely, 'although in all other respects she seemed normal enough and on her good days she could be quite chatty.'

'Can you tell us how long this has been going on?' asked Sukey.

'I've been treating her for depression for a year or two, but about three months ago she turned up in a terrible state of grief and despair and said her fiancé had met with a fatal accident. I sympathized with her, of course, and as she wasn't sleeping I recommended a slight increase in her bedtime dose.'

'Did she ever show any sign of being violent?'

'Certainly not!' said the doctor in astonishment. 'Had she done so I would certainly have referred her to a specialist immediately.'

'Or of suicidal tendencies?'

'Again, no, although treatment with antidepressants has been known to induce suicidal tendencies in some patients, particularly young people – but I certainly never saw any such tendency in Wendy Downie.'

'Did she happen to mention the name of the other woman she held responsible for the death of the fiancé she's supposed to have lost?' asked Vicky suddenly.

'No, but often in her distress she called on her lover's name, which was Laurence. Once she sobbed that by now she should have been Mrs something or other but I'm afraid I can't remember what the surname was.'

'Was it Carmichael by any chance?'

The doctor's eyes lit up in sudden recognition. 'Yes, I believe it was!' he exclaimed. 'That's right, Laurence Carmichael. I always thought it sounded a bit, well, novelettish.'

'Now I understand!' said Vicky in a burst of excitement. 'You know him?'

'In a way. He's a character in a series of sagas by Jennifer Cottrell; he's a bachelor – a country vicar – and he was due to get married, but in the last of the series he came to a tragic end. It was published about three months ago.'

The doctor looked incredulous. 'You're suggesting she became so closely involved with this fictitious character that she actually imagined herself to be his intended wife and was beside herself with grief when he died?'

'Do you think it's possible, Doctor?'

He frowned and pursed his lips. 'It's a bit outside my field, but it's possible, I suppose. Could I ask how you know all this?'

The two detectives gave him an account of Wendy Downie's outburst at the talk by Jennifer Cottrell and the veiled threats she uttered. 'And three days later Jennifer Cottrell was found dead in her bath,' Sukey concluded.

'So the reason you're here is that you suspect Wendy Downie of killing her?' He shook his head in apparent disbelief. 'I find that very hard to credit.'

'According to a neighbour, who admittedly isn't very reliable, she hasn't been seen for several days,' said Vicky. 'Have you any idea where she might have gone? Has she mentioned any friends or relatives?'

'No, she has told me more than once that she is alone in the world – except for this fiancé who now turns out to be a figment of her imagination. This is very disturbing.' The doctor spread his hands in a helpless gesture. 'She has always struck me as a rather sad, lonely person and I believe she regarded her visits to the surgery as social occasions, giving her the opportunity for a chat. I did my best to humour her, although you will understand the time I can spare for each patient is limited. I suggest you do your best to find her as soon as possible.'

'That's what we intend to do,' said Sukey. 'Can you give us a description? When she made that scene at the library she was so muffled up that her face was half hidden. It was as if she didn't want to be recognized.'

The doctor closed his eyes for a moment. 'She's, well, I'd say a bit nondescript really. Mousy, rather lank hair, pale colouring, small, rather sharp features and slight build, height a little over five feet. She has an operation scar on the lower right side of the abdomen. Quite good teeth, very white and even.'

'Thank you, Doctor, you've been a great help.' The two detectives got up to leave. 'We may want to speak to you again.'

'Any time. Could I ask you to let me know if you find her?'

'Yes, of course.'

They left the surgery and Vicky took her mobile phone from her shoulder bag. 'We need to get into Wendy's place and see if she's there,' she said. 'Who knows what she's done?'

'You're going to ask for a warrant?' said Sukey.

Vicky nodded and spoke into her phone. 'Sarge, we've seen Wendy Downie's doctor and he's very concerned for her welfare.' She gave a brief account of their interview. 'Do you think we should get into her house? Is there any chance of a search warrant within the next half-hour or so? That'd be brilliant.' She glanced along the street where they were standing. 'There's a café on the corner of Marley Street. Shall we go and have a coffee and meet you there? Right, see you later.'

It was considerably more than half an hour before Rathbone turned up with the warrant, by which time the two DCs, in response to some rather hostile looks from the café owner, who obviously considered they were taking an unreasonable time over their cappuccino, had decided to order sandwiches. They had almost finished when the sergeant turned up. 'Had a job to track down a magistrate,' he explained. 'How far is it to Wendy's place?'

'It's just up the road.'

'I'll come with you.'

They returned to the small end-of-terrace house and Rathbone inspected the front door. 'It's double locked – no way of getting in without breaking it down,' he said. 'Let's try round the back.'

There was a narrow driveway at the side of the house and Rathbone stopped to inspect it. 'It looks as if she's got a car.' He pointed to a patch of oil. 'That's pretty recent. We'll try and find out from a neighbour what sort of car it is. Meanwhile . . .'

He led the way to the back door, which had two glass panes and was of a far less substantial construction than the front. 'I wonder if she leaves a key on the inside,' he said, peering through the window.

'Or under the mat?' said Sukey as she bent down and triumphantly came up with a key and put it in the lock.

Rathbone shook his head in disbelief. 'In this day and age, people still do daft things like that.'

They went into the kitchen and found a sink full of dirty dishes and the table and draining board cluttered with half-empty food cans. Sukey shook her head sadly.

'She's not been looking after herself lately by the looks of things,' she said.

'So it would seem. Let's have a look round the other rooms.'

The rest of the ground floor consisted of a dining room and a sitting room, both comfortably if plainly furnished, and a small cloakroom. A narrow hallway led from the front door, which Vicky opened. 'She didn't bother to turn the key in the mortise lock,' she reported. 'She obviously wasn't safety conscious, for all her nervous depression.'

'Maybe she just didn't care any more,' Sukey sighed.

'Right, let's not hang about here.' Rathbone led the way up the carpeted staircase to the first floor. There were three bedrooms and a bathroom. The front bedroom was obviously the one occupied by Wendy. The bedclothes were thrown back and a nightdress lay on the floor as if she had got up in a hurry. The wardrobe was open and a random assortment of clothes were scattered higgledy-piggledy here and there as if they'd been dragged out and discarded. 'Seems she couldn't decide what to wear,' he commented. 'Let's look at the other rooms.'

One was a small bedroom that did not appear to have been used lately. It contained a single bed and a chair. Vicky turned back the coverlet to reveal a bare mattress. 'Don't suppose she had many guests to stay,' she commented.

'Well, we don't seem to be getting anywhere at the moment,' said Rathbone. 'Let's have a look at the third bedroom.'

This appeared to have been used as a study and it was obvious the moment they stepped in that their conjectures about the cause of Wendy's despair were correct. It was full of books, most of them by Jennifer Cottrell, one open at a tear-stained page on which had been scrawled the words, 'No, No, No!' in the margin. There were letters strewn all over the desk or scattered on the floor and from the clumsy way the handwriting had been disguised were obviously intended to appear as if written by another. They all began with terms of endearment such as 'My darling Wendy' or 'Wendy, my own sweetheart'. The one bearing the most recent date opened with, 'My adored bride-to-be, Wendy'. Some were smudged with tears, but the most poignant of all was in a more natural-looking hand and simply began, 'I can't, I won't believe it! I can't bear it! Please get in touch to tell me it's all a dreadful mistake.'

'I thought so,' muttered Vicky, brushing her hand across her eyes. 'This is the chapter where Laurence Carmichael dies. And look at this.' She held out another sheet of paper on which, again in Wendy's own writing, were the words, 'She's got to pay for this. When I saw those three vapour trails, all converging on one point, it was like a sign telling me what I had to do.'

Sukey too was on the verge of tears but Rathbone appeared unmoved. 'Well, that appears to clinch it,' he said. 'It looks as if she went off somewhere, probably in her car, in a considerable state of agitation, and my guess is her destination was Woodlands and her motive revenge. It wouldn't surprise me if forensics find prints there that don't match the three members of staff.' He rubbed his hands in obvious satisfaction. 'We'll station an officer in the house in case she comes back, and circulate a description, such as it is,' he went on. 'And you two go and see the doctor and get him to help us compile an EFIT. And try and find a neighbour who can give you a description of the car – and preferably the registration number so we can check if it's been involved in any accidents. I'm going back to the station.'

'What about Maggie?' said Sukey.

'Maggie will have to wait.' He left by the front door, slamming it behind him.

'It doesn't look good for Wendy, does it?' said Sukey.

'Not good at all,' Vicky agreed.

'If the sergeant's theory is right, how do you suppose she found out where Cottrell lived?'

Vicky shrugged. 'I can only think that after driving off in a frenzy on Saturday she came back to the library, lay in wait for her to leave and followed her.'

'But Cottrell wasn't killed until Tuesday, so if Wendy is the murderer, what did she do between Saturday night and Tuesday morning?'

'Maybe she went home in search of a weapon – a knife, perhaps – and then sneaked back in the early hours of Tuesday morning, found Cottrell in her bath and killed her that way instead of using the knife. We know she could easily have got into the bedroom because there's a door into the garden and it wasn't locked.'

'But forensics haven't found anything to show that anyone entered that way.'

'We haven't seen their full report yet.'

'And what do you make of that note about vapour trails?'

Vicky shrugged. 'Search me. Maybe there was some configuration in the sky that suggested a dagger. Unless we find her I guess we'll never know, but it obviously struck some kind of chord with her.'

Sukey shook her head. 'It doesn't quite add up to me,' she said. 'Not that I've got an alternative to suggest,' she added, a little hopelessly.

Seven

Somewhat disconsolately, they relocked the back door and left by the side entrance. As they emerged a woman appeared from the house next door and waylaid them.

'Can you tell me what's going on, please?' she said, a little aggressively.

'Bristol CID,' said Vicky as she and Sukey held up their ID cards. 'And you are?'

'Muriel Lindsay.' She cast an anxious glance, first at Vicky and then at Sukey. 'Has something happened to Wendy?'

'Wendy Downie?' said Vicky. Mrs Lindsay nodded. 'Not that we know of, but we want to talk to her. Do you happen to know where she is?'

The woman shook her head. 'I've no idea, I'm afraid. In fact, I've been wondering about her myself – I know she isn't there because her car's gone, but it's not like her to go away without telling me. Not that she goes away that often, poor soul,' she added. 'She doesn't seem to have many friends.'

'Does she talk to you much, or confide in you?'

The woman shook her head. 'Not really. She seemed quite a lot brighter a while ago and then suddenly she seemed very down and once or twice when I met her in the street I thought she looked as if she'd been crying, but she hurried past me without speaking.'

'Do you happen to know when she left?'

The woman thought for a moment. 'I heard her come home quite late on Saturday and certainly the car was there over the weekend but I didn't see her for the next few days. Not that that's unusual – I don't keep watch on her every movement.' She frowned and put a hand to her brow. 'What's today – Wednesday. It wasn't there yesterday and I'm not sure about Monday – I was out all day.'

'Well, that's very helpful,' said Sukey who had been making notes while Mrs Lindsay was speaking. 'Now, can you tell us what kind of car it was? The make and colour, for example? Or the registration number.'

Mrs Lindsay shook her head. 'It was dark green, fairly old, but I'm afraid I can't give you any details. My Tom would know, he's into cars and he's done a few odd jobs on what he calls Wendy's old banger. I'll ask him when he gets home from work.'

'That would be great,' said Sukey. She gave Mrs Lindsay one of her business cards. 'Would you ask him to ring this number as soon as possible?'

'Yes, certainly.' She went back indoors and the two DCs returned to their car. 'The doctor next?' said Vicky.

'I guess so.'

When they returned to the surgery the receptionist told them that the doctor was out on his rounds and would not be back until his evening surgery began at five o'clock. Having been promised that if they returned shortly before five he would certainly spare them a few minutes, they went back to the café and ordered coffee and cakes.

'This job's not doing my figure any good,' Vicky grumbled.

'You don't have to eat cream eclairs,' Sukey pointed out.

Vicky shrugged. 'I need something to cheer me up. You know something, this is the most frustrating case I've been on for a long time.'

'I know what you mean,' said Sukey. 'It's a bit unreal, isn't it – like a country-house murder in an Agatha Christie novel.'

'Except that there's not much mystery about it because we know who the killer is,' Vicky pointed out.

'There doesn't seem to be any doubt about that. It's something else that worries me—'

'Don't tell me you've got one of your famous hunches,' Vicky taunted.

Sukey felt a shiver run down her spine. 'It's not that, it's just . . . supposing the reason Wendy's disappeared isn't that she's gone to earth somewhere after killing Jennifer, but that she might have decided in her poor deluded mind that she couldn't go on without Laurence and taken her own life. She might have had enough pills to put a lethal dose together.'

'So you're saying it's Wendy's body we're looking for.'

'It's beginning to look that way, isn't it?'

Having returned to the surgery and received the doctor's assurance that he was more than willing to help in the construction of an EFIT picture of Wendy, the two went back to the station. DS Rathbone had already gone home; after completing their report on the meetings with Muriel Lindsay and the doctor and leaving it in his in-tray, Vicky and Sukey did the same.

It was nearly six thirty by the time Sukey reached home. The first thing she did was pour a glass of wine, sink into a chair and put her feet up. Two minutes later her mobile rang. Tom Lindsay was calling about Wendy's car, and as his wife had predicted he was able to give the detailed description that Sukey had hoped for.

'That's really helpful, thank you so much, Mr Lindsay,' she said.

'No problem. I do hope you find Wendy. Muriel and I are really concerned about her.'

'We're doing our best.'

Sukey slowly drank her wine while watching the news on the television and felt the tension gradually slipping away. She was beginning to think about her evening meal when her phone rang again. DCI Jim Castle from Gloucestershire CID was on the line.

'Hi, Sook!' he said breezily. 'Sorry I haven't been in touch for a while.'

Sukey felt a pang of guilt. Despite the fact that they had enjoyed an intimate relationship over a considerable period while she was living in Gloucester, there was no doubt that the move to Bristol had had a considerable effect on her feelings. In fact, she had found herself missing him less as the weeks passed. Just the same, to hear his voice on the line gave her an unexpected surge of pleasure. Apart from the fact that she always enjoyed his company, it would be interesting to have his thoughts on the Jennifer Cottrell murder, which her son Fergus had told her was widely reported in the local press in Gloucestershire as well as nationally.

'Been busy on some special case?' she asked, careful to keep her tone light.

'Er . . . well, yes, in a way,' he said, a trifle awkwardly.

'Meaning?'

'I'd rather not talk about it over the phone. Are you busy on Saturday?'

'Not particularly. What did you have in mind?'

'How about lunch?'

'Fine.'

'Good. I'll pick you up about twelve and we'll find a country pub with a log fire and smoke-blackened oak beams.'

'I'm not too bothered about the beams as long as the food's good,' she assured him.

The following morning Rathbone greeted them with the information that the CSIs had submitted their complete report, which included the fact that they had found traces of earth on the step outside Jennifer Cottrell's bedroom. 'What did I tell you?' he said gleefully. 'Downie came in through the garden door, found Cottrell in her bath, pulled her under the water until she drowned and then scarpered.'

'Without leaving any earth on the carpet?' said Vicky doubtfully.

'And why didn't she use the knife?' objected Sukey. 'It would have been much quicker than drowning her.'

'She could have kicked her shoes off as she came in – probably out of habit,' Rathbone pointed out. 'As for the knife – we're only guessing that she had one with her. But if she did she might have discarded it,' he conceded, 'so I suppose we'd better have a search made.'

'What about prints on the door handle?' said Vicky.

'Several, but very smudged and difficult to identify without further examination. When we catch Downie we'll take hers, of course.' He glanced at his watch. 'Meanwhile, I suppose you ought to talk to Maggie, just to keep the record straight, although I doubt if she'll have much to add. You might as well both go. Have a word with Mrs Norris and ask her what time would be convenient. We don't want to upset the household routine any more than we have to. Meanwhile, I'll arrange to have a talk with Cottrell's solicitor and financial adviser, and also try and contact the guests who attended her latest dinner party.'

Mrs Norris suggested ten thirty, when the staff foregathered in the kitchen for their mid-morning break. When Sukey and Vicky reached Woodlands they found Giles Hickson, Mrs Norris and a somewhat apprehensive-looking Maggie sitting round the kitchen table with steaming mugs and slices of fruitcake in front of them.

'Please join us,' said Mrs Norris. 'The cake is homemade – I baked it yesterday. Would you like tea or coffee?'

'Have you caught the murderer yet?' asked Hickson as the two detectives accepted coffee and slices of cake.

'We're following several lines of enquiry, but I'm afraid we can't discuss the case,' said Vicky. 'We're here because we haven't had an opportunity to talk to Maggie. So when we've finished our coffee and this delicious cake, Mrs Norris, perhaps you could find us somewhere private where we could have a little chat with her. It won't take long.'

Mrs Norris cleared her throat and said, 'Maggie says she'd rather have me with her while you're talking to her.'

Sukey looked at Maggie, who was toying with the crumbs on her plate and avoiding her eye. 'Is that right, Maggie?' she said gently. The girl nodded. 'There's nothing to be afraid of, you know. It's only a formality – we have to ask everyone who was here on Tuesday the same questions. No one thinks for a moment that you had anything to do with Ms Cottrell's death and it will only take a few minutes. How old are you, by the way?'

'Nineteen,' the girl whispered.

'In that case we'd rather see you on your own.'

Maggie still said nothing but shook her head vigorously and looked appealingly at Mrs Norris, who took her hand and said, 'She told me before you came that she wouldn't talk to the police unless I sat with her,' she said firmly. 'That's right, isn't it, Maggie.'

This time the girl raised her head and looked at Sukey and Vicky. 'Yes,' she said.

'All right,' said Vicky, 'but we do need somewhere private,' she added with a meaning glance at Hickson, who stood up and rinsed his mug at the sink.

'I'm going, I've got work to do,' he said.

When he had gone, Sukey said, 'I take it there will be no interruptions? I mean, Ms Brand isn't likely to appear?' Mrs Norris pursed her lips and shook her head. 'All right, Maggie, we just want you to tell us when was the last time you saw Ms Cottrell alive.'

Maggie glanced at the housekeeper, who gave an encouraging nod. 'It were Monday afternoon, about two o'clock,' she said. 'She told me to do the floor in her study while she were having her lunch. I took it up to her and did the study while she was eating it.'

'Can you remember what she had for lunch that day?'

'Course I can.' Maggie looked slightly resentful, as if her memory was being questioned. 'She had chicken soup and a roll and then some fruit salad.'

'What about Ms Brand? When did you last see her?'

'I didn't see her at all on Monday – she were out shopping.'

'What about Tuesday?'

Maggie shook her head. 'I didn't see her on Tuesday either because the police said I could go home.'

'All right, let's go back to Monday. What did you do when you'd finished in Ms Cottrell's study?'

'I cleared away her lunch things and washed them up, and then I went home.'

'What time was that?'

'The usual time – three o'clock.'

'All right. Now, what time did you arrive on Tuesday morning?'

'The usual time – half-past eight.'

'She's always very punctual, I will say that for her,' said Mrs Norris.

Sukey ignored the interruption. 'Did you know then that Ms Cottrell was dead?' Maggie shook her head. 'When did you find out?'

'I can't remember exactly.'

'She came down for her cup of tea as usual at half-past ten,' said the housekeeper, as Maggie seemed either unable or unwilling to continue, 'but instead of sitting and chatting to her and Hickson as usual I poured an extra cup for Miss Brand and went straight back upstairs. Maggie must have seen the police arriving because when I came down again she wanted to know why they were there. I told her what had happened as gently as I could, but she promptly had hysterics and I had to give her a drop of brandy to calm her down. The police said they'd want to speak to everyone but when they saw the state she was in they said she could go home and someone would talk to her later.'

'And that's why we're here,' said Vicky. 'It must have been very upsetting for you, Maggie, but now we need your help, all right? Good girl,' she went on as Maggie gave a wordless nod. 'Now, I understand from Ms Brand that from time to time Ms Cottrell gave small dinner parties for her friends. Did you help Mrs Norris on those occasions, for example with serving the food or clearing away afterwards?'

Maggie hesitated and glanced at Mrs Norris, who gave her a slight nudge and said, 'Answer the officer, Maggie.'

The girl nodded. 'Sometimes,' she said with her eyes on her feet.

'Can you remember the last time there was one of those parties?'

Maggie hesitated and said, 'I don't remember exactly.'

'Was it last weekend?' She shook her head. 'Two weeks ago?'

After another long pause, during which Mrs Norris appeared increasingly impatient, Maggie said uncertainly, 'About a month ago, I think.'

'It was the second Saturday in October, if you must

know,' said Mrs Norris sharply, 'although I fail to see what that's got to do with Tuesday's tragedy.'

'All right, Maggie, just one more question,' said Sukey. 'What did you say to Giles Hickson in the kitchen on Tuesday morning that made him tell you to be careful what you say to us?' Maggie looked startled and shot an anxious glance at Mrs Norris, who looked equally perturbed. 'Well?' said Sukey as neither of them spoke.

After a moment Maggie said, 'Don't know what you're talking about.'

'Are you saying you don't remember talking to Mr Hickson?'

'Might have done, but I don't remember what about. I was upset because of the coppers being here.' She was obviously on the verge of tears. 'I ain't saying no more,' she said with a sudden flash of defiance.

'You heard the girl,' said Mrs Norris. 'She's got nothing more to say and you can see she's upset. I must ask you to go, please.'

'Very well, but we may want to speak to you both again,' said Vicky. 'What did you make of that?' she said to Sukey as they returned to the car.

'They're hiding something,' Sukey replied without hesitation. 'That's why Mrs Norris insisted on being there – she was afraid Maggie might say the wrong thing if we saw her on her own.'

'My impression as well,' said Vicky. 'Just when it all seemed straightforward, it suddenly starts to get complicated.' She took out her mobile and called CID. 'I'd better put DS Rathbone in the picture right away. He isn't going to be best pleased!'

Eight

On their return Rathbone greeted them with the information that they were all to report to DCI Leach right away. 'I've given him an outline of what you've told me, but obviously he's going to want more details,' he said as the three made their way to Leach's office. 'You can do written reports later.'

DCI Leach told them to sit down and said, 'So, it looks as if there's more to this case than we thought.' He looked at the two young DCs, who took out their notebooks and waited. 'You first, Vicky.'

'We've established that Wendy Downie hasn't been seen since the weekend, sir,' said Vicky. 'DS Rathbone obtained a warrant and we searched the house and discovered the reason for her distress.' She gave a brief account of their findings.

Leach nodded. 'I have his report and it seems obvious the poor woman is suffering from serious delusions. Did you find anything else significant after DS Rathbone left?' This time he looked at Sukey.

'Not in the house, sir, but we spoke to a neighbour. She said Wendy's car was there over the weekend; she seemed sure it has been missing since Tuesday but she wasn't so sure about Monday. Her husband rang me later and gave me a detailed description of the car, which I understand has been circulated.'

'What about drugs? Did you find any?'

'No, sir.'

'Did you look?'

'Well, not specifically, sir,' Sukey admitted. 'We found out from the local pharmacist that she had regular prescriptions for antidepressants and it was through her that we found her GP, but we didn't actually search for them in the house. We checked her bedroom and if there'd been any bottles or packets lying around we'd certainly have noticed them. And we went through the drawers in her desk and there was nothing there.'

'But we know she had some, so it's more than likely she took them with her,' said Leach. 'You'd better check with the doctor and find out exactly what she was on and whether an OD could be fatal. Now let's have your report on your visit to Woodlands this morning.'

'We're convinced Maggie and Mrs Norris are hiding something,' said Vicky. Reading from her notes she summarized the interview with Maggie. 'We questioned her about the last time Cottrell gave a dinner party and she claimed she couldn't remember exactly, but when we pressed her she said it was probably some time last month, and Mrs Norris jumped in to say it was the second Saturday, which was the tenth, the date Lillian Brand gave us. We believe Maggie would have said more if we'd been able to talk to her on her own, but we're not in any doubt that it was Mrs Norris who persuaded her to refuse to see us without her.'

Leach nodded. 'Right, so the next job is to find out why.' He turned to Rathbone. 'What about you, Greg – have you got anywhere with your enquiries?'

'I've made an appointment to see Cottrell's lawyer later this afternoon. As for the dinner-party guests, it seems there were only three at the last one – her agent, her editor and a woman who handles her PR. And Lillian Brand, of course.'

'Hardly a social occasion, more like a business meeting,' Leach observed.

'The same thought occurred to me, sir,' said Rathbone. 'I spoke to them all and asked them when it was and they all confirmed the date Lillian Brand gave me. Two of them made a show of consulting their diaries before answering but the editor had it on the tip of her tongue, which struck me as surprising considering it was over a month ago.'

'You believe they'd been primed, and two of them were smart enough to pretend they had to check but the editor wasn't?'

'Yes, sir. My belief is that that party – or whatever it was – took place shortly before Cottrell died and that something very significant was discussed on that occasion that affected all of them. And I think Brand forewarned them that they'd be hearing from the police after the discovery of Cottrell's body and told them what to say if they were questioned about it.'

Leach raised his eyebrows. 'You're suggesting a conspiracy of silence?'

'Maybe not exactly a conspiracy, sir,' said Rathbone, 'but as I said, I do think something's been going on that they all want to keep quiet.'

Leach consulted the file. 'You mention in your earlier report that Lillian Brand said these occasional dinner parties were sometimes held to celebrate the publication of Cottrell's latest book. Did she give any particular reason for this one?'

'I asked her about that and she said it was to celebrate the completion, rather than the publication, of the first book in a new series.'

'Presumably publication will go ahead despite the author's death. I suggest you go back to the editor, Greg, and get a few more details.'

'Will do, sir.'

'And if your conspiracy theory is correct, where do you suppose Wendy Downie fits in?'

Looking utterly perplexed, Rathbone spread his hands in a helpless gesture. 'I'm darned if I know, sir,' he said. 'If we could only find her, maybe we could get some answers.'

'There's also the question of the other Jennifer Cottrell,' Leach pointed out. 'Do you think she knows anything?'

Rathbone shook his head. 'No, sir. I've had a few enquiries made and as far as we can tell there's no connection between Cottrell the writer and any of the agency clients. Wendy mistakenly thought she was the one who'd written the book that had caused her so much grief and that's why she subsequently made those phone calls. Because the Jennifer Cottrell who runs the agency had the sense to check the caller's number and was public-spirited enough to get in touch with us when she heard her namesake had been murdered, we were able to track her down. I think we can safely say that nothing to do with the agency has any bearing on the case.'

'Well, I suppose we should be grateful for that,' said Leach resignedly. 'We seem to have enough complications as it is. All right, let me have your written reports and then get on with your enquiries. And make a point of checking on the drugs,' he added sternly.

Back in the office, Rathbone said, 'I suppose we'd better interview the dinner-party guests face to face to see if we can detect any indication that they're lying, or whether there are any discrepancies in their stories, but they've had plenty of time to compare notes and agree on the details.'

'My feeling is that Lillian Brand is the one masterminding this cover-up,' said Sukey, 'and from what you told us she'll be a tough nut to crack.'

'My feeling too,' he agreed.

'If we could get Maggie on her own we might learn a bit more,' Sukey went on. 'It was plain she was telling porkies, but she wasn't happy about it. Why don't we try and contact her at home?'

'Or better still, find out if she lives with her parents and try and have a word with them while Maggie's at work?' suggested Vicky.

'Good thinking. I'll leave you to get on with that while I give some thought as to how we might get past Lillian's guard,' said Rathbone. 'I take it Maggie's address is on the file?'

'Yes, Sarge.'

A check in the local directory revealed that there was no telephone at Maggie's address, so all they could do was to call at the house some time after three o'clock in the hope of catching Maggie or her parents – preferably both. In the meantime they had a hasty lunch in the canteen before going back to Wendy's house to search for drugs.

'Where do we start?' said Vicky. 'We looked in the bedroom, but I suppose we'd better look a bit more thoroughly.'

'There's no reason why she should conceal them,' said Sukey. 'What about the bathroom – did we look in there?' They exchanged glances and somewhat guiltily searched the bathroom cabinet. The first thing they found was a calendar pack from which the last dose to be taken appeared to be that for Tuesday. 'So she took her regular dose before setting off to Woodlands early on Tuesday morning,' said Sukey, 'which suggests she knew exactly what she was going to do that day—'

'And needed her daily fix to keep her mind on the job,' Vicky finished, 'but never came back to take subsequent doses.'

'Which indicates she wasn't intending to do a runner,' Sukey pointed out.

'Unless in her agitation it didn't occur to her to take her supply with her,' Vicky speculated. 'Now, I wonder if there's any hope of finding out whether she took a weapon of some sort. A knife, perhaps?'

'Considering the mess the kitchen's in we'll have a job to find the answer to that,' said Sukey, 'but I suppose we have to try.'

At first the task seemed hopeless, but just as they were about to give up Sukey spotted a wooden block containing a matching set of knives that had been pushed to the back of one of the work surfaces and partially hidden behind an array of used saucepans. 'There's one missing from there,' she exclaimed, 'and from the look of things the others in the block haven't been disturbed.'

'You're right,' said Vicky, 'and it looks as if the missing one is the largest.'

'So she'd been living out of packets and tins ever since she learned of the death of Laurence Carmichael and not using any utensils or kitchen tools that she'd have needed to prepare proper meals,' said Sukey. 'And then when she saw this pattern of vapour trails she got the idea of how to get revenge on Jennifer Cottrell.'

'After first publicly accusing her of murder—'

'And uttering a thinly veiled threat that she'd suffer the same fate,' Sukey finished. 'Just on a point of interest,' she added, 'I gather you've read the book – is that how Laurence Carmichael died, by being stabbed with a kitchen knife?'

'Nothing so dramatic,' said Vicky. 'He died a heroic death saving one of his parishioners from being run over by a bus and suffering a heart attack brought on by the effort.'

'Ah well, that might have been a bit difficult to stage-manage,' said Sukey with a dry chuckle. She glanced at her watch. 'It's a quarter to three. Shall we see if we can catch Maggie at home?'

They drove to the village of Marfield, a short distance from Woodlands, and after a brief search found Rosewood Cottage. The door was opened by a burly man wearing a string vest and baggy corduroy trousers. His bare arms were heavily tattooed and he wore a gold ring in one ear. 'What d'you want?' he asked abruptly.

The two detectives held up their ID cards. 'We're conducting an enquiry into the death of Jennifer Cottrell,' said Vicky. 'We understand that Maggie Pearce lives here and we'd like a word with her if she's in.'

'I'm her father and she's already answered your questions. Pretty upset she was too, and I'm not having her upset again. Any further questions you can ask me.'

'We'd prefer to put them to Maggie herself,' said Sukey, 'although you're more than welcome to be present while we talk to her.'

'Very kind of you, I'm sure,' he grunted. 'Maggie!' he shouted over his shoulder. 'It's the Old Bill again and they want another word with you.'

There was a pause; after a moment there was a sound of shuffling footsteps and Maggie appeared behind her father's shoulder. 'What d'you want?' she asked fearfully.

'May we come in?' said Vicky, and somewhat grudgingly Pearce stood aside to allow them to step into the tiny square hall.

'You'd better come in here.' He opened the nearest door and they went into what was obviously a little-used front parlour. There were several shabby easy chairs but he did not invite them to sit down. 'You can have five minutes, but if you upset her you leave straight away, OK?'

'Thank you, five minutes is all we want,' said Sukey.
'Maggie,' she went on, 'we know that from time to time Ms
Cottrell gave little dinner parties for a few friends and you've
already told us that you were asked to help Mrs Norris with
the food and clear away afterwards. That's right, isn't it?'

'Sometimes,' said Maggie cautiously.

'And I'm sure she found you a great help. Now, when
we came to see you at Woodlands yesterday we could see
you were still feeling very upset about what happened to
poor Ms Cottrell on Tuesday morning, so perhaps you might
not have remembered everything clearly. Are you quite sure,
for example, you didn't make a mistake in the time you
went home on Monday? Please think very carefully,' she
went on as Maggie moved close to her father, who put an
arm round her, 'are you sure that Ms Cottrell wasn't giving
one of her little dinner parties that evening?'

Maggie shook her head. 'I don't know nothing about no
dinner party that evening,' she whispered.

'Or maybe a couple of days before that? Saturday,
perhaps?' Maggie shook her head even more vigorously.
'So when was the last time that you remember?'

Maggie drew a deep breath and said, 'The tenth of
October.'

'You're quite sure about that?' said Vicky.

'I can vouch for it,' said Pearce. 'There was some lovely
grub left over and Mrs Norris said she could bring it home.'
He smacked his lips at the recollection, and then gave a
mournful shake of the head. 'I don't suppose there'll be
any more,' he said. 'So sad about what happened to the
poor lady.'

'You're absolutely sure about the date, Mr Pearce?'

'Quite sure. We ate the nosh together while watching the
late movie on the box. We often watch a movie, don't we,
Mags? What was this one called – something about
kipping?'

'*The Big Sleep*?' suggested Vicky.

He snapped his fingers and said eagerly, 'That's right,
and it had that posh detective in it, what's his name? Morse,
is it?'

'It's Marlow, Dad,' said Maggie, who was looking extremely uncomfortable.

'Yes, that's right. I knew it began with an M.' He gave her shoulders a squeeze. 'My girl remembers all the details,' he said proudly.

'Mr Pearce,' said Vicky, 'I'm afraid your memory is a little inaccurate. We're talking about the tenth of October and it so happens *The Big Sleep* was shown last Sunday. I know because I watched it.'

'Look, we watch a lot of movies and I can't remember every little detail from that far back,' he said angrily, suddenly becoming aggressive. 'They might have run the same film again for all I know. Anyway, you've had more than your five minutes. We're not saying no more.' He marched out of the room and wrenched open the front door. 'That's the way out – and don't come back!'

Back in their car, the two women exchanged meaning glances. 'So they've got at him as well,' said Vicky.

'It looks like it,' said Sukey. 'I suppose we'd better check what films were showing on the tenth of October, but even if he got it wrong he's not exactly a reliable witness, is he? What I'd like to know is, what in the world are they covering up?' At that moment her mobile phone rang. She listened for a moment in silence and then said, 'Right, sir, we'll be there in ten minutes. Guess what,' she said as she switched off the phone. 'They've found Wendy Downie's car, hidden away in some woods adjacent to the Woodlands estate . . . and,' she added after a moment's pause, 'they've found a woman's body a quarter of a mile from the house.'

Nine

Sukey and Vicky arrived at Woodlands to find the front drive cluttered with police vehicles and the place buzzing with activity. Crime scene investigators were taking their equipment out of their vans and another team was preparing to erect a tent and lighting round the body. The two followed them as they carried various pieces of equipment along a path that ran behind the house and across a meadow towards some woods and put them down a short distance from where DS Rathbone and Dr Hanley were just visible among the trees. It was evident that the ground fell away sharply, as only their heads and shoulders could be seen; when the pathologist crouched, presumably to examine the body, he disappeared completely from view. When Rathbone saw the two women he scrambled up the slope and came towards them, picking his way carefully over the uneven ground, which was partially covered by undergrowth.

'It looks as if she was coming away from the direction of the house, possibly running so she didn't see how the ground suddenly sloped. It's muddy and slippery as well, so she must have tripped over, fallen face downwards into a shallow pool at the bottom of a dip and for some reason didn't get up again. Let's hear what Doc Hanley has to say,' he added as the pathologist stood up and approached them, brushing pieces of wet grass from the knees of his trousers.

'There are traces of vomit, which could have been caused by the shock of the fall or some other factor we don't know about. Why she just lay there instead of getting up is anyone's guess. She could have hit her head on something in the water – a piece of rock for example – and knocked herself out, or choked on the vomit. There's no way of establishing the cause of death until I get her to the morgue and I imagine you'll want the CSIs to record the scene before she can be moved.'

'Any idea how long she's been dead?' asked Rathbone.

Hanley pursed his lips and considered. 'The weather's been cool and damp for the past week or so and there's not much sign of decomposition detectable in the small areas of the body that are exposed. Again, when we get her to the morgue we'll have a better idea, but if you want a rough guess I'd say two days, three at the most.'

'Thanks, Doc, that's a great help,' said Rathbone. He stood aside to let him pass and then signalled to the two women. 'You don't need me to tell you to avoid disturbing the ground, so just observe what you can from a safe distance.'

Treading gingerly on the slippery ground, they moved forward a few paces and stood in silence, committing the details to memory. The body lay sprawled face downwards, the features almost entirely hidden and only a small area of exposed flesh visible between the collar of a padded anorak and the woollen cap pulled low over the ears. The arms were outstretched, the bare hands almost entirely concealed beneath the surface of the muddy water. After a moment Sukey said, 'The clothes look like the ones the woman we believe to be Wendy Downie was wearing at the library last Saturday.' Vicky nodded in agreement and after a few moments, by mutual consent, the two rejoined Rathbone and reported their observations.

'There doesn't seem much doubt that it's her, but we'll have to get a positive ID, probably from her doctor,' he said. 'OK, you can get started now.' He signalled to the group of CSIs, who had followed them along the path and were now standing a short distance away. 'Get as much as you can while the daylight holds and then move out of the way to let the techies put up the tent and the lights. Right,' he added as the group moved in to obey and he set off towards the house, signalling to the two women to follow him, 'now we'll go and look at the car. So far everything seems to support my theory: Downie came here, possibly on Monday night or most likely in the small hours of Tuesday morning, and parked her car where we found it. She probably lay in wait until it got light and then went to the house, found the door unlocked, saw Cottrell in her bath, dragged her under the water and held her down until she was sure she was unconscious. Then her one idea was to get away as soon as possible and that's when she came unstuck – she must have tripped over a tree root or maybe slipped on the wet grass, pitched forward and landed face down in the pool.'

'What puzzles me,' said Sukey, 'is how she knew where to come. How did she locate the house?'

'She must have followed Cottrell home after the meeting in the library,' said Rathbone, unwittingly putting forward the same explanation as Vicky had suggested to Sukey. 'By the way, did you learn anything from Maggie?'

'Just that she – and her father – bent over backwards to support the tenth of October story,' said Sukey.

'We're pretty sure they'd been told what to say,' Vicky added, and went on to recount Pearce's blunder over the movie he claimed they had watched on the night in question.

'It'll have to go in the report, although I can't see at the moment what bearing the apparent cover-up has on Cottrell's murder,' said Rathbone.

'Do we know if any of the staff at Woodlands, or any of the other contacts, knew Wendy Downie, Sarge?' asked Sukey.

'I asked Brand that question when I informed her of the discovery of the body and she said the name meant nothing to her,' Rathbone said curtly. His tone implied he suspected her of hinting that the point had not occurred to him, although that had not been her intention. 'Both Mrs Norris and Hickson are out at the moment and I told her someone would be taking statements from them later and asked her not to talk to the press in the meantime. I was supposed to meet the solicitor this afternoon, but had to cancel the appointment. I haven't asked the other three – the editor, the agent and the PR woman. I'm seeing them all next week – that is, if the SIO considers it's worth pursuing. We were called out to investigate a murder and it appears it's been solved, so with any luck he'll decide we can wrap up the case.'

'He'll be lucky,' said Vicky to Sukey in a low voice as Rathbone strode on ahead, 'from what I know about DCI Leach he won't be satisfied until we find out what the staff at Woodlands are covering up.'

While they were speaking Rathbone had led them back to the road running past the entrance to Woodlands House. 'The car's hidden away a bit further on,' he said. 'We're pretty sure it's Downie's from the details the neighbour gave us.' In a short time they came to a spot roped off by the police with a uniformed officer standing guard. 'You'll notice she's backed up among the trees so it's almost hidden from the road. My guess is she came here some time between Saturday and Monday to have a good snoop round to find a place to hide the car and check if there was any way she could get into the house. The fact that Cottrell's bedroom's on the ground floor and she was in the habit of keeping the door into the garden unlocked made it easy for Downie to get in.'

'Why d'you suppose she approached the house through the woods, Sarge?' asked Vicky.

'She probably wanted to avoid the risk of being seen by anyone passing on the road.'

'Who found the body, by the way?'

'We did. Some kids were in the woods looking for trees to climb and they came across the car. One of them had seen the details we circulated in the media and rang us on his mobile to report it. He gave very clear directions how to get here and when he was told not to touch the car or get too close he made a great point of saying that they were keeping well away from it, "so's not to disturb any clues".'

'Smart kid,' Sukey commented. 'I'll bet he watches police-procedurals on the telly.'

'Could be. Anyway, they've been given a pat on the back and gone home very pleased with themselves.'

'They'll be the heroes in their class at school,' chuckled Vicky.

A couple of CSIs were working on the car, a somewhat

battered Ford Fiesta about seven or eight years old. One
was taking shots of the surrounding ground while the other
examined the bodywork and the interior. 'She'd left the key
in the ignition, Sarge,' one of them told Rathbone.

He nodded. 'Facing the road, ready for a quick getaway.
What about fingerprints?'

'As you'd expect, there are several on the door handle
and steering wheel, probably the driver's. There's one set
of shoe prints leading away from the car towards the road
but no sign of them coming back. At a guess they're trainers,
most likely a woman's. There are two or three other sets
in the mud some distance away.'

'Left by the kids, no doubt, but we'd better check their
shoes to make sure.'

They returned to the house and Rathbone called the
station. After a short conversation he said, 'Well, there's
nothing more we can do here today,' and snapped off the
phone. 'DCI Leach is out and won't be in until late tomorrow
morning. Be ready with your reports by eleven thirty sharp.'

'So, Greg, I understand you've found a body and the indications are that it's that of the missing woman,' said the
DCI when they foregathered in his office the following day.
'I'll study these later,' he added, indicating the reports they
had handed over. 'Meanwhile, perhaps you'd care to fill
me in about yesterday's drama.'

'The fact that she was found lying face down in the water
made a positive ID difficult in situ,' said Rathbone, after
sketching in the circumstances of the discovery. 'Sukey and
Vicky never got a clear view of her face when she jumped
up to make her accusation at the library meeting, but they
confirm that the clothes are the same as, or very similar to,
what the woman who made that disturbance was wearing
– plus of course the fact that the car found half-concealed
a quarter of a mile or so away corresponds to the description a neighbour gave us of Downie's car.'

Leach nodded. 'Go on.'

'The CSIs have found what appear to be prints left by a
woman's trainers on a patch of moist earth just outside the

door to Cottrell's bedroom. There are also traces of what appear to be the same earth on the outside stone step,' Rathbone continued. 'The indications are that she crossed the lawn, opened the door, kicked off her shoes – hence no earth on the carpet – sneaked across the bedroom, probably on hearing splashing sounds from the bathroom, found Cottrell in her bath and pulled her under the water by her feet. That would account for the bruises on her legs; judging from the bruises on the wrists Cottrell struggled, probably reached for the grab handles on the side of the bath to try and pull herself upright. Downie must have taken hold of the wrists and then shoved her head under the water and held her there until she lost consciousness.'

'And then beat it?' said Leach.

'I imagine so, sir.'

'Presumably there are prints leading to and away from the house?'

'Nothing identifiable, sir – just indentations on the grass,' said Rathbone, 'but there are indications that someone landed heavily about three feet from the door. It may be that in her anxiety to get away she took a flying leap, hit the ground running and pelted across the lawn, presumably heading for the place where she'd left her car. In her panic she must have forgotten about the slippery slope, tripped over and landed on her face in the water, knocking herself out in the process. We'll probably find a submerged rock or something similar once the body's been moved.'

Leach sat for several seconds in silence while studying the file that lay open in front of him, apparently deep in thought. Then he said, 'Vicky and Sukey, I see from your report on your return visit to Downie's house that you think she may have taken a knife with her because there was one missing from a set of four?'

'Yes, sir,' said Vicky, 'although bearing in mind the state of the kitchen it's quite possible that the missing knife is hidden somewhere among all the dirty pots and pans.'

'And this note you found on Downie's desk about vapour trails forming what seemed to suggest a dagger to her – are you suggesting that her original intention was to stab Cottrell?'

Vicky nodded. 'It did appear that way to us, sir, on the surface at any rate.'

'I have ordered a search to be made for a knife, sir, but none has been found,' said Rathbone.

'It's probably not significant,' said Leach with what appeared to be a hint of reluctance. Sukey recalled hearing someone say of him that he liked all the 'i's dotted and all the 't's crossed. His next remarks therefore came as no surprise.

'There's obviously plenty of circumstantial evidence to suggest that Cottrell was killed by the woman whose body was found on her land, although we have to wait for the PM report and also forensics may come up with something more positive. It's certain that as things stand we'd not have been in a position to charge Downie if she'd survived the fall and we can only speculate as to the reasons she might have given for being at Woodlands. We know that she lived in a fantasy world and was under the delusion that Cottrell was responsible for the death of her imaginary fiancé. On the face of it, therefore, since we can't question our suspect, we might be justified in considering the case closed – were it not for the question of the mysterious dinner party that everyone seems so anxious to convince us never took place, plus the fact that there's an almost unnatural consensus as to the date of the most recent one. Have you any theory about that, Greg?'

'Bearing in mind who attended, sir, it struck us that it could have been more a business discussion than a social occasion. It was probably something to do with Cottrell's writing, since they all have an interest in it. The only concrete evidence of some kind of cover-up – if you can call it concrete – is that snatch of conversation overheard by Sergeant Rosy Brookes on the morning of Cottrell's murder, something that both parties claim not to recall having taken place.'

'So Brand, the editor, the publisher and the PR woman agreed on their story and Brand made sure the rest of the staff backed them up? You think she wields sufficient influence over them to make them do what they were told?'

'We all believe so, sir.' At this point Rathbone gestured towards his two junior officers, who nodded in agreement. 'I think,' he went on, 'that when Cottrell was found dead, someone – probably Brand – must have seen it as a golden opportunity to conceal whatever unwelcome fact emerged during the dinner party and made a snap decision to conceal the fact that it had taken place. She would have made sure the gardener, the housekeeper and the maid – and later the maid's father – all told the same story. She must have contacted the others and set it all up before we had time to check on the dates.'

'And there's no connection you've been able to establish between Downie and any of the people involved?'

'No, sir.'

'Right.' Leach closed the file and stood up to indicate that the discussion was over. 'We'll leave it at that for now, at least until we have the result of the post-mortem, get Downie's ID confirmed and so on. I take it the coroner's been informed?'

'Of course, sir,' said Rathbone.

'And meanwhile, I'd like you to dig a little deeper among the dinner-party guests. It seems pretty certain there's a cover-up, but of course there's nothing at this stage to suggest that there's anything illegal going on. Just the same, I don't think the Super will want us to leave it at that.'

Ten

'Have you anything special lined up for the weekend?' asked Sukey as, after spending the rest of the day in consultation with Rathbone on a strategy for detailed questioning of the dinner-party guests in an attempt to find weaknesses in their story, she and Vicky cleared their desks and prepared to go home.

Vicky shrugged. 'Nothing special; Chris is working over the weekend so maybe I'll give the flat a bit of a clean and do some washing. How about you?'

'Likewise, I suppose.' Sukey said resignedly. 'Go to the supermarket and stock up my freezer, and maybe do a workout in the gym.' She suddenly stopped short in the act of shutting down her computer and put a hand to her mouth. 'Heavens, I'd almost forgotten – Jim's coming tomorrow to take me out to lunch. He's got something to tell me that he wouldn't talk about on the phone.'

Vicky gave her a curious glance. 'I've noticed you haven't mentioned him lately,' she commented. 'I've been wondering if you'd fallen out or something, but I didn't like to ask.'

'No, we certainly haven't fallen out – but neither have we been in touch for quite a while. No particular reason,' she went on, as if anticipating her friend's next question. 'Thinking about it, I haven't really missed him the way I did for the first few months after I moved to Bristol, although hearing his voice on the phone the other day did give me a kind of warm feeling.'

'Maybe he's engaged on some secret mission – or,' Vicky suggested, with a sudden twinkle in her eye, 'maybe he's been plucking up courage to ask you to marry him. Just kidding,' she added in response to Sukey's cynically raised eyebrow, 'but perhaps you'd better do your report tonight in case tomorrow's announcement is so momentous that you're too gobsmacked to remember anything!'

It was true, Sukey reflected as she drove home, that after the initial feeling of pleasure on hearing from Jim and a natural curiosity to hear what he had to tell her, her mind had been so focused on the Cottrell case that from then on thoughts of tomorrow's meeting had gone to the back of her mind. As she tried to recall his exact words she found herself thinking – a little uneasily – of Vicky's mischievous suggestion that he might at last be about to ask her to marry him, but all she could remember of the conversation was that he had seemed a little evasive when she asked what he had been doing recently. On further reflection it occurred to her that he had not asked her the same question, which was unusual. Recalling occasions in the past when she had half-expected him to suggest a more permanent commitment, she found herself mentally lining up the reasons why she would have been reluctant, even when their affair had been at its most intense, to agree. After her husband deserted her and Fergus – only five years old at the time – she had developed an independent streak that had more than once been the cause of friction because of Jim's habit of being overprotective.

She stopped off at the local supermarket to buy provisions for her evening meal, making sure she chose something quick and easy to prepare so that she could concentrate on writing her report. By the time she had eaten, written the report and watched the late news on the television, she was ready for bed. She half expected to lie awake for a while, speculating what tomorrow would hold, but she was so exhausted that she fell almost immediately asleep.

Next day, Jim arrived on the stroke of twelve, almost concealed behind a huge bunch of flowers. 'How beautiful!' she exclaimed as he handed them over. 'I hope I can find enough vases for them,' she added as she closed the door behind him and led the way upstairs to her sitting room. 'Would you like to make some coffee while I put them in water?'

'Never mind coffee, just put them down anywhere for
the moment,' he said. 'Come and sit down.' He indicated
the pair of armchairs that she kept in front of the television and she obeyed, curious to know what lay behind
his uncertain, almost apprehensive manner.

'You know,' she said after a pause that seemed to go on
for an unusually long time, 'I'm beginning to think you
must have been up to no good. First you hint at something
that can't be spoken of on the phone and then you offer to
buy me a sumptuous lunch and turn up with a massive
bouquet. I can't believe this is all because you haven't been
in touch lately.'

'You're right.' As if on an impulse, he suddenly reached
across the space between them and took her hand. 'Sook,
you and I have had some good times together, haven't we?'

'Yes, of course.'

'And a few differences as well?'

'That's because you're such a bossy-boots,' she teased
him, 'but they've always blown over very quickly. And I've
always appreciated the support you've given me, and the
interest you've taken in Fergus. He thinks a lot of you.'

'It's mutual. He's a great lad and you must be very proud
of him.'

'I am.' There was another silence and Sukey gave his
hand, still clasping hers, an impatient shake. 'Oh, come on,
Jim, I know you've got something to tell me so please get
on with it.'

'All right, but this isn't easy for me. Sukey, do you
remember how we got together in the first place?'

'I remember we were a pair of humble PCs pounding
the beat together in Gloucester about twenty years ago; we
might have become an item except that I met Paul and fell
for him rather heavily. We had a whirlwind romance and
got married, and soon after that I got pregnant and left the
force. After Paul and I were divorced and when Fergus was
old enough I rejoined as a SOCO and we met up again, by
which time you were a DI and—'

'And like you I'd also been married and divorced,' he
continued, 'the reason being that Tanya couldn't cope with

the stress of being a copper's wife. So it seemed natural that you and I should get together. Then you moved to Bristol and we saw less of each other and—' he took a deep breath, 'Tanya and I met up again a couple of months ago. She's never remarried and . . . well, to cut a long story short, we—'

'You're together again!' Sukey exclaimed, as once again he appeared tongue-tied. To her surprise, she suddenly became aware of an enormous sense of relief. 'Jim, I'm really happy for you.'

'Truly?' His anxious expression gave way to a smile of mingled astonishment and pleasure. 'You really mean that?'

'Truly.' She jumped up and kissed him on the cheek. 'I do hope it works out for you both.'

In reply, he got to his feet and gave her a hug. 'Thank you so much, Sook,' he said huskily. 'I really believe it will. And I hope you and I can stay friends.'

'Of course we can.' Gently she disengaged herself from his embrace and said, 'Now, what about that lunch you promised me!'

That evening, Sukey called Vicky and invited her for coffee the following morning.

'So, have you learned the solution to the great mystery?' asked Vicky when the two were settled with their coffee.

'I haven't solved the Cottrell case single-handed, if that's what you mean,' said Sukey, knowing full well what her friend had in mind.

'You know jolly well what I mean,' said Vicky with a hint of exasperation. 'Did Jim come clean?'

'He came clean, all right. He's dumped me in favour of his first wife. They're going to remarry.'

Vicky's jaw dropped. 'The rotten bastard!' she exclaimed and then, detecting the twinkle in Sukey's eye, she said, 'You don't look all that upset.'

'I'm not upset at all; on the contrary I suddenly felt liberated and I really hope they'll be happy. We had a great time together but after his call last week I got to thinking and it began to dawn on me that the old magic wasn't there any more. Your suggestion that he might be going to ask me to marry him scared the pants off me.'

'So long as you're not hurt.'

'Not in the least, honestly.'

'That's great. Now, as we've got some time together, shall we compare notes and see if we can come up with something constructive to offer DS Rathbone tomorrow?'

On Monday morning, Rathbone greeted them by saying, 'So, have you two had some bright ideas over the weekend about how to set about breaking this conspiracy of silence?'

'We've given it a lot of thought, and we believe Maggie is the weakest link, Sarge,' said Vicky. 'The problem is getting her on her own. It seemed obvious when we interviewed her that her father had been got at as well – probably bribed – to confirm the date of the dinner party, and he made darned sure she repeated to us what they'd both been told to say. We don't know anything about the three other people at the so-called dinner party they all claim took place in October, except that they're all involved in the production of Cottrell's books, so of course they'll have to be interviewed.'

'We think they got Lillian Brand to mastermind the cover-up because she was in a position to make sure the rest of the staff told the same story,' Sukey continued. 'She's a pretty tough cookie and probably capable of lying through her teeth when it suits her.'

'You're assuming that something happened at that party that for some reason they didn't want made public?'

'That's right, Sarge. Knowing that questions were likely to be asked on account of Cottrell's unexpected death, they had to act fast.'

'Any theory as to why the staff at Woodlands would agree?' asked Rathbone. 'Money, perhaps? And who do you suppose would offer it, and why?'

'In the case of Maggie and her father, we think money is the most likely explanation,' said Vicky. 'Possibly it applied to Hickson as well. His main concern would be for number one; he was probably hoping to keep his job after Cottrell's death and I don't imagine he'd be particularly scrupulous about keeping his mouth shut if it was made worth his while. As for the housekeeper, we've already come to the conclusion that there isn't much love lost between her and Brand, so why should she lie at her behest? Unless, of course, Brand had some kind of hold over her.'

'What about the motive for buying their silence?' said Sukey. 'We can't know that until we know what happened at that dinner party, or when it actually took place, can we?'

Rathbone gave a nod of agreement. 'My thoughts have been running on similar lines,' he said. 'Right, there's plenty there to chew on, so you can spend the next couple of hours working out a plan of campaign. Maggie's the most likely to sing, so you might begin by figuring out how to catch her without either her father or the housekeeper breathing down her neck. And while you're at it, it might be worth looking into Pearce's background. He sounds the kind of chap who might have form. Hickson too, come to think of it.' He reached for his jacket. 'I'm off to the morgue now to attend the PM on Downie.'

'Do we know for certain it's Downie, Sarge?' said Sukey.

'Oh yes, her GP has identified her.'

'Well, that's a relief,' said Vicky as he left. 'Not that there was much doubt, but we don't need any more complications. With luck, we should soon be able to wind up the investigation into the Cottrell murder.'

Her optimism was short-lived. Less than two hours later Rathbone was back, and from the set of his mouth it was obvious something was wrong. Without taking off his jacket he grabbed the phone on his desk. 'Rathbone here, sir,' he said. 'I need to see you as soon as possible about the Cottrell case . . . In half an hour? . . . Thank you, sir.' He put down the instrument and turned to the two women. 'DCI Leach's office in thirty minutes,' he said. 'Time for a coffee.'

'What's happened, Sarge?' asked Sukey.

'Wendy Downie's death was no accident,' he replied grimly. 'She was murdered.'

Eleven

'We got it right up to a point,' said Rathbone. He tipped sugar into his coffee and stirred it as if he was trying to bore through the bottom of the mug. 'That's to say, the PM hasn't turned up anything to contradict our theory as to how Downie got into Cottrell's room, or that she subsequently beat it in a hurry. Before Hanley got down to business with his carving knife he drew my attention to two things he'd noticed from his external examination of the body: first, there's no sign of an abrasion on the head to indicate that in falling she'd knocked herself out by striking it on a hard object such as a submerged rock and second, there's some quite extensive bruising in the small of the back and some on the abdomen.' He paused to swallow a mouthful of coffee before saying, 'What does that tell us?'

'That the reason she was running away,' Vicky said slowly, 'was not just a sudden panic-stricken desire to get away from the scene as quickly as possible after killing Cottrell, it was because she was being pursued, possibly by the person who saw her do the killing.'

'Such a person would obviously want to catch her, but surely with the idea of preventing her from getting away, maybe even arresting her,' Sukey objected. 'They'd hardly be likely to kill her. Unless . . . '

'Unless what?' he said impatiently, as she hesitated for a moment while assessing the idea that flashed into her head.

'Unless she happened to arrive just in time to witness someone else killing Cottrell,' she said slowly, considering the picture that was taking shape in her mind's eye. 'She'd have been shocked and terrified, probably unable to move for a moment, maybe betrayed herself by letting out a gasp or even a scream before running for her life. The killer heard her, turned and realized she'd seen what had happened. He – or she – must have abandoned the victim and given chase.'

'And then when she fell on her face in the water made sure she couldn't get up again,' said Vicky.

'That's probably it,' Rathbone agreed.

'By holding her head down and putting pressure on her back?' suggested Sukey. 'Is that consistent with the nature of the bruising, Sarge?'

He nodded gloomily. 'So far. According to Hanley, that could have caused the vomiting. The CSI in attendance at the PM is making a record and there'll be some images for us to pick up before we go to DCI Leach's office.' He drained his mug and thumped it down on the table. 'So now the case is wide open again – a whole string of suspects, maybe plus one we don't even know about, with who knows what motive for wanting Cottrell out of the way.' He pushed back his chair and stood up. 'Come on, let's go. I hope this interview won't last too long; I've managed to get another appointment with Cottrell's solicitor and I don't want to have to cancel a second time.'

'So, Greg,' said Leach when they were settled in his office, 'it seems we're in a different ball-game altogether.'

'Yes, sir,' said Rathbone. He took a series of printouts from the envelope that had been delivered to the CID office. 'You'll see from these that only Downie's face and her outstretched hands were under the water. The rest of her was lying on the slope and there are signs that the grass on either side of the torso has been trampled, but unfortunately no recognizable shoe prints, only some odd sections where Downie's and the pursuer's feet skidded in the mud. That suggests to me, sir, that her killer stood or knelt on her body using his own weight to keep her down while pressing her face under the water with one or both hands.'

'You said "his own weight" – does that mean you're assuming the killer was a man?' asked Leach.

Rathbone hesitated a moment before saying, 'Not necessarily, sir. Downie was slightly built and if someone only a few pounds heavier knelt on her the way I've suggested it would probably be enough to hold her until she lost consciousness under the water.'

'And the cause of death?'

'As in Cottrell's case – drowning. Not that I think that's anything more than a coincidence, sir.'

'I'm inclined to agree with you there,' said Leach. 'I'd say that whoever killed Cottrell saw Downie, realized she'd caught him or her in the act, and had to kill her as well. A murder of expediency, in fact.'

'That's how I see it, sir.' He omitted to give credit to his two DCs for suggesting this probable sequence of events.

'How far is it from the house to the place where the body was found?'

'Quite a distance, actually. You have to cross a wide lawn and beyond that there's a largish field and then the patch of woodland where she was lying. I imagine there'll be a plan of the estate with the deeds and my guess is Cottrell's solicitor will be holding it. I'll ask him to let us have a copy when I see him – that should give us an idea of scale.'

Leach nodded. 'What time's your appointment?'

'At half-past two, sir.'

'I suggest you call him as soon as we've finished to make sure he's got it and if not, ask him to get hold of it for us as soon as possible.'

'Will do, sir.'

'What other steps are you planning?'

'I've instructed Vicky and Sukey to find some way of catching Maggie Pearce on her own, as we all feel she's the one most liable to drop her guard.'

'Good. That's all for now; report back to me later.'

Back in the CID office Rathbone picked up the phone on his desk and tapped out a number while Vicky and Sukey waited for further instructions. They had earlier agreed on a plan to intercept Maggie when she finished her day's work at Woodlands in order to question her without interference from either Mrs Norris or her father.

When he had finished his call, Rathbone put the phone down and beckoned to them. 'I've left a message for

Mr Fraser, asking him to look out the plan of the Woodland estate before our meeting,' he said. 'I'm going to grab a quick bite to eat now and I suggest you two do the same. Have you figured out a plan to get Maggie on her own?'

'We have, Sarge,' said Vicky. 'We think she cycles to work and . . .' She outlined their plan and he gave an approving nod.

'Good thinking,' he said. 'We'll meet up again later.'

By half-past two they had parked in a lay-by a short distance from Woodlands before approaching the entrance to the long driveway to the house on foot. As on their previous visits, the heavy metal gate stood open.

'Where do you suggest we wait?' said Vicky.

Sukey thought for a moment. 'If we close the gate, Maggie will have to get off her bike to open it,' she said, 'so why don't we hide behind the hedge outside and jump out and nab her before she has time to hop on again and make a dash for it?'

'Good idea,' said Vicky. She gave a quick glance round. 'It's lucky the bend in the drive means we can't be observed from the house. Let's do it.'

The gate was heavy and from the grinding and squeaking of the rusty hinges it did not appear to have been moved for some time. 'I hope no one hears this racket and comes to investigate,' panted Vicky as they heaved it into place before retreating to their hiding place.

'I suggest we wait till she's got the gate open just far enough to let us nip through and grab her before we show ourselves,' said Sukey, 'otherwise she might rush back into the house and take refuge with Mrs Norris.'

They did not have to wait long. Soon Maggie appeared on her bicycle, leaning low over the handlebars so that it was several seconds before she realized the way was barred. She skidded to a halt, dismounted, leaned the machine against a convenient bush and began struggling with the gate. She was slightly built and it was some time before she managed to drag it open a short distance. As soon as the gap was wide enough, Sukey and Vicky emerged from their hiding place and stepped through it.

'Can we give you a hand, Maggie?' said Vicky.

The girl gave a little scream and the colour drained from her face. 'What d'you want?' she said in a hoarse whisper.

'A little word with you,' said Sukey.

Maggie swung round as if intending to dash back to the house, but the two detectives each took hold of an arm in a gentle but firm grip. 'You can either come and sit quietly in the car with us and answer a few questions there,' said Vicky, 'or if you prefer you can come down to the station for a formal interview.'

'I answered all your questions – I've got nothing more to tell you,' the girl protested, but her words lacked conviction.

'We think you have,' said Sukey. 'We think you'd been told what to say to us when we came to talk to you before and we think you were told not to talk to us without Mrs Norris being present.'

'And we would remind you that withholding information from the police is a serious offence,' Vicky continued.

'Even more serious when it's a murder enquiry,' Sukey added.

Maggie looked from one to the other, shaking with terror. 'I didn't murder Miss Cottrell and I don't know nothing about it, honest!' she said tearfully.

'We believe you, but we still think there's something you've been told not to tell us and we want to know what it is, and who told you,' said Vicky.

Maggie looked from one to the other and there was fear in her eyes. 'Please let me go,' she pleaded, 'me dad will wonder why I'm not home.'

'Won't he be at work?' said Sukey.

'He can't do a regular job, he hurt his back.'

'Then the sooner you tell us what we want to know, the sooner you can get home. You don't have to tell him you've been talking to us. You can make up some excuse for being late – I'm sure it won't be the first time you've done that.'

Maggie's resistance crumbled; they led her to their car and put her in the back seat between them. Still tearfully protesting her innocence, she nonetheless made a full statement, which Sukey wrote on pages from her note-book and got her to sign. They then put her bicycle in the boot of their car, drove her to Marfield and dropped her at the end of her road before returning to the station.

Rathbone joined them in the office a few minutes later. 'Any joy from Maggie?' he asked.

'Yes, Sarge,' said Vicky. 'She doesn't know a great deal, but what she had to tell us could be very useful.'

'Good. Likewise with Cottrell's solicitor, Paul Fraser.' Rathbone picked up the phone and asked for DCI Leach. 'A few developments in the Cottrell case, sir. May I come and see you with DCs Reynolds and Armstrong? Fine.' He put the phone down. 'Come along, you two, let's go and report to our SIO.'

Leach's PA had just brought him his afternoon tea and at a sign from him she brought three further cups. 'Right, Greg,' he said. 'You first.'

Rathbone put an A4 envelope on Leach's desk and said, 'That's a photocopy of the plan of the Woodlands Estate, sir,' he said. 'I've marked the point where we found Downie's body and if you refer to the scale you'll see that it's approx-imately a hundred and fifty metres from the house. It looks as if her pursuer was close enough behind her when she fell to grab her before she had a chance to get up.'

Leach studied the plan for several minutes with evident interest. 'I see what the surveyor meant when he described the house as an architectural nightmare,' he observed. 'The kitchen and the housekeeper's room were apparently added at a later date, and because of the lie of the land there had to be some extensive excavation. That accounts for the differ-ence in levels.' He passed the plan back to Rathbone and said, 'He was between the devil and the deep blue sea, wasn't he?'

'Sir?'

'The killer. He had to make a snap decision: should he go after the person who'd caught him in the act of murdering Cottrell and make sure they wouldn't be able to give evidence against him, or should he make sure that Cottrell was dead before going after a witness to the killing?'

'Yes, I take your point, sir,' said Rathbone. 'It seems more than likely that Cottrell knew her killer, because an opportunist thief who saw the open door, for example, would be more likely to nick whatever he could lay his hands on and then scarper. And if Cottrell was soaking in her bath with the door shut he might not even have known she was there. But if his intention was to kill her, then if she was still alive when he realized he'd been spotted, she would be the one whose testimony was the more damaging. Unless Downie recognized him, of course. I suppose we can't rule that out.'

'Right, leave that with me to mull over for a while,' said Leach. 'What else did you learn from Fraser?'

'This is really interesting,' said Rathbone. 'First of all, apart from a few legacies to charity, a modest annuity to Mrs Norris and two grand to Hickson, Lillian Brand is Cottrell's sole heir. The house and estate alone must be worth several million, plus a life interest in royalties on the books.'

Leach gave a soft whistle. 'How's that for a motive?' he exclaimed.

'Except for one thing, sir. When Cottrell made her will, she swore Fraser to secrecy, told him that under no circumstances should Brand be told until after her death. Her reason was, to quote her own words, "I've no reason to mistrust her, but I don't believe in putting temptation in people's way." Fraser assured me that only he and two old-established members of his staff, whom he trusted absolutely, knew the contents of the will.'

'That doesn't rule out the possibility that she managed to find out somehow,' Leach pointed out. 'I assume she's been told about it now?'

'No, sir; Fraser was away in France on business and didn't return until Thursday. He was of course very shocked to learn of his client's death and in the circumstances decided to wait until he'd seen me before saying anything.'

'Quite right too,' said Leach. 'How long has Cottrell dealt with this firm of solicitors, do you know?'

'Since she moved to Woodlands about fifteen years ago, according to Fraser – he's the senior partner, by the way.'

'Hmm.' Leach chewed his lower lip. 'It seems this will was made after the move, then. Does Fraser know why she left everything to Brand?'

'He says he asked her that very question at the time, sir, and she said something to the effect that she had no living relatives and Brand was the only employee she'd ever had who was a hundred per cent loyal. Incidentally, his receptionist told me that Cottrell rang his office the day before she died, asking to speak to him. When she was told he was away until the end of the week, she said she'd call again when he got back.'

'Without giving any indication of what it was about?'

'No, sir.'

Leach turned to the two DCs. 'Right, let's have your report.'

'First of all, sir,' Vicky began, 'there almost certainly was a dinner party over the weekend before Cottrell died. Maggie wasn't asked to help with the serving, possibly because of the small number of guests, but when she reported for work on the Monday she found a lot more dishes than usual in the dishwasher. It seems the normal routine is for Mrs Norris to run the dishwasher after cooking for Cottrell and Brand over the weekend and leave it for Maggie to unload on the Monday morning. The day before Cottrell died, Maggie noticed that as well as the usual assortment of everyday dishes, cutlery and so on, there were some of the special plates, dishes and wine glasses that only came out when they were entertaining. When she remarked on this to Mrs Norris she was told rather sharply to mind her own business, which she said wasn't like her as she was usually so pleasant.'

'And then, when we arranged to go and interview Maggie at Woodlands,' said Sukey, 'she said that before we arrived Mrs Norris told her that if we asked her she was to say the last dinner party was on the tenth of October.'

'Did she say why?' asked Leach.

'No, sir, and when Maggie asked her she said, "Never mind, just do as you're told." '

'So how was it that when you went to see her at home

that time, her father went out of his way to back up her story?'

'This is where it gets really interesting, sir,' said Vicky. 'It seems Pearce used to give Hickson a hand on the estate from time to time until he hurt his back while working on his regular job. That was some time last year; he's been off work ever since except for the odd light job, and Cottrell, out of the kindness of her heart, used to supplement his benefit. When she died Maggie said something to her father about losing the money and it seems he told her not to worry, everything would be all right so long as she did what she was told. She asked him what it was all about but he just repeated what Mrs Norris had said, that it was none of her business.'

'And those are the words Hickson used during that snatch of conversation between him and Maggie on the morning of the murder, sir,' said Rathbone. 'I take it you questioned her about that, Sukey?'

'We did, sir. It was something she'd overheard on the Monday when passing by Brand's office. The door wasn't properly shut and it seems Brand was saying something like "there might be trouble". She didn't wait to hear any more and didn't think about it at the time, but when uniformed turned up the next day she threw a wobbly and asked Hickson if it might have anything to do with what she'd overheard. As we reported earlier, he told her to keep out of it.'

Leach frowned. 'I wonder if there was another reason for her being upset at the sight of the police,' he said thoughtfully. 'Have you run a check on Pearce, Greg?'

'I instructed the girls to do that, sir.' Rathbone turned to them. 'Did you come up with anything?'

'Yes, Sarge,' said Sukey. 'Pearce doesn't actually have form, but DC Pringle recalls him being questioned about some dodgy deals in builder's equipment that we were asked to investigate some time ago. There was no evidence against him, but the investigating team had their suspicions all the same. You asked us to run a check on Hickson as well, but we've nothing on him. He's worked on the estate for years, and his father before him.'

'I wonder how widely the Pearce business is known?' mused Leach. 'Something else we should bear in mind, I suppose. Let's consider how many suspects we've got. I think we're agreed we eliminate Maggie?' he finished with a faintly rueful smile.

Rathbone was counting on his fingers. 'I make it seven, sir – the housekeeper, Hickson, Pearce, Brand and the three guests at the dinner party.'

Leach nodded. 'It strikes me that it all hinges on that dinner party, Greg. Who arranged it, and why? What happened that for some reason it was decided – and by whom – to conceal the fact that it ever took place? And why did everyone go along with the cover-up? Any ideas?' His glance included all three detectives facing him. When there was no immediate response he continued, 'This needs a larger team. I'll be thinking who else to put on the case and meanwhile you can all go away and think up some ideas. And Greg, get forensics to blow up the images of the prints in the mud. Smudged or not, we might be able to pick up something useful.' He closed his file and got to his feet. 'Meet me here at nine tomorrow morning.'

Twelve

Punctually at nine the following morning, DS Rathbone, Vicky and Sukey presented themselves in DCI Leach's office. Already there were three other detectives of whom one, DC Mike Haskins, had worked on a case on which they had all previously been involved and a second, DC Tim Pringle, had provided such information as was already known about Maggie Pearce's father. The third, DC Penny Osborne, had only recently joined the department after completing her CID training. On Leach's desk was the complete file on the Cottrell case, plus a sheet on which he had written what Sukey guessed was a list of questions to which he wanted answers.

'Right,' said Leach, 'Penny, Tim and Mike will be joining your team as of now, Greg, and I've given each of them a copy of every report on the Cottrell file to put them in the picture. As they're bringing fresh minds to the case, I'm going to begin by asking them in turn if anything stands out as particularly significant. You first, Tim.'

'Well, sir, seeing as I'd had dealings with Bill Pearce before and knew him to be a dodgy character, I began by asking myself how he might fit into the picture and how he might be prevailed on to back up the story about the date of the dinner party – assuming, of course, that the suggestion of a cover-up we got from Maggie's statement is correct and there was one just before Cottrell was killed. Just to refresh your memory, sir, and put the others completely in the picture, before he injured his back he worked as a driver for a firm of builders' merchants, delivering everything from bricks to scaffolding to various construction sites over a fairly extensive area. We were called in to investigate a series of thefts of equipment and materials from a number of such sites, to all of which supplies from Pearce's employer had recently been delivered. We managed to recover some of the stuff and in practically every case it turned out he was the driver who made the delivery. We suspect that whenever he spotted something particularly valuable – incidentally, it was mostly heavy machinery that went missing – he would take the opportunity of sussing out security measures at the site and tip off the thieves, probably getting a rake-off from whatever was stolen. We could never pin anything on him, but it was significant that the level of thefts dropped off significantly after he injured his back and had to give up the job.'

Leach nodded. 'I remember the case. I think we can take it that he's up for anything dodgy provided it's worth his while. Anything else?'

'It's interesting that Maggie told Vicky and Sukey she'd happened to mention to her dad when Cottrell died that he'd lose the money she'd been giving him to make up his sick pay, and he'd replied that it would be OK "so long as she did what she was told". Exactly what did he mean by this? Had someone given him that assurance – perhaps to encourage his cooperation – and if so, who? And how could that person be in a position to give it anyway?'

'Good point,' said Leach. 'Now you, Mike.'

'The same thought occurred to me, sir,' said Haskins. 'So far, there hasn't been an opportunity for face-to-face interviews with the three people other than Brand who were present at the crucial dinner party, so we don't know whose idea it was to arrange it, let alone deny it ever took place. We suspect that it was Brand who made sure the other people at Woodlands, i.e. Norris, Hickson and Maggie – and by extension Maggie's father – all told the same story, but we don't know if it was on her own initiative, on the orders of someone else or a joint decision. More significantly still, we don't know what happened to bring them to that decision. Was it something so crucial to all of them that Cottrell had to die to prevent it becoming public?'

'Another sound bit of reasoning.' Leach ticked off a

second point on the list in front of him. 'Do you reckon there may be someone else in the background whose existence we don't know about?'

'I suggest we bear that possibility in mind, sir.'

'We'll certainly do that.' Leach turned to DS Rathbone. 'What about you, Greg?'

'First of all, sir,' Rathbone began, 'I've checked on the partial shoe prints in the mud near the Downie murder scene and there is a slight irregularity in one of them, but it's only a fragment. There's trampled grass right up to the edge of the puddle and only a small muddy area where prints could be left, and if the killer knelt on Downie to hold her down he might simply have sat back on his heels once the job was done and stood up without actually standing in the mud or leaving any recognizable prints. In any case, the body lay there undiscovered for two or three days and there was some heavy overnight rain during the period, which didn't make forensics' task any easier. The kids who found the car were all wearing trainers and the prints we found there have been checked and are either from theirs or from those Downie herself was wearing when we found her. Incidentally, the socks she had on were wet, even though her feet were clear of the water when we found her, so she must have trodden in it on her way to the house. Most of the identifiable fingerprints on the car were hers, although there were others that were probably left by the neighbour who used to do odd jobs on it for her. He's very kindly allowed us to take his prints for elims and I'm waiting for a report on them.'

Leach nodded and made another tick. 'Anything else?'

'It was suggested that Downie's original plan was to stab Cottrell as there appeared to be a knife missing from a set in her kitchen,' Rathbone continued. 'An extensive search failed to find it at Woodlands. I've ordered a further search of her kitchen, but so far it hasn't been found. Regarding the other witnesses, it seems to me there's a question mark over Mrs Norris and her apparent willingness to move with Cottrell out of London. I had a strong impression from her manner that the move wasn't to her liking, so why did she agree to go? She was only about thirty-five at the time, and with her qualifications and experience it would not have been difficult for her to find another job. She was shocked at Cottrell's death, of course, but she hasn't shown any sign of the personal grief that you might expect from a devoted servant of long standing mourning the death of her mistress. And there's a certain edginess to the relationship between her and Brand; she made a particular point of emphasizing how much longer she'd been in Cottrell's employ, while Brand appears to regard her as slightly lower down the social scale to herself by referring to her – and even addressing her – as "Norris". Incidentally, Hickson referred to Brand as a stuck-up cow who thought she was in charge of the staff.'

'So although the household at Woodlands appears to run smoothly, not everything beneath the surface is sweetness and light,' Leach remarked, 'plus it seems that everyone either has something they want to hide, or is not averse to backing up a phoney story so long as it's made worth their while.' He made another tick and then turned to Sukey and Vicky. 'Right, let's hear from you two.'

'We wondered what lay behind Pearce's willingness to cooperate as well,' Vicky began. 'Like Tim and Mike, we want to know how he could assure Maggie that Cottrell's death wouldn't affect the money she'd been giving him.'

'And if that was the case, how did he know?' Sukey continued, reading from her own notes. 'Did Lillian Brand give him that assurance? Was she able to buy his silence because she knew about the legacy Cottrell was leaving her in her will, and if so how? If she didn't know what was in the will, was whatever happened at the dinner party that they insist never took place so important that they were prepared to stake their own money? If not, who else could have told him? He's hardly the type you'd expect to have a contact in a solicitor's office.'

'True,' said Leach. 'Can you suggest any answers to those questions?'

'Supposing Brand had occasion to talk from time to time to someone in Fraser's office on her employer's behalf, for example on some routine matters?' Sukey suggested. 'Did she perhaps strike up a friendship with that person? Did he or she tell her in confidence that she was to inherit the bulk of Cottrell's fortune? And did she know that Cottrell was planning to see Fraser and has she any idea why?'

Leach nodded and made more ticks before he turned to DC Osborne, who appeared to Sukey to be a little nervous, as if fearing that any contribution she might make would seem weak compared to her more experienced colleagues. 'How about you, Penny? Have you anything to add to that?'

Penny hesitated for a moment before saying, 'Well, sir, I get the impression from the early reports that Lillian Brand is a stronger, possibly more forceful character than Jennifer Cottrell, whereas Sukey specifically describes Jennifer Cottrell's private persona as "intensely feminine", and I just wondered if there was a lesbian relationship – or at least an attraction on Cottrell's side amounting to love that was strong enough to make her decide to name Brand as her principal heir.'

Leach tapped his pen against his teeth and considered before turning to Sukey and Vicky. 'Did this thought occur to either of you?' he asked.

'No, sir,' said Vicky.

Sukey shook her head. 'Nor me, sir. I'd describe Brand's personality as brisk and businesslike, which is what you'd expect from an efficient PA, but there's nothing about her that struck me as . . . well, *masculine*.'

'Greg?'

Rathbone shook his head. 'It did cross my mind for a moment, sir, but on reflection it seemed unlikely.'

Leach added a note to his list. 'It could be significant,' he said. 'Well spotted, Penny. I think we might ask Fraser if he's ever picked up anything to suggest it. I'll leave that with you, Greg. As to the other points you've all made, they're very sound and call for further investigation, but there's one more that none of you has mentioned so far and I think we need to bear in mind. According to Maggie, she overheard that snatch of conversation on the telephone between Brand and someone else the day before Cottrell was killed. When Brand referred to the possibility of trouble, was it because of something that arose during or after the dinner party? Was it for the same reason that Cottrell called Fraser's office on Monday, the first working day after the party? And we need to check the discrepancy between Hickson's version of what Maggie said to him in the kitchen and Maggie's own.' He put down his pen and sat back. 'Right, Greg, you now have a team of six including yourself and I want you to follow up all these questions and also to organize face-to-face interviews with Cottrell's editor, her agent and the person who handles her PR. You're now in a position to challenge them over the tenth of October story and it will be interesting to compare how the different witnesses react. With any luck you'll come back with enough ammunition to make a serious dent in Brand's statement.'

'I wonder if they've heard about the second murder?' Rathbone speculated. 'Even if they read about it in the papers or saw it on the box I'd say it's unlikely they made a connection with Cottrell's murder, especially as we haven't released Downie's name. I suppose someone might have picked up on the fact that Downie's body was found on the Woodlands estate, but I don't recall seeing any reference to that in the press.'

'That's a point,' said Leach. 'Are any of them based locally?'

'The agent lives in Torquay,' said Rathbone. 'Cottrell's books are published by Handover Press in London so that's where the editor works. The PR woman is based in Oxford, but she used to travel down to Woodlands if she was arranging an important promotion for Cottrell such as a signing tour to coincide with the publication of a new book.'

'So there's a fair chance they won't know about the second murder.' Leach made another note. 'It might be interesting to observe their reactions when you tell them.'

'I take it these interviews won't be under caution, sir?' said Rathbone.

'Not at this stage, but if anyone asks for a solicitor to be present it could be significant, so use your own judgement. Thank you, that's all for now.'

Thirteen

'OK, coffee in interview room one in fifteen minutes,' said Rathbone as he and his newly enlarged team returned to the main CID office. He went to the coffee machine, filled a mug and carried it out of the room.

'He probably wants time to organize his plan of campaign,' Tim Pringle remarked as the rest of them filled their mugs and stood around in a group. 'What's the betting he'll kick off with an interview with Lillian Brand? The fact that Maggie admitted she was instructed to give a false account of the dinner parties will be hard for her to explain.'

Sukey shook her head. 'That's true, but I doubt if he'll want to start with Lillian,' she said. 'We've already agreed that she'll be the toughest nut to crack and I reckon he'll want to start by chipping away at the lesser characters in the cast until we've built up a bigger stick to beat her with.'

'In any case, it wasn't Lillian who told Maggie what to say,' Vicky pointed out, 'it was Mrs Norris and we don't know for certain that it was on Lillian's instructions.'

'That's true as well,' Sukey agreed. 'We've managed to open a chink in their armour by getting Maggie to come clean about the dinner party, so if we can get Hickson, Pearce and Mrs Norris to admit they've been telling porkies, and who instructed them to, it'll open the chink even wider.'

'Yes, I can see what you're driving at,' said Tim. 'It was just . . . I was wondering about Penny's suggestion of a lesbian element in the relationship between Brand and Cottrell. Mike and I don't know either of them but Sukey and Vicky have met them both. On reflection, have you anything to add to what you said just now?'

Sukey shook her head doubtfully. 'Lillian certainly

showed some emotion over Jennifer's death, especially when she was told it was murder, but I would have said it was as much shock as grief. And remember, she'd worked for her for five years when she decided to move to Woodlands so she must have had some feeling for her to agree to go with her.'

'To give it a try, and in return for a substantial increase in salary,' Vicky reminded her.

Sukey nodded. 'That's right, and having moved she simply stayed on. I remember I asked her about that and she said she "supposed she got used to it". So far we haven't turned up anything to suggest she was thinking of leaving. After all that time she was bound to have had some feeling for Cottrell; I can't say I noticed any sign of anything deeper, but of course, she may be one of these people who keep a tight rein on their emotions. What do you say, Vicky?'

'I agree the two women were very different types, but I'd say the arrangement suited them both – Lillian the efficient organizer was exactly what Jennifer the writer with the artistic temperament needed to run her household and ensure that she wasn't bothered with day-to-day details, and Lillian didn't want to lose a well-paid job and a comfortable home. And from what Lillian said they shared some out-of-office interests like theatre and travel and watching films on the telly and so on. But it's certainly surprising that a paid companion cum personal assistant should inherit the bulk of such a large fortune and I agree it would be a good idea to get the solicitor's slant on the relationship. It's interesting that he queried the reason for the bequest at the time Cottrell made the will, and that she didn't want Brand to know about it.'

'Of course, we don't know whether she's told her since,' Sukey pointed out. 'She did deny knowing anything about the will, though,' she added as an afterthought. She glanced at the clock on the wall. 'Right, shall we go and see what the Sarge has got lined up for us?'

They found Rathbone sitting in the interview room, fiddling with his empty coffee mug and contemplating a sheet of scribbled notes on the table in front of him.

'OK, troops,' he said as they entered. 'Here's the programme for the next stage in the investigation. Tim, I want you and Penny to interview Giles Hickson; get him to repeat his recollection of what Maggie said when she threw her wobbly after seeing the police and then throw the alternative version at him – without of course revealing where it came from. We don't want to drop the girl in it, especially as I suspect she's more than a bit scared of her father. Mike, you and Vicky tackle Bill Pearce. Make sure you see him when Maggie's out of the way at Woodlands and of course be even more careful not to let him know we got our information from his daughter. I suspect he'll be the one to sing first as he's not particularly bright and it shouldn't be hard to trip him up. Hickson strikes me as being smarter and therefore probably more capable of thinking on his feet – I think we agreed on that a while ago, didn't we, Sukey?'

Sukey nodded. 'We did, Sarge.'

'Plus Maggie may have accidentally let something slip about the police having questioned her again,' Tim remarked. 'In that case, he'll have had time to think up another version that might or might not be plausible.'

'So be on the lookout for that,' said Rathbone. 'Sukey, you and I will go and have a chat with Paul Fraser. Apart from getting his impression of the relationship between Cottrell and Brand, it'll be interesting to find out the last time his client went to consult him, and what about, and how long ago she made the will leaving almost everything to Brand. He might on reflection be able to make an intelligent guess about why she rang his office asking for an appointment the day before she was killed.' He folded his sheet of notes and stood up. 'Any questions?' There was a general shaking of heads. 'Right, everyone. Get on with it, and keep me in the picture every step of the way.'

While the others went off on their respective assignments, Rathbone called Fraser and Partners and after a short delay an appointment was made for two o'clock that afternoon. 'By the way, Sukey,' he remarked after putting the phone down, 'I remember seeing a reference in one of your reports

that on the day you and Vicky went to Woodlands to interview Mrs Norris and the others you took a quick look round
Jennifer Cottrell's study?'

'That's right, Sarge, but it was as much out of interest
in seeing her working environment as a search for clues to
her death. It appears that she worked sitting at her desk –
incidentally it looks like an antique and was probably used
by the previous owner – and wrote her books by hand. We
looked in the drawers and found hardly anything but reams
of blank lined paper and loads of pencils and a couple of
erasers. Oh, there was a pad of writing paper and a book
of stamps, so presumably she wrote personal letters from
time to time.'

'Was there an address book or a personal phone directory?'

'We didn't see any.'

Rathbone frowned. 'If she wrote personal letters, then
it's unlikely she had all the addresses in her head. For
someone who spent most of her time in the imaginary world
of her own books to have a memory for that sort of detail
would be a bit unusual. And surely she must have made
personal phone calls from time to time, or did she get Brand
to make them for her?'

'There are three land lines to the house – one for business with an extension in both offices and the other with
extensions in both women's private quarters plus one in the
sitting room where they used to watch television or sit and
chat in the evening, but of course neither is private although
they are ex-directory. The third is in the kitchen with an
extension in Mrs Norris's sitting room.'

'So when Jennifer made that call to the solicitor's office,
it's possible Lillian overhead it,' said Rathbone.

'Unless she had a mobile for any personal calls that for
some reason she wanted to keep private,' said Sukey.

'Like making that call to her solicitor,' said Rathbone.
'We'll check on that as well, and I think we'll go and have
a closer look in her study. In fact,' he went on, glancing at
his watch, 'we might as well do it now. There's plenty of
time for a quick trip to Woodlands. We won't give them
advance warning of our intention.'

'Tim and Penny will probably be there already, talking to Hickson,' remarked Sukey as the two of them went down to pick up a car. 'It'll be interesting to see the reaction when we turn up half an hour later.'

In the event it was Maggie who answered their knock and the minute she saw them she gave a little gasp and put a hand to her mouth. 'What's going on?' she asked shakily. 'There's two coppers here already, talking to Mr Hickson. You've not come to arrest me?' she went on in a sudden panic. 'I've told you everything I know, honest. Me dad'll kill me if he finds out I've been talking to you.'

'It's all right, Maggie, it's not you we've come to see,' Sukey assured her. 'In fact, we aren't here to see anybody; we just want to have another look round Ms Cottrell's study. Would you tell Ms Brand we're here, please?'

'She's not here, she went out, and so did Mrs Norris,' said Maggie. 'Miss Brand said she'd be back by about twelve,' she added helpfully.

'Well, we don't want to wait outside for an hour, and I'm sure there'll be no objection if you let us in,' said Rathbone coaxingly. 'In any case, we won't be staying long.'

'I s'pose it'll be all right.' After a momentary hesitation the girl held the door open for them and then closed it behind them. 'D'you know the way?'

'Yes, thank you, Maggie, you go and get on with your work,' said Rathbone and the girl scuttled away, evidently relieved that her presence was no longer required.

The walls of Jennifer Cottrell's study were entirely lined with bookshelves, apart from the tall sash windows and the heavy oak door. The majority of the books looked old; many of them were leather bound and most gave the impression of not having been disturbed for years. In contrast, Jennifer's own books, amounting to some fifty or so titles plus paper-back and large-print editions, occupied several of the shelves closest to the desk, and there was also a considerable number of titles by other contemporary authors.

'I suppose she had to keep up with what the competition was doing,' said Sukey. 'According to what I've read in the papers, writers are very touchy if they suspect a rival of pinching their ideas. They threaten to sue at the drop of a hat.'

Rathbone grimaced. 'Not only writers,' he complained. 'OK, let's have a hunt around. If she had a mobile, the obvious place to keep it would be in her handbag, but we didn't find one there.'

'Or an address book,' Sukey reminded him. 'Vicky and I looked in all the desk drawers, but as you can see, there's very little in any of them apart from writing paper, manuscript paper and stamps. I wonder if she kept them hidden for some reason,' she went on. 'Maybe there were some contacts she wanted to keep private. Or, did someone – in other words, the killer – steal and maybe destroy them because they contained information he or she didn't want made public?'

'In which case there must be someone she mistrusted,' said Rathbone. 'Could this be the reason why she wanted to speak to her solicitor?' He took a last look round the room, closed all the drawers of the desk and made for the door. 'Come on, we've seen all there is to be seen here.' He glanced at his watch. 'I wonder how Tim and Penny are getting on. I doubt if they'll be through with Hickson yet so the best thing we can do is grab some lunch before going to see Fraser.'

'What the hell's this all about?' demanded Giles Hickson as he was escorted into the kitchen at Woodlands and politely invited to sit down. 'I told the sergeant and the woman he had with him all I knew about the day Miss Jennifer died.'

'Yes, we have your statement here, sir,' said DC Tim Pringle. 'Just one or two points we want to check with you again. You were asked about a short conversation between yourself and Maggie that morning. About what time was this?'

'Round about ten thirty, I suppose. I was in the kitchen for my tea.'

'I understand the girl was in obvious distress and evidently told you something, to which you replied, "You'd best forget you heard that, Maggie. It's none of your business." Do you remember?'

'I remember she was getting her knickers in a right old twist, but I can't say I recall every word that passed between us,' Hickson said.

'Do you remember what it was she overheard?'

Hickson shook his head. 'Not exactly, except it was Miss Brand talking on the phone and she was saying something about "trouble". Maggie didn't think anything of it at the time, but when the police turned up the next day she jumped to some wild conclusion that something bad had happened.'

'And she was right, wasn't she?' said Tim.

'Yeah, as it turned out, but even then I didn't see why there should be a connection with the phone call. At the time I thought it was probably something to do with Miss Jennifer's writing affairs and I just told Maggie not to be a silly little cow and to mind her own business. After all, neither of us even knew then why the police were here.'

'And which day did she say this phone conversation took place?'

'I can't remember exactly.'

'Mr Hickson,' Penny interposed, encouraged by a glance from Tim, 'I think you do remember because a moment ago you said, "when the police turned up the next day", implying that the conversation took place the day before the murder.' Hickson looked uncomfortable and remained silent. 'Mr Hickson?' Penny persisted.

He shifted in his chair and said reluctantly, 'I suppose it was the day before the murder. I don't see what difference it makes.'

'All right, let's talk about something else,' said Tim. 'We understand that Ms Cottrell used to give dinner parties for her friends from time to time.'

Hickson shrugged. 'If you say so. How would I know? I was never invited,' he added with a laboured attempt at humour.

'You never heard any mention of such an occasion between the other members of staff – perhaps during the tea break in the kitchen? A discussion of the menu, perhaps, or Mrs Norris telling Maggie she'd be needed to wait at table on such-and-such a day?'

'I suppose there might have been some talk on those lines, but I wouldn't have taken any notice. Anyway, I've got better things to do with my weekends.'

Tim leaned forward and looked Hickson straight in the eyes. 'So you know these events took place at weekends?' he said smoothly.

For the second time, the man looked away in confusion, but quickly made an effort to pull himself together. 'That's when people normally give parties, isn't it? Miss Jennifer worked at her books all week and she was probably tired in the evenings.' Unexpectedly, his features distorted and he put his hands over his eyes. 'She was a lovely lady, and she didn't deserve to die like that,' he whispered.

'Then you'll want to help us find her murderer,' said Tim.

Hickson lowered his hands and raised his head. 'I would if I could, but I can't tell you anything,' he said.

'Can't or won't?' There was a pause. 'Mr Hickson,' the detective continued, 'I believe you know more than you have admitted to us.'

Hickson took a deep breath and said defiantly, 'I'm not answering any more questions. I want to see a solicitor.'

Fourteen

The offices of Fraser and Partners were in Whiteladies Road. After parking in a nearby side street, Sukey and Rathbone went into a café a few doors away where they bought sandwiches and coffee and sat down at a corner table.

'What age is Paul Fraser?' she asked.

Rathbone shrugged. 'Fiftyish perhaps, but it's hard to say. He's got one of those smooth faces that have a kind of ageless look about them. He's starting to lose his hair – which of course doesn't necessarily mean anything. Lots of men start going bald quite early.' A hint of a smile flitted across his own features, suggesting that he derived some satisfaction in his own abundant head of hair despite the approach of middle age. 'Any particular reason for asking?' he added.

'I was just wondering . . . Penny was speculating about the possibility of a lesbian relationship between Jennifer and Lillian, but perhaps we should also consider whether there might be something going between Fraser and Lillian. She must be forty-something so they might be in a compatible age range. Anyway, age seems to matter less in relationships nowadays.'

Rathbone looked dubious. 'I thought we'd already agreed Brand has a very businesslike personality that some might describe as a bit unfeminine.'

'Yes, but being businesslike goes with her kind of job. She might be like her employer – assumes a different persona when she's on duty.' Sukey chewed thoughtfully at her sandwich before saying, 'I know this is pure speculation, but supposing Brand and Fraser are an item? Fraser knows Brand stands to inherit a pile if Cottrell dies. They'd have to keep it very quiet, of course, but . . . could they have hatched a plot between them in which Brand does the killing and she cleans up and—'

'And when the dust has all settled the pair of them run off to the Bahamas on their ill-gotten gains?' Rathbone jeered. 'You don't expect anyone to take that seriously, do you?'

Sukey nibbled at a piece of lettuce from her side salad. 'I suppose I didn't expect *you* to, Sarge,' she said with a grin, 'but should we rule anything or anyone out at this stage? I suppose your money's on Hickson?' she finished, seeing the mockery in his eyes.

'He seems the most likely at the moment, but I'm not putting my shirt on it.' Rathbone finished his sandwiches and drained his coffee cup.

'Wendy Downie seemed the most likely killer of Jennifer Cottrell,' Sukey pointed out.

'Touché,' he admitted, 'but you have to admit you thought so at the time.' He pushed back his chair and stood up. 'Come on, let's go.'

Paul Fraser received them cordially in his office, offered them chairs – which they accepted – and coffee, which they politely declined.

'We'll try not to take up too much of your time, Mr Fraser,' Rathbone began, 'but we think you may be able to give us some help in our enquiries into Jennifer Cottrell's death.'

'Of course, I'll be glad to do anything I can to help catch her killer,' Fraser said earnestly. 'Incidentally, Sergeant, I read a report of the body of another woman being found on the Woodlands estate. Is this a tragic coincidence, or is there some connection?'

'We have an open mind about that, sir,' said Rathbone. 'We are here on another matter entirely. You may recall that at our first meeting I asked who inherited the bulk of the lady's estate. At the time you said Ms Cottrell made a particular point of confidentiality – that is, Ms Brand was not to know she was the heiress until after her death. You also said her reason for the bequest was that Ms Brand was the only person in her employ on whose loyalty she could depend.'

Fraser nodded. 'That's right.'

'When was the will made?'

'Ten years ago last month.'

'That would be about five years after she moved to Woodlands?'

'Approximately, yes.'

'Was it her first?'

'No, it superseded one made about ten years earlier. Before you ask, Sergeant, I have no idea what was in that will as Ms Cottrell had not yet moved to Woodlands and it was drawn up by her London solicitor.'

'Mr Fraser,' said Sukey, 'I wonder if you could cast your mind back to the time the latest will was being drawn up. Apart from the reason for the bequest and the condition of confidentiality, is there anything else that struck you about Ms Cottrell's demeanour when speaking of Ms Brand?'

Fraser pressed his fingertips together and closed his eyes for a few moments. 'She certainly spoke of her with great warmth, in fact, I might say affection,' he said. 'This did not really surprise me; she would hardly have made the bequest to someone for whom she had no personal regard.'

'Have you – or had you at the time – met Ms Brand?'

'At the time, no. I admit to a certain curiosity about her, but it was some while before she had occasion to call here on some routine business for her employer.'

'What was your impression, sir?'

Fraser hesitated and appeared faintly embarrassed. 'To be honest, from the way she was dressed and from her very brisk, almost authoritative manner, she did not appear to be a very feminine woman.'

'In other words,' Rathbone said bluntly, 'it occurred to you that there might have been a lesbian relationship between the two women.'

'Well, yes,' Fraser admitted, 'but I must make it clear, it was only a possibility and nothing occurred at any time later to make it appear . . . well, more than just that.'

'So how often did Ms Brand have occasion to call on you, and for what reason, sir?' asked Sukey.

'For the most part, it was to deliver a contract for a new book or a new edition of a title already published. The usual procedure was for her agent to negotiate the details and send two copies of the document to Ms Cottrell for signature. One copy would come back in due course, signed and dated on behalf of the publisher, and Ms Brand would bring it in for safe keeping in our strong room. Ms Cottrell preferred important documents to be delivered to me personally rather than sent by post.'

'That sounds a little unusual. Surely she had to rely on the post quite a lot of the time?'

'For routine correspondence, I'm certain she did, but for important documents she obviously felt it was more secure.' Fraser smiled and spread his hands. 'We have to accept our clients' little foibles,' he said, almost apologetically.

Sukey nodded. 'Of course. By the way, how often did this happen?'

'Several times a year. Ms Cottrell was a very prolific writer.'

'I presume the document was normally handed to your receptionist?'

'No, Ms Brand would phone in advance to make sure I was there so she could hand it to me personally.'

'So you saw Ms Brand on each occasion?' said Rathbone.

'Yes.'

'Did she give a reason for this?'

'She explained that Ms Cottrell wanted her personal assurance that every contract was put in safe custody; she even insisted on accompanying me down to our strong room while I locked them away.'

'So Ms Brand would make an appointment, come to the office and watch this procedure?'

'Correct.'

'And then return to Woodlands?'

'I usually offered her coffee before she left.' Fraser hesitated and cleared his throat before adding, 'It's normal to allocate half an hour to each client visit, and the locking away of the document would take only five minutes so—'

'So as you were going to charge Ms Cottrell for half an hour anyway it seemed only courteous to offer hospitality to her representative?' said Rathbone smoothly.

'It's normal business practice, Sergeant.'

'Quite. I imagine that over the years you've come to know Ms Brand quite well?'

A guarded expression came over Fraser's face, but he met Rathbone's keen eyes without flinching. 'We've had some quite interesting chats on various topics over the years,' he said, 'more often than not about current affairs. She has some very forthright views,' he went on with a hint of a smile, 'but I can't say we've exchanged many personal details. She did mention a sister in Australia once, and I have the impression that she has no other close relatives.'

'You're certain that she never knew – until you informed her, that is – that she had been Ms Cottrell's heir for a number of years? '

'As certain as one can ever be of anything.'

'And you've never met her other than in a professional capacity?'

'Certainly not!' There was a hint of annoyance in Fraser's tone and he cast a meaningful glance at his watch. 'Sergeant, I am expecting a client in five minutes so if you have no more questions—?'

'Not for the moment, Mr Fraser,' said Rathbone. He got to his feet and Sukey did the same. 'Thank you for your time, you've been most helpful.'

They left Fraser's office and went back through the reception, where Rathbone went over to the desk and spoke to the receptionist, a petite blonde in an advanced stage of pregnancy. 'Just a quick word,' he said, 'was it you who answered the telephone to Ms Cottrell when she rang the day before she was found dead to ask for an appointment with Mr Fraser?'

For a moment Sukey thought the woman was about to burst into tears at the mention of Jennifer Cottrell's name; her face crumpled and she put a hand to her mouth, but she managed to control herself and said, 'Yes, officer, I'll never forget it. It was the last time I—'

'I don't want to distress you,' Rathbone said gently, 'but this could be important. Can you recall how she sounded? I mean,' he continued in response to her questioning look, 'when you explained that Mr Fraser was away, how did she react? Take your time, just try to think back.'

'She sounded very disappointed when I told her he was away and said, "When will he be back? I want to see him as soon as possible," and when I explained that he wasn't back in the office until Friday morning she said, "Oh dear, I really wanted to see him before then." '

'And then what?'

'I offered to make an appointment with Mr Nash – that's Mr Fraser's partner – but she said she had to speak to Mr Fraser personally and it was important so I offered her his first appointment on the Friday. And the next day we heard the dreadful news,' the receptionist faltered as once again emotion threatened to overcome her.

'I see. Thank you very much,' said Rathbone and headed for the door. 'Well, what did you make of Fraser?' he asked as they returned to the car.

'I think he's a pretty smart cookie who would make a good criminal lawyer,' she replied.

He raised an eyebrow. 'Now you come to mention it, you could be right,' he said. 'He knew very well what was in our minds when we questioned him about how well he knew Lillian Brand; he might even have anticipated the line we were going to take.'

She nodded. 'My impression as well. And when you asked him how certain he was that Lillian didn't know about her legacy, he avoided giving a straight answer.'

'Exactly.' Rathbone settled in his seat and clipped on his seat belt. 'Let's get back to the station and see what the others have come up with.'

They found the other four members of the team waiting for them in the CID office. 'Right, let's hear how you lot fared,' said Rathbone. 'You first, Tim.'

'Penny and I only had a few minutes with Hickson, Sarge,' said DC Pringle. 'At first he answered our questions fairly freely until he slipped up over a couple of points and

when we challenged him he clammed up and wouldn't say
another word without legal advice. We offered to bring
him back here and put him in touch with one of our duty
solicitors, but he got stroppy and said he'd make his own
arrangements thank you very much. I told him to come
to the station at noon tomorrow, complete with brief, otherwise we'd pick him up and he could take his chance with
whoever was available here.'

'Not sure that was wise,' said Rathbone. 'I hope for your
sake he turns up. Right, Mike, let's hear from you.'

'Pearce wouldn't say a word without a brief, Sarge,' said
DC Haskins, 'so we brought him in and fixed him up with
Arthur Townsend. They're in interview room two.'

'How long have they been together?'

'About twenty minutes.'

'Right.' Rathbone stood up. 'Tim, you and Penny go and
write your reports. Mike, you and Vicky come with Sukey
and me to see Pearce.'

They found Maggie's father sitting at a table in the interview room beside a shabbily dressed grey-haired solicitor
with a slightly world-weary expression. As soon as Rathbone
had gone through the preliminary formalities Townsend
said, 'Sergeant, I have had a full discussion with my client
and he is prepared to give frank answers to your questions,
but he wishes to begin by stating categorically that he played
no part in the death of Jennifer Cottrell and knows nothing
at all of the circumstances of her murder.'

'We are prepared as things stand at the moment to accept
that assurance on behalf of your client,' Rathbone replied.
'Our concern for the moment is to clear up what appear to
be some inconsistencies in his earlier statement.' He
consulted the papers in his hand before continuing. 'Mr
Pearce, it is a fact, is it not, that when Ms Cottrell enter-
tained friends to dinner it was the practice for your daughter
Maggie to assist with preparing the food and waiting at
table?'

Pearce nodded and muttered, 'That's right.'

'And that when DC Armstrong and DC Reynolds here – '
Rathbone indicated Vicky and Sukey sitting either side of

him – 'called at your house to question your daughter, you admitted them only on condition that you were present. Why were you so insistent on this point? She is not a child and does not need to have a responsible adult with her.'

'She's easily frightened and I wasn't goin' to 'ave 'er bullied,' said Pearce.

'That's the only reason?' Pearce shifted uneasily and glanced at Townsend, who responded with a slightly non-committal gesture with his hands. When Pearce made no response Rathbone said, 'All right, we'll come back to that in a moment.

'Now, referring to these occasional dinner parties, Maggie stated categorically that no such party had taken place at Woodlands over the weekend before Miss Cottrell died.' Again, Pearce muttered assent. 'She further stated,' the detective continued, 'that in fact the most recent time such a party took place was on the tenth of October. Do you remember?'

Pearce shot a nervous glance at Townsend, who this time gave a positive nod. 'That's right,' he repeated.

'And you confirmed her statement that the most recent of such parties had taken place on the tenth of October' – at this point Rathbone leaned forward and emphasized each word by tapping a forefinger on the table – 'and that you particularly recalled the occasion because Maggie brought surplus food home and you enjoyed it together while watching the late-night movie.' Pearce shifted uneasily, nodded, and had to be requested to speak his response for the tape before Rathbone, after referring to his earlier statement and reminding him of the inconsistency concerning the film he claimed they had watched that night, continued, 'We now have every reason to believe that Ms Cottrell gave a party at Woodlands on either Saturday the twelfth or Sunday the thirteenth of November for which your daughter helped prepare and serve the food, that you were aware of this and that you were knowingly giving false information to the police.'

Pearce fiddled with his earring, drew a deep breath and said, 'Yes, Sergeant.'

'Perhaps you would like to tell us why.'

Little by little the story came out: Maggie's brush with Hickson over the phone call she had overheard, and later with Mrs Norris over the quantity of crockery and cutlery in the dishwasher, both of whom had instructed her to 'mind her own business' and tell the false story if questioned, but refused to give any reason. He hastened to assure the detectives that he didn't like the idea of lying to the police, but Hickson had come to see him and promised he'd be well paid to keep his mouth shut if questioned.

'So the real reason why you insisted on being present while Maggie was questioned was to make sure she stuck to the official line?' said Vicky.

Pearce nodded. 'I s'ppose so,' he admitted grudgingly. 'Giles also 'inted there'd be trouble if I wouldn't play ball. I couldn't afford to fall out with 'im 'cos I've depended on 'im for light jobs on the estate since I 'ad to leave Newtons,' he pleaded.

'I understand that was on account of an injury to your back,' Tim observed. 'It doesn't seem to have kept you entirely incapacitated,' he added dryly.

'Like I said, I can do light jobs.'

'I take it you declare such earnings to the social security?'

'Sergeant, there is no need for my client to answer that question as it is quite irrelevant to your present enquiry,' Townsend interposed.

'I'm not entirely convinced of that, but we'll leave it for the moment,' said Rathbone. He stood up. 'All right, Mr Pearce, you can go for now, but we may need to see you again.'

Back in the office, where the other members of the team had just finished their reports, he gave them a résumé of the interview.

Tim whistled and exchanged glances with Penny. 'No wonder Hickson wants a brief!' he said.

Fifteen

'So,' said DCI Leach, glancing round the semicircle of detectives seated before him, 'I see you've made some cracks in their armour. Well done.'

It was Wednesday morning and the team working on the Woodlands Estate case were once again assembled in the SIO's office.

'Small ones, admittedly, sir,' said Rathbone, 'but enough to make it pretty certain that there was a cover-up in which the entire staff as well as the four outsiders – Pearce plus Jennifer Cottrell's three business associates – appear to have colluded. I haven't actually interviewed the financial adviser, but I've spoken to him on the telephone and he's sent me copies of his quarterly reports on Cottrell's portfolio for the past couple of years. In total it represents quite a substantial investment; I've had it vetted by one of our own financial whiz kids and she assures me it appears to have been well managed with no unusual or suspect movements in or out. The FA – his name's Bicknell, by the way – assures me that his client left her affairs entirely in his hands and that she always signed without question anything he sent, such as contracts for the sale or purchase of shares, but otherwise took no interest. He understands she passed his reports to Lillian Brand, who sent formal acknow-ledgements but never passed on any comments from her employer or made any of her own.'

'I see.' Leach made a note on his own file and moved on to the next item on the list on his desk. 'Now, I have the report of your latest interview with Fraser. I see Sukey has raised a tentative point about a possible relationship between Fraser and Brand. Would you like to enlarge on that, Sukey?'

'It was just a thought that came into my head before our
– that is, DS Rathbone's and my – interview with Fraser,
sir,' Sukey said. 'You could describe it as brainstorming I
suppose, but it was something I bore in mind during the
interview.'

'And?'

'All I can say is that he said nothing that would have
suggested that possibility until I asked him if he had ever
met Lillian Brand in other than a professional capacity. For
some reason the question appeared to irritate him.'

Leach turned to Rathbone. 'Was that your impression,
Greg?'

'Yes, sir, but I'd already noticed he was beginning to
watch the clock and it was at that point he said he was
seeing a client in five minutes, so—'

'So that could have been behind the hint of tetchiness?'

'That's what I put it down to, sir.'

'Sukey?'

She hesitated for a moment before saying, 'I'd like to
keep an open mind for the moment, sir.'

'Very well.' Leach made another tick and turned to
Rathbone. 'It seems from your report on the interview with
Pearce that unless he's an exceptionally clever liar – which
according to what you say about him here seems unlikely
– you're inclined to accept his insistence that he had no part
in the murder nor knew anything about the circumstances.'

'Yes, sir, I do accept it,' said Rathbone. 'My opinion is
that like his daughter he's a pawn in the game. There's a
very intelligent brain behind these murders, which rules
Pearce out right away.'

'And that brings us to Hickson,' Leach observed. 'I see
he's been given a deadline of midday today to turn up with
a brief. Not the best decision in the circumstances, Tim –
I just hope for your sake that he keeps to the arrangement.'

The young DC coloured to the roots of his hair and said
nervously, 'So do I, sir.'

'While you're waiting, Greg,' Leach went on, 'I suggest
you use the time to get your team to set up appointments
with Cottrell's editor, agent and PR person.'

'With particular reference to the dinner party they all deny took place, sir?'

'Right. Needless to say, you give them as few details as possible about your reasons for wanting to see them. Your checklist should include: who set up that little gathering and why; what took place; whose decision it was that, if questioned, they were to say the tenth of October was the most recent time they all met and for what reason; who made sure Hickson, Mrs Norris and the Pearces all sang from the same hymn-sheet; and by what means they were persuaded. That should do to be going on with – plus of course anything else that crops up during the conversations that you consider relevant or significant. Oh, one other thing: was it to one of them that Brand was speaking during the conversation that Maggie overheard and if so, what was meant by the reference to "trouble". Got all that?'

Rathbone scribbled in his notebook. 'Yes, sir, I'll get to work on it right away.'

'And be sure to check whether they've been in touch with Lillian Brand or with each other since they first agreed on the cover-up date and, if so, who initiated the contact.'

'Right, troops,' said Rathbone when they re-mustered in the CID office. 'Who fancies a trip to the seaside and who'd like a bit of culture? Sukey and I will go to London to have a chat to Cottrell's editor.'

It was agreed that Tim and Penny should go to Oxford to inquire into the mysteries of Jennifer Cottrell's PR arrangements while Mike and Vicky would visit her agent in Torquay. It was almost half-past eleven by the time the appointments, the one to London for the next day and the other two a day later, were set up. 'Time for a coffee,' Rathbone remarked as he made for the machine. 'When Hickson and his brief arrive we'll assume they've had plenty of time for their preliminary chat so we'll get to work on him straight away. You and I in the front line, Sukey; the rest of you sit in during the interview but remain observers unless any of you wants to make a particular point, in which case you can give me a signal to that effect. Understood?'

'Yes, Sarge,' they all responded dutifully and wandered off to drink their coffee and await Hickson's arrival. But by one o'clock there was still no sign of him. Instead a man who gave his name as Bentley Thorne of Thorne Brothers, solicitors, telephoned at one fifteen asking to speak to the officer who had been expecting a visit from Giles Hickson. DS Rathbone took the call.

'Yesterday afternoon I received an urgent request for advice from Hickson,' said Thorne. 'He wouldn't give any details over the phone except to say that he had to report to police headquarters by midday today, so I arranged an appointment with him at my office here in Portishead at eleven. He left me his mobile number and when he had not arrived by twelve I rang but got no reply. It's now gone one and I decided I should inform you what has happened.'

'That's very helpful, Mr Thorne,' said Rathbone. 'Didn't he give you any information at all about the nature of his request?'

'Only that he insisted it was urgent.'

'Nor where he was calling from?'

'No.'

'I see. Perhaps you'd be kind enough to let me have his number.' After jotting it down, Rathbone said, 'Thank you. Well, I can confirm that we were expecting a Giles Hickson to report here by midday in the company of a solicitor, that we have received no word from him since making the arrangement and that he has not kept his appointment. I may need to call on you later for a statement, sir, but in the meantime thank you very much for the information.'

Rathbone put down the phone and looked round the circle of questioning faces.

'What now, Sarge?' asked Mike.

'Looks like Hickson's done a runner,' Rathbone said glumly. 'Another headache for DCI Leach.' He tapped out a number, spoke for a couple of minutes and put the phone down. 'Back upstairs, folks. He was on the point of going out, so get your skates on.'

There were no formalities or invitations to sit down when they reached Leach's office. 'So Hickson's made monkeys out of you,' he said grimly. 'I'll have more to say about that later. You know what to do, Greg. Circulate a description and issue an order for him to be picked up and brought in for questioning as soon as apprehended. Meanwhile, all of you go to Woodlands right away and question the staff as to what if anything they know about his movements since he was interviewed yesterday. And see if you can get hold of a photograph in case we need to issue a press release. Make sure I'm informed immediately of any developments. Any questions?' There was a general shaking of heads. 'Let Lillian Brand know you're coming and ask her to make sure all the staff who are in today are available to answer a few questions. They may already have realized Hickson's missing and twigged that's what's behind the visit. OK, get moving.'

'Well, Sarge, it looks as if your hunch is spot on,' Sukey remarked as they trooped downstairs again.

'Can you think of another reason why Hickson should vanish, Sukey, unless he's responsible for one or both murders?' Rathbone's mouth twitched in a humourless grin.

'Offhand, no,' she admitted, 'and before you say anything else I don't think there's any likelihood of a Fraser and Lillian show either.'

'Well, you can't win 'em all,' he chuckled. 'Now, when we get there we'll speak to all the staff separately, find out what they know and inform them that any sighting of Hickson is to be reported immediately. You and I will have a chat with Lillian and the others can share Mrs Norris and Maggie between them.'

Rathbone called Lillian Brand, informed her of his intention of bringing his team to Woodlands to interview all the members of staff and asked her to make sure they were all present. She informed him icily that it was most inconvenient as she had an important appointment that afternoon, to which he replied, 'Ms Brand, this is a very serious matter which concerns everyone at Woodlands.'

'May I ask what this very serious matter is?'

'Serious enough to ask you to be kind enough to postpone your appointment.'

After a futile effort to persuade him to arrange his visit
for the following morning, she finally said sulkily, 'Oh,
very well.'

Rathbone put down the phone and said, 'Right, everyone,
if you want a bite to eat on the way I suggest you pick up
a sandwich in the canteen and then we'll get going.'

Fifteen minutes later, with Rathbone and Sukey leading
and the other four behind them in a second car, the team
headed for Woodlands. Maggie, looking even more apprehensive than on their previous visit, admitted them and
escorted them to the kitchen, where Mrs Norris was waiting
for them. It was quickly established that Hickson had not
come in to work that day, whereupon Rathbone, accompanied by Sukey, set off for Lillian Brand's office, leaving
the rest of the team to question the two women.

There was no mistaking the hostility in Lillian Brand's
manner as Rathbone rapped on her office door and entered
without waiting for a summons. He pulled up a chair and
signalled to Sukey to do the same.

'Good afternoon, Sergeant, do sit down,' she said sarcastically. 'You'll excuse me if I don't offer you tea.'

'It's not tea we want, but information,' was Rathbone's
blunt response. 'I asked to interview all the staff, but only
Mrs Norris, Maggie and yourself appear to be present. It's
our understanding that you are responsible for the staff here
at Woodlands, so perhaps you can tell me whereabouts on
the estate Giles Hickson is working this afternoon?'

Lillian assumed a haughty expression. 'I'm not a nursemaid and I don't follow the staff around to make sure they're
doing their work properly,' she said disdainfully. 'I suggest
Norris would be of more help than I can. He normally goes
to the kitchen for tea at around ten thirty and for tea some
time in the afternoon; why don't you ask her?' There was
a rasping edge to her voice – irritation, Sukey wondered,
or could it be nerves?

'At the moment I'm asking you.'

'And I'm telling you I don't know. Have you any more
questions?'

'What time did Hickson go home yesterday?'

'I've already made it clear that I do not keep track of his whereabouts. I assume he went home at the usual time yesterday and arrived at his usual time this morning, but as I had no reason to see him today I was unaware whether this was the case or not.'

'He has not been in touch with you to say he would not be in today – perhaps on account of illness?' said Sukey.

'No.'

'So you were not aware that he has not been seen today and you—?'

'I thought I had already made it clear—' she broke in, but he in turn interrupted her by continuing, 'Have no idea of the reason for his absence?'

'No and no!' she snapped. 'I suggest you question the household staff.'

'Some of our officers are already interviewing both Mrs Norris and Maggie,' Rathbone replied.

'Then I hope they can be of more assistance than I can. For my part, I should like to ask *you*, Sergeant, why you are here asking pointless questions instead of pursuing your hunt for the killer of Jennifer Cottrell.'

'I assure you our presence here is entirely relevant to the case.' There was an edge to Rathbone's own voice that told Sukey he was having difficulty in hiding his frustration. 'For your information, we interviewed Giles Hickson yesterday and he said he needed legal advice. I can now inform you that we gave him until midday today to report to our headquarters in the company of a solicitor. He did not keep the appointment and a little under two hours ago we received a call from a solicitor who told us Hickson had made an appointment with him this morning but failed to keep it. Ms Brand,' Rathbone adopted his favourite tactic of leaning forward and gazing directly into her eyes, 'have you any idea at all why Hickson should consult a solicitor, or why, having made an appointment with one, he should fail to keep it?'

Lillian shifted uneasily under that unwavering stare. 'Why on earth should I?' she said defiantly. 'I'm not his keeper.'

'Isn't that what Cain said when God asked where his brother was?'

She gave a start, but recovered her poise immediately and said angrily, 'What on earth are you suggesting, Sergeant?'

'I'm suggesting that you are not being completely honest with us, Ms Brand. In fact, even if you do not know where Hickson has gone, you either know or at least have a shrewd idea of the reason for his absence. To put it another way, I believe you are covering up for him.'

'How dare you!' Lillian's colour rose. 'What possible reason could I have for doing such a thing?' she demanded indignantly.

'That's what we'd like to know,' Rathbone replied.

She stood up. 'I have nothing more to say. Unless you are going to charge me with an offence, I must ask you to leave immediately.'

'There is no question of a charge at present; we are merely seeking information. I have one more question, so please sit down.' She did so with obvious reluctance. 'Now, I should like you to cast your mind back to the day before Ms Cottrell died. Did you on that day make a telephone call to someone during which you referred to the possibility of some kind of trouble?'

She made an impatient gesture. 'Really, Sergeant, I can make up to a dozen calls during a normal working day. Do you expect me to recall every detail of every one of them?'

'So the reference to "trouble" on that particular day doesn't strike a chord?'

'No.'

'You're sure.'

'Quite sure.'

'Very well, I have no further questions for now, but I must make it clear that we have further enquiries to make, after which we shall want to speak to you again. And in the meantime, please do not leave the district without informing us, and be sure to let us know immediately if you have any further information on Hickson's whereabouts.'

Sixteen

Rathbone and Sukey left Lillian Brand's office and walked along the corridor that Sukey had already dubbed 'the long gallery', resembling as it did – albeit on a small scale – a comparable feature in an historic stately home. As they approached the far end they saw their four colleagues awaiting them on the settle on which they found Lillian awaiting their arrival on the day of Jennifer Cottrell's death.

'Any joy?' asked Rathbone.

'Not from Maggie, Sarge,' said Tim. 'She knows that her dad has already come clean about the date of the dinner party and why they told the phoney story. He obviously didn't know she'd already told us and she's very relieved it's all out in the open as far as they're concerned, but she's adamant they agreed between themselves they wouldn't say a word to anyone else and they've stuck to it.'

'She doesn't seem to have much time for Hickson,' said Penny. 'Without any prompting on our part, she said he fancies himself as a bit of a ladykiller, but went on to make it clear – in no uncertain terms – that he's not her type. The only reason she confided in him about the conversation she overheard was that she was very upset at the time because of the police being here and she had to tell someone. Of course, she didn't know at the time that Cottrell was dead.'

'Did she say why the sight of the police upset her?'

'She admitted, after a bit of coaxing, that her dad had once had "a spot of bother" as she called it with the police – which of course we already knew – but she hastened to assure us that he had a clean record.'

'She told us the reason she panicked when she saw uniformed here on the day of Cottrell's murder was that she thought what she overheard might in some way be connected with the fact that he works at Woodlands from time to time and that Brand had found out about his record and had reported him about something suspicious,' said Tim. 'We told her neither of them had anything to fear from us today and she's beginning to believe that not all police officers are big bad wolves.'

'Going back to Hickson,' Penny said, 'I got the impression Maggie believes he might have had something to do with the other girls not staying at Woodlands very long.'

'I think you could be right,' said Sukey. 'He struck me as a bit of a Jack the Lad the first time we interviewed him. I seem to remember him saying rather scornfully that Maggie wasn't his type either, but maybe that was a bit of face-saving on his part. He might have tried it on with her and been given the brush-off. Maggie might be a bit nervous of the police, but I get the feeling she could see off unwanted attentions without too much difficulty, with or without Daddy's help.'

'Does she know Hickson's gone AWOL?' said Rathbone.

'No, Sarge. As far as she knows he was still here when she went home at three o'clock yesterday, and she hadn't realized he didn't come in today. Not that she seemed too bothered by the fact that he didn't appear this morning, but she did say Mrs Norris seemed surprised he wasn't there.'

'Did you ask her if Mrs Norris mentioned it to Lillian?'

'Yes, and she said it would be Lillian he'd inform if he was going to be absent for any reason but nothing had been said to her – or if it had, she didn't let on to Maggie.'

'OK. Now you, Mike. Was Mrs Norris any help?'

'She claimed to be surprised that Hickson hadn't shown up. He hadn't said anything to her about not coming in today, but she says she hadn't realized he was absent until he didn't show up for his morning coffee.'

'We asked her if she'd made any attempt to find out where he was and she said she hadn't,' said Vicky. 'She said it wasn't up to her to chase round after him and anyway if he'd told anyone it would have been Brand, but if so the message hadn't reached her.'

'And then she went on to say something rather strange,' said Mike. 'What were her exact words, Vicky? I saw you making a note.'

Vicky consulted her notebook. 'She said, "I'm not a party to everything that goes on between those two." '

'I asked her what she meant by that and after a bit of persuasion she said she thought once or twice during discussions about household and estate matters she'd detected what she thought was "a kind of atmosphere" between them. We couldn't get anything more specific out of her and in the end she said, "Perhaps I shouldn't have mentioned it." '

'It's a very good thing she did,' said Rathbone. 'We both have a gut feeling that Brand knows more than she's prepared to admit about Hickson's non-appearance.'

Sukey nodded. 'She got quite ratty when you suggested she might be covering for him, didn't she, Sarge?'

'You can say that again!' said Rathbone dryly. 'After that, I didn't see much point in asking if she had a picture of him. She'd probably have bitten my head off! What about you, Mike? Did you get any personal details from Mrs Norris? Does she know where Hickson lives, and whether he's married or lives on his own?'

'She said very firmly that she has no interest in his private life, but as far as she knows he still lives in the house in Marfield that he shared with his father until the old man died some years ago. She was quite scornful when I mentioned a photograph. "What would I want with a picture of *him*?" she said and gave a sniff as if she had a bad smell up her nose.'

'It seems our man isn't universally loved. I presume we have his address, Sukey?'

'Yes, Sarge, it's in Marfield, but right on the edge of the village.'

Rathbone glanced at his watch. 'Well, we'd normally leave house-to-house to uniformed, but as we're just up the road from Marfield and it's on our way back to the station anyway, we might as well have a quick look round while it's still light. If there's no sign of Hickson and none of the immediate neighbours can help, we'll send a team out tomorrow to cover the whole village. In the meantime I'll apply for a warrant to search the house.'

They returned to their cars and set off. The only address they had was the name of the house – Stony Cottage – and they had to ask at the village shop for directions. By the time they found it – a substantial stone cottage at the end of a narrow lane leading off the main road through the village – the light was beginning to fade, but there was still enough remaining for them to realize that Hickson had no near neighbours. 'We might as well leave the enquiries in the village until tomorrow,' muttered Rathbone, 'but as we're here it won't do any harm to bang on his door. No lights on, but there might be someone else at home.' He switched on the flashlight he had taken from the car, pushed open the gate, marched up the path and pounded on the solid oak door with the heavy iron knocker.

No one was surprised that there was no reply. Rathbone knocked again, then bent down, shone his flashlight through the letterbox and shouted, 'Open up – police!' several times with no result. As he rejoined the others they heard the sound of approaching footsteps and through the gathering gloom saw a middle-aged man approaching. He wore a dark overcoat, a muffler and a grey cloth cap, and a black and white collie trotted along at his side.

'I heard a shout of "police" – is anything wrong?' the man asked.

'I'm Detective Sergeant Rathbone and these are five of my colleagues.' Rathbone held out his warrant card. 'Would you mind telling us your name, sir?'

'Ned Turndall. I'm a friend of Giles . . . is he all right?'

'Do you live in Marfield, Mr Turndall?'

'That's right – School House, next to Dr Blaines.'

'Do you walk this way often?'

'Meg and I often come this way for our evening walk – there's a footpath across the fields behind Giles's cottage and now and again we drop in on him on our way back for a bevvy and a chat. He's usually in at this time, but sometimes he goes out. He must be out at the moment – his truck's there but his car isn't.' Turndall nodded in the direction of an open trailer parked on the verge.

'Have you any idea where he might be now?'

'No, but—'

'But you say he sometimes goes out in the evening. You must have some idea where he goes.'

'Sometimes he goes to the Feathers – that's the pub in the village – for a drink and a game of darts, and I think he goes to the pictures now and again. He likes a bit of skirt, I do know that, so maybe he's gone out with a lady friend.'

'Do you know anything about his lady friends?'

'Why should I? I'm not interested in fancy women. Anyway, we find more interesting things to talk about. Football, for instance – he supports City and I—' He appeared to be about to hold forth on a favourite topic and Rathbone hastened to stem the flow.

'Have you seen him lately, Mr Turndall?'

'Not for a couple of days.'

'Or spoken to him?'

Turndall shook his head. 'I know he's on the phone and he's got one of those newfangled things you carry around with you as well, but I don't even have one in the house. If I don't see him, we don't talk.'

'So when was the last time you saw him?'

Turndall thought for a moment. 'I haven't been this way for the past two or three evenings so it might not have been since the weekend. Look, officer, if that's all I'd like to be going. I'm later than usual and it'll soon be dark. You know where to find me if—'

'Yes, thank you, Mr Turndall, you've been very helpful,' said Rathbone and the man went trudging on his way.

'Bit of luck him turning up,' said Rathbone. 'We might as well go back now; there's nothing to be gained from hanging about here. Make a note of the registration number on the trailer, Sukey,' he added as they retraced their steps. 'It should be the same as the towing vehicle so we can add

that to the description of Hickson. As soon as we get back
I'll see about getting a search warrant for Stony Cottage.
When we come back tomorrow one of you can nip out to
School House in Marfield and see if Turndall can give us
a description of Hickson's car; he probably hasn't a clue
what make it is but he might at least know the colour.'

A little wearily, they returned to their cars, drove back
to the station and made out their reports. DCI Leach had
already gone home, so Rathbone left a brief message
requesting a meeting first thing in the morning. He then
arranged for a party of uniformed officers to carry out house-
to-house enquiries in Marfield the following day and
contacted a local magistrate with a request for a warrant to
search Hickson's house, after which he dismissed the team
until the morning.

The first thing Sukey did when she reached home was
check for messages on her answering machine. There was
just one – from Fergus, and she was touched as much by
the note of concern in his young voice as by his words.
'How are you, Mum?' he began. 'We haven't spoken since
you told me about you and Jim breaking up. Are you OK?
Would you like me to come down at the weekend? Please
call back soon.'

She felt a pang of guilt as she switched off the machine
– not because she had not spoken to Gus for three days, but
because she had hardly given a thought to Jim since the
previous Saturday when he told her he and his ex-wife were
planning to remarry. Looking back, it seemed a lifetime ago
when three days without a word from him would have
seemed like three days lost. Now, she recalled the sense of
liberation she felt when he broke the news. She smiled at
the thought of his embarrassment, and wondered if perhaps
his pride had been a little hurt at her calm acceptance and
warm wishes for his and Tanya's future. Had he been
expecting her to throw a wobbly, to burst into tears, to show
at least some sign of distress?

She took from the refrigerator the evening meal that she
had taken from the freezer before leaving home that
morning, put it in the oven and poured out her customary

glass of red wine. The weather was surprisingly mild for late November and on impulse she stepped out on to the patio and leaned on the balcony, sipping her wine and enjoying the panorama of the city, its buildings dramatically outlined by a myriad lights against the dark backdrop of the sky. A plane droned overhead, its lights winking. She watched its slow descent as it headed for the airport. She felt relaxed, at peace.

She called Fergus on her mobile. 'Got your call,' she said when he answered. 'It'd be great to see you at the weekend. It'll do me good to do some proper cooking for a change – I've been living on instant meals all week. And you don't need to worry about me, honestly,' she went on. 'In fact, I haven't had time to think about Jim; we've been too busy over the Woodlands Estate murders. Unfortunately we've had a setback – our main suspect appears to have done a runner!'

Her son roared with laughter. 'That's the second you've lost in this case! To misquote the immortal Oscar, "to lose one suspect is unfortunate, losing two looks like carelessness".'

'That thought had crossed my mind,' she admitted.

'Let's hope this one doesn't turn up dead like the last one,' he taunted her.

'No problem, there are plenty more to choose from,' she joked back. 'See you Saturday, usual time at the bus station?'

'I'll be there. Ciao!'

Seventeen

When the five DCs working on the Woodlands case mustered on Thursday morning, DS Rathbone greeted them with the information that he had already spoken to DCI Leach. 'I've told him what I'm proposing to do today and he doesn't want to see any of us until we've got something definite to report,' he said. 'He's in a pretty tetchy mood,' he added in a low voice to Sukey as they trooped downstairs to collect their cars. 'It's obvious he's putting Hickson's disappearance down to incompetence on our part.'

Sukey was about to pass on the quotation from Oscar Wilde that she and Fergus had chuckled over when she remembered that literary allusions were not the sergeant's strong point. So she hid her smile and said, 'I hope on reflection he'll accept that it wasn't entirely your fault,' but he merely grunted by way of a reply.

In the yard the party of uniformed officers detailed to carry out house-to-house enquiries in Marfield were climbing into a van. Rathbone spoke briefly to the sergeant in charge and then told his own team to forget about calling on Turndall for a description of Hickson's car. 'The woodies should get that between them in the village while we get on with a search of Stony Cottage,' he said.

The team of detectives parked their cars in the lane leading to Hickson's house. The trailer gave no sign of having been moved and there was no car to be seen.

'Mike, you and Vicky check the outside; the rest of us will go in,' Rathbone ordered. As before, he hammered on the door and shouted through the letterbox before signalling to Tim to force an entry. A few blows with a ram sent the door flying open and the four of them piled in. They found themselves in a small square entrance hall that led into a passage with white-painted doors on each side and a staircase at the far end. The walls were painted a pale biscuit and were hung with a few good-quality watercolours of local landmarks, all apparently by the same artist. A tobacco-brown carpet covered the entire floor area and continued up the stairs. Sukey was immediately struck by the contrast between this dwelling and Rosewood Cottage, where Maggie lived with her father. Although the Pearce's home was clean enough – doubtless thanks to Maggie's efforts – she remembered noticing the cheap rugs on the floors, the shabby furniture and the generally down-at-heel appearance of the place. Stony Cottage gave the impression – heightened as they moved through the various rooms – of having been decorated and furnished by someone with an eye for colour and design.

As if the same thought had occurred to him, Rathbone said, 'D'you reckon he got one of his lady friends to do his decor?'

'Could be,' said Tim. 'She might have made sure he kept it in good order as well,' he added. 'It's all very clean and tidy, almost unnaturally so, not like your average bachelor's pad.'

'He doesn't seem to have been pushed for money,' Penny remarked as they entered the living room. 'Not that there's anything wildly expensive, but it's all very well coordinated,' she went on, casting an appraising eye over the furniture. 'I like the design of those curtains . . . and the view from the French window is superb.'

'OK, we're not planning to buy the place, so let's get on with the search,' said Rathbone impatiently. 'You know what to look for – letters and anything else that might give a clue as to who his friends are for a start, and maybe a personal phone directory. We know he's got a mobile; see if you can find the most recent account so we can check his calls. And any indication that he's had anyone staying here recently. Tim, you and Penny take the upstairs; Sukey and I will do the downstairs. Oh, and by the way, something's just occurred to me. You're right, Tim; it is unnaturally tidy.

Maybe he made a point of putting things away before scarpering, but it could be someone else did it for him.'

'Like who, Sarge?' said Sukey curiously.

'I'm not thinking of anyone special. Perhaps he's a naturally tidy chap and gets someone from the village to do a bit of cleaning for him. To be on the safe side we'll wear gloves and take care when touching anything and get forensics to give the place a going-over.'

As the team scattered to begin the search, Rathbone pointed to a bureau standing against the wall to the left of the French window and said, 'Have a go at that while I tackle the sideboard and bookcase.'

In the top of the bureau were a number of pigeonholes; in one was a chequebook and the others contained accounts from several credit-card companies, all neatly secured in separate bundles by elastic bands, each bearing a pencilled note of the date they were paid. A quick glance through the accounts for the past three months showed that most of the payments were to filling stations or supermarkets, with occasional items from department stores and several from restaurants, none of which she recognized. She put them back and pulled out the top drawer, where she found two manila folders, one containing bank statements and the other accounts from water, gas and electricity companies. Scanning the most recent bank statements she found monthly direct-debit payments to the three utilities and payments by cheque to the various credit cards and a mobile-phone company. She opened the second drawer down; it contained nothing but a prospectus from a local college of further education and another from the Open University. The bottom drawer was empty. She recalled hearing that he had left school early to help his father, the previous estate manager at Woodlands, when his health began to fail. Perhaps he was thinking of studying for a degree, maybe to get a job more in line with his true inclinations.

Another thought struck her. 'Sarge,' she said.

Rathbone put down a book he had taken from the bookcase. 'Found something?'

'I found all these.' She reopened the top of the bureau

and indicated the bundles of accounts, all neatly filed and dated.

'Either he's got a secretary or he's as meticulous in his financial affairs as in his domestic arrangements,' he commented. 'What's special about that lot?'

'Payments to all the people he has regular dealings with appear on his bank statement as made either by cheque or direct debit. There are accounts going back several months from all of them except one – his mobile-phone company.'

Rathbone whistled. 'I get what you're driving at – he's guessed that sooner or later we'll be searching this place so he's taken them with him or destroyed them.'

'That's what I was thinking, Sarge. He's obviously really methodical; you'll see he even checks every item on the credit-card statements and ticks them off.'

'He could have shredded them, I suppose, but there doesn't seem to be a shredder in here. It's no problem; his bank will be able to tell us which mobile system he's on. We might as well take this lot with us.' With a grunt of satisfaction Rathbone took a plastic bag from his pocket, opened it with his gloved hands and held it out while Sukey packed the accounts inside. 'I haven't found anything in the bookcase other than books,' he said after sealing and labelling the bag, 'and the sideboard only contains things like glasses and bottles of booze. Let's have a look in the kitchen.'

Like the living room, the kitchen was immaculate. There was milk, a few items of salad and fresh provisions in the refrigerator; the cupboards were stocked with canned food and cereals and there were several ready meals and packets of frozen food in the freezer. In a rack near the sink were several bottles of red wine; by the back door, which led into the garden, was a cupboard containing a vacuum cleaner and cleaning materials.

'He seems to live quite well,' Sukey commented. 'He eats out regularly too – according to one of the credit-card accounts he visits restaurants several times a month and the amounts suggest he didn't eat alone.'

'Entertaining a lady friend, no doubt,' said Rathbone.

'Perhaps he's taken refuge with one of them.' He went out into the hall and took a quick glance into the cupboard under the stairs, which contained little apart from a few pairs of shoes, an overcoat and an anorak. 'Not much in there,' he commented. 'Let's see how the others have been getting on.'

While he was speaking the other four members of the team appeared and they foregathered in the sitting room to compare notes. 'Well, we've made one interesting discovery,' Rathbone said and told them about the missing mobile-phone accounts. 'I don't suppose you came across them upstairs, Tim?'

'No, Sarge.'

'So what did you find?'

'On the face of it, everything seems normal. His clothes are all neatly put away, either hanging in the cupboard or folded in a chest of drawers in what is obviously his bedroom. We didn't see a suitcase or travel bag of any size, which suggests he might have packed one before leaving, and there's no toothbrush or shaving gear in the bathroom, so it seems pretty obvious he's gone away.'

'As far as having guests is concerned,' said Penny, 'there are just two bedrooms and the second doesn't seem to have been used recently, but in the bed in the main one there are stains that might be semen. If he had sex with his lady friend, and forensics find two separate samples of DNA on the bed linen,' she went on, her voice rising in intensity as she pursued her theory, 'with any luck one of them will be Brand's and that will prove she's been lying. And there's a bottle of Casbah perfume in the bathroom cupboard which is sure to have prints on it.'

'So, we could finally be on to something,' said Rathbone. 'OK, bag up the sheet and the perfume – and be careful to avoid any chance of contamination. Anything else? Right, Mike and Vicky, let's have your observations.'

'There's a small garden at the back that's mostly given over to growing vegetables and all very well cared for,' said Mike. 'There's also a single garage that he seems to use as a workshop and storage for logs and gardening tools and so on rather than to keep his car in. No patches of oil on the floor, for example.'

'It's all very neat and tidy,' Vicky commented. 'There's even a row of hooks on the wall with a clean suit of overalls hanging on one of them.'

'It all seems in keeping with the state of the house,' Mike went on, 'but one thing struck us as odd. On the floor below the hooks is a plastic bin with one suit of dirty overalls in it, and beside it a pair of slip-on shoes. Having heard what a fastidious chap Hickson seems to be, it suggests that when he comes home from work he usually takes off his overalls and drops them into the bin to be washed, and then takes off his boots and puts on the shoes before going indoors. For some reason or other he didn't take off his boots last time he came in.'

'And the dirty overalls could be from the previous day and he never came home on Tuesday night,' said Vicky.

'So how do you account for the stuff missing from the bathroom?' asked Rathbone.

'We don't know, Sarge; it just seems odd.'

Rathbone thought for a moment and then said, 'OK, include it in your report. We'll get back to the station now and see what the house-to-house team have come up with.'

The house-to-house team had a great deal to report, much of which was potentially of value in the search for Hickson. As Rathbone had suspected, Turndall was unable to give any useful information about his car, but this hardly mattered as Hickson was well known to – and on the whole well liked by – many people in the village who were only too willing to talk to the police. The owner of the garage where his car, a grey Honda four-by-four, had recently been serviced was able to confirm that the registration number was the same as that on the trailer; he also gave a description of some damage to the front passenger door for which he had given an estimate earlier in the week.

Hickson himself was variously described as 'a bit of a lad' and 'having an eye for the birds', but no one had been able to find a witness who had seen him in the company of a woman. The impression had apparently been gained more from comments he was apt to make in the bar of the Feathers after a few drinks than from any actual sighting.

'In fact,' said Sergeant Partridge, who had been in charge of the house-to-house team, 'a few people wondered whether all the big talk was a cover-up for the fact that he didn't have much luck with women. One man even went so far as to suggest he might be gay and was scared someone would find out.'

The most promising witness they spoke to was a Mrs Pritchard, who not only went into Stony Cottage once a week to clean and do the laundry, but had also 'noticed' a few things around the house from which she had drawn her own conclusions. When pressed, she appeared reluctant to give details and the young officer who called on her – PC Atkins, known to his colleagues as Tommy – suggested that it might be due to embarrassment and that she might respond more openly if interviewed by a woman.

'She went all fluttery and coy, Sarge,' Tommy told DS Rathbone. 'Sort of nudge-nudge wink-wink, if you know what I mean.'

'She's certainly worth another visit,' said Rathbone. 'OK, thanks, lads, you've given us quite a bit to work on. Let me have your reports ASAP.' Partridge and the uniformed officers dispersed but Rathbone signalled to his team to remain, saying, 'Wait while I have a quick word with the SIO before we break, in case he's got any questions of his own.' He picked up the phone and spoke briefly before putting it down. 'He'd like to see us at two o'clock.' He ran his eyes over some notes he had been taking. 'So,' he said, 'we've got two witnesses so far who haven't yet told us everything they know. Let's try and get a bit more out of them after we've reported to DCI Leach. Vicky, you and Penny go to Marfield and have a chat to Mrs Pritchard. Find out which day she cleans for Hickson, when she last changed his bed linen, how often she washes his overalls and how many she'd expect to find in the bin at her next visit. Mike, you and Tim go to Woodlands and see if you can get Mrs Norris to be more forthcoming about her somewhat cryptic comment about Hickson and Brand – and at the same time see what Brand herself has to say on the subject. Sukey, have a word with Jennifer Cottrell's editor and tell her we're liable to be late for this afternoon's interview. OK everyone? Back here at two with your reports.'

Eighteen

Mrs Pritchard was a short, slight woman with apple cheeks and bright darting eyes. When Vicky and Penny knocked on her door and asked her if she would be kind enough to give them some further help with their enquiries into the Woodland Estate murders, she welcomed them into her neat cottage and plied them with coffee and home-made cakes, all the time chattering away like a cheerful sparrow and evidently eager to talk for as long as they were prepared to listen. She revealed, as she bustled about, that most of her clients were out at work while she was cleaning their homes – 'they know I'm as honest as the day is long so they trust me with their keys' – and was delighted with the opportunity for a chat. It was several minutes before the two detectives managed to pin her down to the subject of their visit.

At the mention of Hickson's name she gave a knowing smile that was almost a wink and said, 'Oh yes, Mr Hickson; he's a funny one, he is.'

'What do you mean, funny?' asked Vicky.

'Well, he's a very tidy gentleman for one thing.'

'You find that unusual?'

'Gentlemen living on their own without a woman to tidy up after them tend to be a little careless with their things and leave them lying about,' she said with an indulgent smile. 'Not Mr Hickson. He's very fussy about all sorts of things. Never comes into the house in outdoor shoes ... told me on day one I have to change into my slippers before I come in. He takes off his overalls and his boots in the garage so's not to bring dirt indoors. Oh yes, very particular is Mr Hickson.'

With very little encouragement and no sign of the reticence reported by PC Atkins, she was only too ready to answer their questions. Her regular day for cleaning Stony Cottage was Friday – 'I think he likes to have it all spick and span in case he has any *visitors*,' she said, putting a meaning emphasis on the last word. 'Not that I ever *saw* anyone,' she assured them in response to Vicky's request for elaboration, 'but of course I wouldn't, would I? I mean, he's always at work when I'm there, but – ' she leaned forward, her eyes darting from one to the other – 'you can always *tell*, can't you?'

'Tell what?' said Vicky.

'When someone's been in a house . . . someone besides the person who lives there.' She pursed her lips and gave a mysterious nod, at the same time refilling their coffee cups without asking. It was evident that she wanted to milk the interview for all it was worth. 'Maybe you wouldn't know yourselves, but when you've had my experience of cleaning for people—'

'How do you tell?' asked Penny.

'You *notice* things.'

'What sort of things?

'Things that aren't in their usual place, for example. Now, Mr Hickson, he's what I'd call a creature of habit. "A place for everything and everything in its place," my mother used to say, and that describes Mr Hickson to a T. And I can remember times when certain things were in different places and I'd say to myself, "Aha, Mr H. has had a visitor." '

'Can you say what kind of things had been moved?'

'Sometimes it would be things in the kitchen – saucepans, cooking utensils and things like that. And there's something else I've noticed from time to time—'

'Yes?' Penny prompted as Mrs Pritchard paused, coffee cup held dramatically aloft.

'In the bathroom . . . a different *smell*!' she said in a stage whisper.

'How do you mean – different?'

'Not the kind of smell that's usually in his bathroom – like soap and aftershave, that sort of thing.'

'Do you mean perfume?'

'Yes, I suppose you could call it that. Fancy stuff, not the sort a man uses. And sometimes there's been –' she broke off and wrinkled her sharp little nose in apparent disgust – 'a different *kind* of smell . . . in the bedroom. Maybe you don't know what I'm talking about, you being single ladies,' she added after searching glances at the women's left hands, 'but I can tell you, I always put gloves on to change his bed linen.'

'Are you suggesting he sometimes had a woman visitor?' asked Vicky.

'Well, what else could it mean?'

'Do you happen to remember any particular time recently?' asked Vicky.

'Now, it's funny you should say that.' Mrs Pritchard's bright eyes lit up. 'I'm pretty sure it was last Friday. I remember saying to myself, "I do believe Mr H. has had his lady friend here again." '

'When you say "lady friend", does that mean you think it's always the same one?'

'Well, it's always the same smell, perfume that is, in the bathroom.'

'Going back to last Friday, did you change the sheets that day?'

'Of course, like I do every week.' It appeared, from Mrs Pritchard's slightly scornful smile, that while she would not expect respectable 'single ladies' to recognize the smell of semen, she had assumed they were familiar with the procedure for changing bed linen in civilized households.

'Have you seen or spoken to Mr Hickson since Friday?'

'No.' The woman's eye went to the clock on the mantelpiece. 'I don't want to rush you, ladies,' she said with evident regret, 'but I've just realized, I'm due at my next job in fifteen minutes.'

'We have just one more question,' said Vicky. 'What happens about Mr Hickson's laundry? Do you do it and if so, at his house or do you take it home?'

'I don't take in washing.' Plainly she took the suggestion as an affront. 'I put his soiled things into a bag and take it to the laundry on my way home and collect it and bring it back the next week.'

'His overalls as well?'

'Yes, although in a separate bag, of course. He leaves those in a bin in the garage, but everything else goes in the linen basket in the bathroom.'

'How often does he change the overalls?'

'It depends – once or twice a week depending on how dirty they get.'

'Well, thank you, Mrs Pritchard, you've been really helpful. If you should hear from Mr Hickson, will you ring this number and let us know?' Vicky held out her card.

The woman hesitated before taking it. 'He's not in any trouble, is he?'

'We need to talk to him, that's all.'

DCs Tim Pringle and Mike Haskins arrived at Woodlands and parked at the end of the drive. Tim was about to knock at the front door when it opened and Mrs Norris appeared. She was evidently on the point of going out; she was dressed in a smart red woollen outdoor coat and a grey fur hat, a black leather handbag swung from her shoulder and she had what looked like a car key in her gloved hand. At the sight of the two detectives she appeared startled; she gave a gasp, opened her mouth as if about to speak and then shut it again.

Tim gave a friendly smile and said, 'Good morning, Mrs Norris. It seems we've come at an awkward time. We'd like a word with Ms Brand, if she's in, and then—'

'She went out half an hour ago and I've no idea when she'll be back,' the housekeeper replied tartly.

'Never mind, we can see her another time. I see you're about to go out as well but I wonder if you could spare us a few minutes?'

'There were two of your people here earlier on and I told them everything they wanted to know,' she replied without returning the smile. She pulled back the sleeve of her coat and made a great show of consulting her watch. 'I'm meeting my daughter in Bristol,' she said hurriedly. 'We're going shopping in the Galleries and then having something to eat before going to the theatre and—'

'This won't take long,' said Tim, 'but if you're anxious not to keep your daughter waiting perhaps you could call her before we start to let her know you might be a little late.'

After a moment, when she appeared to be deciding whether or not to comply, she reluctantly stood aside and admitted them, but made no attempt to invite them beyond the hall or to sit down. 'It won't matter, Kate's usually late anyway,' she muttered. 'We might as well get on with it.'

'So why don't we find somewhere a little more comfortable?' said Tim.

'This is as good as anywhere, I suppose.' She sat down on the settle and they had no option but to do the same. There was a short silence, broken by the sound of a vacuum cleaner starting up; evidently Maggie's services were still required.

'Well? What do you want to know?' said Mrs Norris.

'We'd like you to cast your mind back to the day your employer, Ms Jennifer Cottrell, died,' Tim began. 'You were interviewed on that day, first by Detective Sergeant Rathbone and Detective Constable Reynolds, and later by Detective Constable Armstrong, accompanied by Police Constable MacCall. No doubt you remember?'

'Of course.'

'According to your statement, you have been in Ms Cottrell's employ longer than either of the other full-time members of her household, namely, her secretary/companion Ms Lillian Brand and her estate manager Giles Hickson.'

She gave an impatient movement of her head. 'That's right. I really don't see why we have to go over all this again.'

'And during that interview,' Tim continued as if she hadn't spoken, 'the officers gained the impression that relations between you and Ms Brand were not exactly cordial.'

A guarded look crept into the housekeeper's eyes. 'I'm sure I don't know what gave them that impression. I'm sure I never said anything against Miss Brand.'

'It was perhaps your body language more than anything you said. And later, when DC Reynolds asked you why village girls who came daily to do the housework seldom stayed very long, you seemed unwilling to give a definite reason.' There was another silence, but this time it was left to the detective to speak again. 'Mrs Norris, will you tell us why you think a number of village girls left Ms Cottrell's employ after only a few weeks?' Again there was no answer. 'Did you find their work unsatisfactory?'

'Not that I remember.'

'Did they complain about anything – or anybody – here?'

'Not to my knowledge.'

'Did it perhaps occur to you that they might have left because another member of the staff paid them unwelcome attentions? Giles Hickson, for example?'

Mrs Norris gave a slight shrug. 'All right, it did cross my mind. I've always thought he had an eye for a pretty face, but I never saw anything untoward between him and any of the girls. Maybe he said something they took exception to . . . I don't know. I don't want to be unfair to the man.'

'What about Maggie? How long has she worked here?'

'Just over a year.'

'It would seem that she never took exception to anything he said, then?'

Mrs Norris appeared to relax. 'I imagine that girl can take care of herself,' she said with a hint of a smile. 'In any case, Giles is friendly with her dad, and it would be more than his life's worth to take liberties with his daughter.'

Mike took up the questioning. 'Now, DC Armstrong and I asked you yesterday if you knew of any reason for Hickson's non-appearance. You replied that it would be Ms Brand he would inform if he intended to be absent and you had heard nothing from her. We both noticed a hint of, shall we say, disparagement in your manner when making this statement, and you went on to say,' he quoted from the open notebook in his hand, ' "I'm not a party to everything that goes on between those two." We'd like you to tell us exactly what lay behind that remark.' Once again, the housekeeper remained silent, and after several seconds Mike said sternly, 'Mrs Norris, we wish to speak to Mr Hickson; he arranged to come to the station to be interviewed, but he failed to keep that appointment. He is not at work and he is not at home. I must remind you that we are conducting a murder inquiry and it is an offence to withhold information from the police,' he added as she remained silent. 'Do you understand?' She nodded. 'So, once again, what prompted that slightly cryptic remark?'

'All I can say is,' she began with evident reluctance, 'I've seen him go into her office now and again and wondered . . . but on reflection it was probably to talk about something that needed to be done on the estate. Now I come to think of it,' she hurried on, 'if she wanted to discuss anything with me she never came down to the kitchen – I always had to go to see her. It was probably the same with Giles.'

'Would you say she considered herself a little, shall we say, superior to the rest of you?'

Her mouth set in a firm line. 'I'd rather not say.'

'You're sure there's nothing else you want to tell us?' said Mike.

'Quite sure.'

'All right – one last question. Have you any idea where we might find Giles Hickson?'

'None at all.'

'Can you suggest anyone who might have that information?'

'I thought I had made it clear that I know nothing about his private life, and I have no idea who his friends are.' She consulted her watch and stood up. 'I really must go now to meet my daughter. If you want to see me again, perhaps you would have the courtesy to make an appointment.'

'Thank you for your time,' said Tim politely, receiving a stony stare in response. She held the door open for them before stepping outside after them, closing it behind her and disappearing behind the house.

'What d'you reckon?' asked Tim as they went back to their car. 'She seemed pretty jumpy when we arrived and I'm pretty sure she hasn't told us everything she knows.

Mike nodded. 'Me too,' he said. 'If she's questioned again it will have to be under caution.' He buckled his seat belt and inserted the key in the ignition but without starting the engine. 'We'll wait till she leaves and see where she goes,' he said. 'In any case, it won't hurt to see what she drives.'

A few moments later a silver-grey Toyota appeared with Mrs Norris at the wheel. Ignoring their politely raised hands as she passed them, she turned into the lane and drove at a moderate speed through the village until she reached the main road, after which she quickly accelerated. They followed at a discreet distance until it appeared that her destination was the main shopping mall in the city centre, after which they abandoned the pursuit.

Nineteen

The offices of Handover Press were situated in a modern office block in Richmond. DS Rathbone and DC Sukey Reynolds were directed to the fourth floor, where a woman, whom Sukey judged to be in her early forties but at first sight looked younger, greeted them as they stepped out of the lift. She had shoulder-length straight blonde hair falling on either side of a heart-shaped face, and blue-grey eyes behind a fashionable pair of dark-framed spectacles.

'Isla Bain, Jennifer Cottrell's editor,' she said in response to Rathbone's introductions. Despite the smile that accompanied her words, Sukey sensed that she was not entirely at her ease. 'My office is just along the corridor,' she continued. 'Follow me, please.'

She ushered them into a small room with a tall window overlooking the river. All the available wall space was lined with shelves crammed with books, leaving just enough room for a computer workstation. More books were stacked on the floor, leaving barely enough space for two additional chairs.

'Please sit down,' she went on. 'I apologize for the clutter; this lot are waiting to be collected for despatch. Would you like some tea?'

'No, thank you,' said Rathbone without giving Sukey a chance to speak. 'We don't want to take up any more of your time than is strictly necessary, so I'll come straight to the point. As you know, we are investigating the murder of Jennifer Cottrell.' She gave a brief nod. 'Now,' he resumed after a glance at his notebook, 'according to the statement you made on the telephone two days after her death, the last time you saw her was on the tenth of October, when you, her agent and her PR manager, along with her companion Ms Lillian Brand, were guests at a dinner party at Woodlands. Do you still stand by that statement?'

A wary expression crept into Isla Bain's eyes and she hesitated. As Sukey remarked later to Rathbone, she seemed to lose her youthful look; plainly she was on her guard. After a moment she said, 'It's over a month ago and I have a very crowded diary.'

'So perhaps you'd like to refer to it now?'

She swivelled round in her chair and began searching among the papers on her desk, then pulled out first one drawer and another before saying, 'That's funny, I can't seem to lay my hand on it. I must have left it somewhere – what a nuisance, I'm lost without it.' The Scottish accent, barely noticeable until now, seemed to strengthen in proportion to her agitation.

'What about your handbag?' Sukey suggested.

'Oh aye, it's probably in there.' She rummaged for a few moments in a capacious leather bag, apparently without success. 'I can't understand it,' she muttered, 'I know I—'

'It can't be far away,' said Rathbone. 'You must have consulted it recently as you were obviously expecting us at the time DC Reynolds suggested when she called you earlier today.'

'The time was only put forward by an hour so there was no need—' she began lamely, but Rathbone cut short her excuses.

'Ms Bain,' he said sternly, 'when I spoke to you two days after Jennifer Cottrell's death to ask for some information about this dinner party, you told me, *without hesitation*,' he paused for a moment, 'I repeat, without hesitation, that it took place on the tenth of October. At the same time you said that the reason for the party was to celebrate the completion of a new book. That conversation took place exactly a week ago, and I imagine that you have in the meantime relived many times – and probably discussed with your colleagues – the shock you undoubtedly experienced at Ms Cottrell's death. You are now asking us to believe, firstly that you cannot recall with any certainty the last time there was a party at Woodlands, and secondly that you cannot lay hands on your diary. That's a rather convenient coincidence, don't you think?'

'Coincidences do happen from time to time,' she said in a voice that lacked conviction.

'Quite so, but in this case I put it to you that you are deliberately trying to mislead us, and I must remind you that knowingly giving misleading information to the police, especially in a murder case, is a serious matter. Ms Bain,' he continued as she remained silent, 'we have now received information from two sources that the last time there was a party at Woodlands was either Saturday the twelfth or Sunday the thirteenth of November – that is one or two days before Ms Cottrell's death, and that you were among the guests. And it so happens,' he went on, 'the same date – the tenth of October – was quoted to me by all the other guests at the party and confirmed by members of Ms Cottrell's staff when we were making our initial enquiries. So you all gave the same earlier, but incorrect, date, which makes it appear that you agreed between you to conceal the truth. Have you anything to say about that?'

For a moment she seemed to be on the verge of tears. Her shoulders sagged and she bit her lip, took off her spectacles and dabbed her eyes with a handkerchief. Then she straightened herself and looked Rathbone in the eye.

'I thought it was a bad idea all along and I said at the time we'd never get away with it, but by then it was too late,' she said. 'All right, I'll tell you everything, but we were only trying to protect Jennifer. I swear I had nothing to do with her death and I can't believe any of the others—'

'We'll leave them to answer for themselves, shall we?' Rathbone cut in. 'So perhaps you'd like to begin by telling us exactly when this party took place and whose idea it was to call it.'

'Lillian phoned earlier in the week to say Jennifer had told her to arrange it as she had something important to tell us. It was for lunch on Sunday the thirteenth.'

'And you attended along with Ms Cottrell's agent and the lady who handles her PR – and of course Ms Brand?'

'That's right.'

'And what was this something important?'

Isla spread her hands in a gesture of bewilderment. 'We couldn't believe it – we thought at first it must be Jennifer's bizarre idea of a joke, although it wasn't like her. Up to then she seemed to be her usual self; we'd had a nice meal and were drinking our coffee when she suddenly said, "Right, now let's get down to business. I know what you've been up to, all of you." She then launched into a tirade, accused Handover Press of falsifying her sales and fiddling her royalty accounts and making similar accusations against her agent, Robbie Lang, and Lizzie Holt, who handles her PR. We all sat there with our mouths open. I remember Lillian saying something like, "You can't be serious, Jennifer. You know I keep a very careful eye on your affairs and I've never had any reason to think—" and Jennifer said, "Don't lie to me, I know what you've been up to as well." Then she stood up and said, "It's all going to be in my next book – and as for you lot, you're all fired," and stalked out of the room.'

'And what happened then?' asked Rathbone.

'We sat there for a while in utter bewilderment, trying to figure out what had come over her. I told the others that so far as I knew there was nothing whatsoever in her allegations against Handover Press. The others gave similar assurances and Lillian said Jennifer had never said anything to her to indicate that she suspected us – or her either – of any kind of deceit or dishonesty, and she'd certainly never hinted that she was going to put her allegations in a book. It came out of the blue and we wondered if she'd had some kind of brainstorm. Lillian said she'd keep an eye on her for the next few days and let us know if she showed any other signs of . . . well, paranoia I suppose you could call it.'

'Go on,' Sukey prompted gently as Isla fell silent.

'The next thing that happened was that Lillian rang on Tuesday morning to tell us there'd been an accident and Jennifer had drowned in her bath. She was in a terrible state; she said she and the housekeeper, Mrs Norris, had dragged her out of the water and tried desperately to revive her but they couldn't so they'd called the ambulance and the paramedics said she was dead and they were waiting for the doctor.' Isla lapsed once more into silence and sat staring into space for some moments, as if reliving the shock on hearing the news.

'And what was your reaction to that?' asked Sukey.

She gave a little start. 'Sorry, I was miles away. As you can imagine, I was absolutely stunned. My first thought was that possibly Jennifer really was unbalanced and had killed herself, but some time later Lillian rang again to say the police said she'd been murdered. It didn't make sense – who on earth would want to kill Jennifer? Lillian said the police had asked a lot of questions about her lifestyle and the way she ran her household including her social life. She'd mentioned the little parties she gave from time to time to celebrate the publication of a new book and thank us for our work on it. They wanted to know when was the last time and what were we celebrating. Lillian said she'd decided on the spur of the moment not to say anything about the latest one because if the media got to hear of Jennifer's outburst there'd be hordes of journalists asking loads of questions and that would mean a lot of adverse publicity and possibly suggestions that one of us might be responsible – I remember her saying, "You know what the paparazzi are like" – so she gave them the date of an earlier party. She asked us to say the same if we were questioned and said she'd make sure the rest of the staff did as well.'

'Did she give you any indication as to what she was going to say to them?'

'I wondered about that,' Isla replied. 'As far as I remember, she just said, "Don't worry, just leave them to me." You must believe me,' she went on earnestly, 'although we all felt with hindsight that it wasn't a very bright thing to do, we understood why Lillian had done it and we had to back her up. In any case, we wanted to protect Jennifer's reputation. We've all worked with her for years and we can't think who—' Her voice wavered and she brushed more tears from her eyes.

'It didn't occur to you that you might be protecting a murderer?' said Sukey.

Isla shook her head. 'I suppose . . . I just didn't think,' she said.

'Ms Bain,' Sukey continued, 'I imagine you and your colleagues at Handover Press have made enquiries through your contacts in the publishing world to try and find out if Jennifer Cottrell has offered elsewhere a book you knew nothing about – a book containing some damaging revelations?'

'What do you think? Of course we have, and so have Robbie and Lizzie, but so far we've drawn a blank.'

'No doubt, if such a book were published, it could represent a considerable threat to your company's reputation – and that of her other business associates?'

Isla hesitated before replying, 'That's a hypothetical question and I don't think I can give an answer. There might be questions of possible libel actions – I'd say it could be difficult to find a publisher.'

'I can understand that,' said Rathbone, 'but what would be the effect on your company if Ms Cottrell, had she lived, started selling all her work elsewhere? She is a prolific writer whose books are regularly in the bestseller lists.'

'It wouldn't have affected our contracts for her existing books, but of course we'd lose out on future titles.'

'Naturally,' he said, 'and it would be illogical to kill a writer merely because she was threatening to sell future books to another publisher. But going back to the possibility of a particular book containing some very damaging revelations which would cause financial harm and possibly lead to criminal proceedings against certain companies or individuals – that would be a very different state of affairs, wouldn't it?'

From the look of horror that came over Isla's face it was evident that she had grasped the implication of his question, but she was spared the need to answer immediately by a ring from Rathbone's mobile.

With a gesture of apology he stepped outside the office and the two women waited in silence as he moved out of sight and hearing. When he returned he said, 'Ms Bain, you've had time to consider my question. May I have your answer, please?'

'I understand what you're saying, Sergeant,' she said in a voice that shook. 'All I can do is repeat my assurance that I had nothing to do with Jennifer's death.'

'Very well, we'll leave it there for the time being. I'm afraid we have to end this interview as there has been an unexpected development in the case, but we shall certainly want to speak to you again. Thank you for your time.'

As he and Sukey were on their way back to the car he said, 'That call was from the station. Hickson's car has been found abandoned on the drive of a derelict house in a side street near Clifton Down train station. Enquiries among the locals so far indicate that it was first noticed some time yesterday. Forensics are on the scene and a recovery team is standing by.' He gave a sour chuckle. 'It could have been worse; imagine if it had been left at the top of a multi-storey. Getting a low-loader round those tight corners would have been a challenge!'

Twenty

'I knew letting Hickson make his own arrangements was a mistake,' muttered Rathbone as he clipped on his seat belt. 'A bad decision on young Pringle's part; he should have taken the bugger down to the nick and let him call his brief from there, but once he was off the hook it was too late to do anything about it. He's had a forty-eight-hour start and he could be anywhere. Abroad even – we didn't find a passport when we searched the house. He must be laughing his head off, thinking how clever he's been to outsmart us.'

'It confirms what you said about there being a very shrewd brain behind all this, Sarge,' said Sukey. 'I remember we agreed when we first interviewed him that Hickson came across as an intelligent, well-educated chap. I'll bet he could hardly believe his luck at being given such a golden opportunity to do a runner. He probably—'

'Went straight home,' Rathbone continued as Sukey broke off to negotiate a roundabout, 'packed a bag, drove into town, dumped his car, maybe had a meal somewhere and then took a bus or a train, or a plane even – but where to?'

'He'd need money if he was planning to go far,' she pointed out. 'He could pay cash for a bus or train ticket, but if he was leaving the country he might have used a card . . . and maybe bought currency at the airport.'

'And on top of all that we've got yet another new line of inquiry to follow,' Rathbone went on gloomily. 'Was that a brainstorm on Jennifer's part or did she have genuine cause to suspect her associates of ripping her off? Was she really writing an exposé . . . the sort of thing that might cause them to panic? We'll have to go over her study and private apartments with a toothcomb to see if we can find a hidden manuscript. Ye gods, what a can of worms we've uncovered this time!'

They continued to speculate as they joined the motorway and headed west. It was the height of the rush hour when they reached Bristol and well after seven o'clock when they got back to the station to find a message awaiting them. 'The SIO wants to see you two, Sarge, and he's not best pleased,' a young uniformed constable informed them.

'Don't blame him,' muttered Rathbone as he and Sukey made their way upstairs.

DCI Leach was not alone in his office. DCs Tim Pringle and Penny Osborne, both looking somewhat crestfallen, were standing in front of his desk. They turned their heads as Rathbone and Sukey entered; there was a hopeful look on both their faces, as if expecting their sergeant to say something in their defence, but they were soon disillusioned.

'This is a bit like "Ten Green Bottles",' said Leach. His grim expression belied any hint of humour in the words. 'I'm beginning to wonder how many suspects are going to slip through our fingers or get themselves murdered before we close this case – if we ever do. I suppose it was your idea to let these two rookies interview Hickson for a second time, Greg?'

'I'm afraid it was, sir,' Rathbone admitted. 'I told them afterwards it was a bad idea to leave Hickson to make his own arrangements instead of bringing him down to the station, but by then the damage was done.'

'Not necessarily,' said Leach. 'If you'd gone straight to his house when you'd learned what a bloody cock-up they'd made of it, it's odds on you'd have found him packing his bag and you could have nicked him on the spot.'

Rathbone nodded. 'Point taken, sir. As to Pringle and Osborne, all I can say is I hope they've learned their lesson.'

'I hope you all have. To bring you up to speed, the minute the news came in about the discovery of his car we sent out a nationwide alert including airports. It won't surprise you to hear there's been no sighting so far. Now, I understand you and Sukey have been interviewing Cottrell's editor, so as you're here you might as well give a preliminary report.'

'Well, sir,' Rathbone began, 'she tried at first to stick to the script, but as soon as we told her we had evidence that she and the others had been telling us a load of porkies she broke down and confessed.' He gave a brief résumé of the interview with Isla Bain.

Not unexpectedly, Leach's reaction to her revelations was the same as Rathbone's own, although expressed in what was, for him, unusually colourful language. 'So what's your next move?'

'The agent and the PR woman are being interviewed tomorrow, sir, and will no doubt be ready with the same story. It's possible of course that Isla's already let them know she's spilled the beans.'

'I'd have said it's a dead cert,' said Leach. 'What about Brand? I seem to recall a suspicion on your part that she might be covering for Hickson.'

'I did put it to her, sir, but it was a shot in the dark and there was no evidence. She emphatically denied it, of course.'

'Well, she would, wouldn't she? Has she been seen today?'

'Unfortunately, she was out when Haskins and Pringle called. We'll get her tomorrow even if we have to issue a warrant for her arrest. They've been pulling the wool over our eyes long enough.'

'You can say that again,' Leach grunted. 'You'd better see Brand yourself, Greg – under caution this time – and if she wants a brief you know what to do. And I suggest DCs Pringle and Osborne sit in as they're obviously badly in need of a refresher course in interviewing. The house-keeper will have to be seen again in the light of this new situation. Meanwhile, we'll wait for forensics to complete their report on the vehicle, although I'm not hopeful it will tell us much.' With an impatient gesture he closed the open file on his desk and pushed it into a drawer. 'All right, give me a further update ASAP – sooner if possible. And try not to lose any more suspects.'

'Should we see Lillian right away, Sarge?' asked Sukey as, feeling considerably chastened, they left Leach's office. Rathbone considered the question and consulted his watch. 'It's nearly a quarter to eight,' he said morosely, 'and I'm darned if I want to risk another fruitless visit to Woodlands. Just the same, I suppose you'd better check if she's back.'

Sukey called the Woodlands number and waited. After a few moments she said, 'There's no reply, Sarge – shall I leave a message?' He gave an emphatic shake of the head and gestured to her to break the connection.

'Let's think for a moment,' he said. 'Brand was already out when Mike and Tim called and spoke to Mrs Norris, who claimed to have no idea where she'd gone or when she'd be back. That number you called, Sukey; I imagine that would be the one to the office with extensions to the private apartments?'

'That's right, Sarge.'

'I remember you mentioned there was a phone in the kitchen. Do you happen to have that number?'

'Yes, Sarge.'

'Try it. If Mrs Norris is there, I'll have a word with her.'

Mrs Norris was there. Sukey handed over the phone and Rathbone, after apologizing for calling so late, said, 'Has Ms Brand returned yet? . . . I see . . . have you spoken to her since my officers called this afternoon? . . . No? . . . All right, thank you. I'll ring again in the morning.' He snapped off the phone and handed it back to Sukey. 'You'll have gathered that according to Norris she's not there and she hasn't been in touch. Norris thinks she's at the theatre and may not be back until late. Does that tie in with what she told you and Mike Haskins, Tim?'

'She said Ms Brand was out and she didn't know when she'd be back, Sarge,' said Tim. 'She didn't mention the theatre, but she wasn't best pleased at being delayed when she was just going out herself, so maybe she didn't feel like being helpful.'

'She sounded amenable enough on the phone, but I doubt whether she was telling the truth when she said Brand hasn't been in touch.' Rathbone thought for a few moments, frowning, and then said, 'If Brand carries a mobile – which I'd say is almost certain – I think we can assume that by now she's heard from Isla Bain and it's ten to one she's warned Norris to expect a call from us. If she really has gone to the theatre and maybe supper afterwards, it could be midnight by the time she gets back to Woodlands.' He thought for a few more moments before coming to a decision. 'Right, Sukey, you and I will present ourselves at Woodlands first thing tomorrow morning. We'll bring her down to the station, caution her and let her call a brief from there if she wants to. If she cuts up rough, too bad. That means you and I get here by eight o'clock – OK?'

Sukey hesitated. 'If you say so, Sarge,' she said doubtfully.

'Right, let's get home.'

'What about us, Sarge?' asked Tim Pringle tentatively. 'DCI Leach wants us to sit in when you interview Brand, but Penny and I have a date with Jennifer Cottrell's PR woman in Oxford at ten tomorrow.'

'Put it off till the afternoon,' Rathbone snapped. 'Goodnight, all.'

'Something's just occurred to me, Sarge,' said Sukey as they went down to the yard to collect their cars. 'If Hickson intended all along to do a runner, why bother to make the appointment with Mr Thorne?'

'Maybe he did intend to keep the appointment, but something happened to make him change his mind. We'll know when we find him – if we ever do. About Brand,' he added in a low voice, 'you think I'm taking a risk, don't you?'

'All I can say, Sarge, is I don't like to think what DCI Leach will say if she isn't there when we go to pick her up in the morning.'

He gave a humourless bark of laughter. 'If she isn't, I'll hand in my resignation. See you tomorrow.'

There was a marked change in Lillian Brand's demeanour on Friday morning as she sat facing DS Greg Rathbone and DC Sukey Reynolds in the interview room. At her side was a clean-shaven man of about forty, formally dressed in a grey suit with a white shirt and striped tie, whom she introduced as her solicitor, Owen Franklin.

'Before we go any further, Sergeant,' she said after the tape was switched on and she had been formally cautioned, 'I feel I owe you and your colleagues an apology.' Her voice and expression were full of contrition as she continued, 'I quickly realized it was a mistake to give you false information, but I assure you it was a snap decision for which my sole motive was to protect the reputation of someone for whom I had a very high regard.' Her voice dropped a tone on the final words. 'I suppose we should have realized . . . I mean, it should have been obvious that sooner or later the truth would come out, but all we – that is Isla, Robbie, Lizzie and I – could think of at the time was that Jennifer was dead and the police thought she'd been murdered. That in itself was bad enough, but it would have been so awful if this breakdown she'd had – it was almost a brainstorm in fact – had become public. The press would have had a field day and she didn't deserve that.'

'So you hoped you could get away not only with giving misleading information to the police yourselves,' said Rathbone, 'but also causing Ms Cottrell's employees to do the same, thereby putting them in an invidious position. As a result of your actions a great deal of police time has been wasted and an important witness – of whose present whereabouts you have previously denied all knowledge – has disappeared.'

'Sergeant, unless you have evidence to the contrary,' Franklin interrupted, 'my client can hardly be held responsible for the subsequent actions of anyone else in this case.'

'That remains to be seen,' said Rathbone. He turned back to Lillian. 'Do you still deny knowing where Hickson has gone?'

'I most certainly do. If I knew, I would have told you.'

'So tell me, Ms Brand, exactly what pressure did you put on Mrs Norris, Giles Hickson and Maggie Pearce to persuade them to lie to the police?'

She made a small, helpless gesture. 'It was hardly pressure; I simply appealed to their sense of loyalty to Jennifer.

She was a good employer and I knew they all had a high regard for her.'

'Mrs Norris, the housekeeper at Woodlands, had been in her employ even longer than yourself, hadn't she?'

'That's right.'

'What was her reaction when you told her what you had done?'

'She was taken aback, of course, and she seemed reluctant at first, but when I explained the circumstances she quite understood why I had done it and agreed to back me up.'

'I see. Now, when my officers called yesterday, Mrs Norris was on the point of leaving the house to have lunch in town. Did you know of this arrangement?'

'Why should I? She comes and goes as she pleases and as long as the place is properly looked after I don't interfere.'

'She also mentioned that she was going to meet her daughter.'

'So?'

'You don't appear surprised.'

'Why should I?'

'Ms Brand, on the day of Jennifer Cottrell's death I and DC Reynolds asked you for some background information about her household. No doubt you remember?'

'Of course.'

'I remember commenting on Mrs Norris's wedding ring and asking you if she was a widow. You claimed at the time to know nothing about her personal circumstances.'

Lillian appeared for the moment nonplussed. She hesitated for several seconds before saying, 'The fact is, Sergeant, when I first went to work for Jennifer in London I learned – through another member of her staff who was an incorrigible gossip – that although Norris wore a wedding ring she was not married and was in fact the mother of an illegitimate child. She – Norris – had unwisely confided in this person that she became pregnant after working for Jennifer for two or three years, but had been deserted by the father. Because she was such an excellent cook Jennifer was reluctant to sack her so she allowed her to keep her job on condition she had the child fostered. I understand it was all arranged privately and when the child was of an age to start school she even paid for her school uniform and other expenses.'

'Mrs Norris has never mentioned her daughter to you?' Lillian shook her head. 'Never.'

'Not even when Ms Cottrell announced her intention of moving to Woodlands? Leaving London might have caused her some problems.'

'She never discussed her personal affairs with me, although I do remember noticing that she was far from happy over the move.'

'So although the two of you have been working for the same employer for about fifteen years it would seem you have never been on particularly intimate terms?'

Lillian gave a slight shrug and made a vague gesture with her hands. 'From the outset she seemed to have a veiled hostility towards me. Perhaps she was jealous because Jennifer and I . . . right from the start, we hit it off so well. It's hard to believe—' For a moment she appeared on the point of breaking down.

'All right,' said Rathbone, showing no sign of being affected by this momentary show of grief, 'I'd like to return to the matter of the pressure you put on your colleagues to give false statements to the police. You say you appealed to Mrs Norris's sense of loyalty; what about Giles Hickson? He was already working on the estate during the time of the previous owner, wasn't he? Did you appeal to his sense of loyalty to Ms Cottrell as well?'

'Not so much to Jennifer as to the rest of us,' said Lillian. 'I explained the situation to him and told him that we were all very anxious to protect her reputation. Just the same,' she added, apparently as an afterthought, 'Jennifer often spoke quite warmly about him, saying he appreciated her interest in his work, especially on the garden. She loved the garden.' Her voice ended on a sad note that sounded genuine.

Rathbone nodded and assumed a sympathetic expression

before saying in a deceptively casual voice, 'You didn't tell him by any chance that the next owner of the estate was yourself, and that whether or not he kept his job depended on—'

'Really, Sergeant, I must object to this line of questioning unless you have proof that my client knew that she was to inherit the estate,' Franklin interrupted. 'My client informs me that according to the late Ms Cottrell's solicitor, who drew up her will, the terms of that will were to be revealed to no one until after her death.'

'All right, we'll leave that for the moment,' said Rathbone calmly. Observing them both closely, Sukey detected a distinctly uneasy look on Lillian's face, which quickly turned to relief when she was spared the need to reply. Knowing Rathbone's methods, she had a shrewd idea that he had anticipated her reaction and was not in the least fazed by the solicitor's intervention. Meanwhile, he calmly resumed his questioning.

'That leaves Maggie, one of a succession of village girls who have done domestic work at Woodlands over the years. Maggie has I believe been the housemaid there for a little over a year. Hardly a long-service employee, would you say? How did you persuade her to join in the deception?'

'I didn't speak to Maggie. In fact, to be honest, I never gave her a thought. I suppose Norris told her what to say.'

'Did Mrs Norris tell her father what to say as well?' asked Sukey.

Lillian stared at her in obvious surprise. 'I don't understand what you mean. What has her father got to do with this?'

'Ms Brand,' Sukey continued, 'when my colleague and I called at the Pearces' house to interview Maggie her father refused to allow us to see her alone. We have subsequently learned that the reason was to make sure she told the same story as the others about the date of the party. What inducement was offered him?'

'I've no idea what you're talking about.' For the first time a hint of her defiant manner during previous interviews returned. 'I have never had any contact with Pearce – I wouldn't know the man if I met him in the street. If you think he was encouraging his daughter to give false evidence I suggest you ask him yourselves.'

'We've done exactly that,' said Rathbone. 'He has made a full statement, admitting that pressure was put on him to support the false story. What do you have to say about that?'

'Sergeant, my client has already stated that she has never met this man Pearce,' said Franklin. 'She can hardly be expected to comment on anything he has said to the police or any other third party.'

'All right, let me put my question another way. Have you any idea, Ms Brand, who might have put pressure on Pearce to support his daughter when she gave us incorrect information?'

'All I can say is that it was not I,' said Lillian. Her voice was firm, but her face was pale and she showed signs of being uncomfortable at the direction Rathbone was taking.

'Or who might be in a position to offer, for example, a financial inducement?'

'How should I know? Pearce was not employed at Woodlands.'

'No? You are not aware that after he lost his regular job because of injury he helped out on the estate from time to time under Hickson's direction or,' Rathbone pressed on relentlessly as she flinched and drew a sharp breath, 'that if there was no work for him at Woodlands your employer, Ms Cottrell, occasionally gave him sums of money to supplement his benefit?'

She compressed her lips for a moment and then glanced at Franklin, who gave a brief shake of his head. 'No comment,' she said.

'Ms Brand, you informed us when we interviewed you on the day of Ms Cottrell's death that she left everything to do with the administration of her household to you. Are you now telling us that it was Ms Cottrell herself who handled the arrangements I've just outlined without saying a word to you?'

'No comment.'

'Very well, if you refuse to answer I'm sure Mr Pearce will give us the information we need.'

Sensing that he was about to close the interview, Sukey leaned forward and said quietly, 'By the way, Ms Brand, do you have a favourite brand of perfume?'

Lillian's look of surprise at the question seemed to be tinged with unease. 'What an extraordinary question,' she said.

'I notice you don't wear perfume in the office, but perhaps you use it on special occasions?'

She shook her head. 'I used to, but when I came to work for Jennifer she told me she was allergic, so I only used it on my evenings out.'

'And has that been the arrangement ever since?'

'Yes, except that as we became closer I went out without her less and less often.'

'So, do you have a favourite brand?'

'I'm afraid I'm not familiar with all the names – there are so many.'

'But you do use it now and again?'

Once again Franklin intervened. 'Really, Sergeant, I fail to see what bearing this line of questioning has on the subject of Giles Hickson's whereabouts. Unless you can show that it is relevant to your investigation, Sergeant, I shall advise my client to answer no further questions.'

'Very well, perhaps she will answer this one,' said Rathbone. He turned back to his witness. 'Ms Brand, in the course of our investigation into Hickson's disappearance we obtained a warrant to search his house. I presume you know where he lives?'

Her lips tightened, but she met his gaze without flinching. 'Of course I do. I know where every member of staff lives – it's part of my job.'

'Have you ever been inside Hickson's house?'

She took a deep breath and a faint colour rose in her pale cheeks. 'Why on earth should I have been?' she said in a show of defiance.

'Ms Brand, I'm not asking for reasons, I simply want to know if you have ever visited Hickson at his home.'

She cast a desperate look at Franklin, but before he had a chance to respond to her mute appeal Rathbone added, 'It would save us trouble if you answered the question, but if you prefer to remain silent I would remind you that we took your fingerprints, and those of the rest of the staff at Woodlands, as a matter of routine. Our forensic team have gathered a considerable amount of evidence in Stony Cottage which they are at present examining with a toothcomb.'

Her flush faded, leaving her face ashen. 'No comment,' she said and added, in a barely audible whisper, 'I wish to confer with my solicitor.'

Twenty-One

'So what do you reckon?' asked Rathbone. 'Is she telling the truth or is she lying through her teeth? In other words, is she Hickson's mistress and does she know where he's gone?'

The four detectives were in an adjacent interview room, having left Lillian Brand alone with her solicitor. There was a short silence before Sukey said, 'My feeling is, yes and yes, Sarge, and it seems pretty obvious that she was behind the financial inducements given to both Pearce and Hickson.'

'Do you think she knew about her inheritance before Jennifer Cottrell was murdered?'

'She might have done, but even if she didn't she could have pledged her own money if they weren't prepared to play ball unless there was something in it for them. She's admitted to being well paid and she may have quite a nest-egg tucked away.'

'You're saying it was essential from her point of view that they confirmed her story?'

'It looks like it.'

'You don't believe her claim that she gave the false date out of loyalty to Cottrell's memory?'

'No, Sarge, I don't. I think she's a very plausible liar who had her own reasons for keeping Cottrell's outburst a secret. Remember how she reacted when you put it to her that she was covering up for Hickson? It crossed my mind at the time that she might have been having an affair with him, although on the face of it they seemed an unlikely couple. And if Cottrell had got wind of it she might have suspected the pair of them – along with the others – of ripping her off, which could account for her outburst.'

He nodded. 'It's pretty obvious now that you were right – about the affair, at least. Whether that was the sole cause of Cottrell's outburst we may never know.'

'Of course, it might be genuine affection on both sides,' said Sukey, feeling it was only right to give them the benefit of the doubt, 'but she is quite a bit older than he is and he could have been leading her up the garden path, knowing she had money. It's not exactly unheard of.'

'A gigolo, in fact.' Rathbone considered this line of reasoning for a second or two before saying, 'So it could be infatuation on her part and an eye to the main chance on his. As you say, she probably has money of her own and she may have been happy to splash it out on him in return for sex. She managed to bluff it out until I started asking her if she'd ever been to his house, and it was pretty obvious then that I was on the right track.'

'I thought she was going to break on the spot at the suggestion we might find her prints there, but she had the presence of mind to ask for permission to consult her brief,' said Sukey.

'And now she's covering for him – which we've suspected all along.' Rathbone struck the table with his fist in exasperation. 'And we let the bugger slip through our fingers!' he fumed.

'You reckon Hickson's the killer then, Sarge?' said Tim nervously.

It was obvious that until that moment Rathbone had temporarily forgotten his presence. As if he'd been stung, he rounded on the unfortunate young detective. 'Of course he is, you prat!' he shouted. 'And Lillian Brand knows it. She cooked up that story about the date of the dinner party because she didn't want us to know Cottrell had rumbled them. My guess is she somehow knew she was going to inherit Cottrell's fortune and is so besotted with him she was stupid enough to confide in him. Maybe he was in urgent need of money to pay gambling debts, for example, or maybe he has a drug habit and owed a lot to his dealer – or maybe he's just greedy and decided he didn't want to wait until Cottrell popped her clogs from natural causes.'

He clenched his fist and for a moment Sukey seriously wondered if he was going to lash out, but all he did was say, through gritted teeth, 'When I think of all the garbage he told us about how fond he was of the old biddy – if it hadn't been for your and Penny's bungling we'd have had the pair of them in the cells by now and the case as good as sewn up. A fat chance you two have of getting promotion!'

He had become red in the face and was breathing heavily. Sukey waited until he had calmed down before saying, 'About the Pearces, Sarge, do you think Lillian was lying when she denied putting pressure on them?'

'She was hardly likely to admit it, was she?'

'But she denies ever having met Pearce,' she pointed out, 'and I had the impression that she was telling the truth at that point.'

'She was saying what Hickson told her to say,' he fumed. 'He's a plausible bugger with the kind of charm a lot of women fall for and like I said, she's probably so besotted with him she'd do whatever he asked her.'

'Or it could have been Hickson himself,' Sukey suggested. 'Pearce was obviously scared to reveal who'd twisted his arm to back up his daughter's story. Now Hickson's disappeared he might be more willing to talk.'

Rathbone nodded and made a note. 'It's possible. We'll go and see him again.' He glanced at the clock on the wall. 'Lillian's had enough time with her brief; let's see if she's ready to start talking again. Yes, what is it?' he said irritably as a young uniformed constable put his head round the door.

'Message from Inspector Collins, Sarge, calling from the mobile station at Marfield,' he said. 'He wants to speak to you, please – says it's urgent.'

Rathbone rolled his eyes in exasperation. 'He sure knows how to choose his time! OK, I'll have a quick word. Sukey, go back to Lillian and hold the fort while I see what it's about.' He hurried out and Sukey returned to the interview room with the other two DCs trailing behind her.

'I'm afraid there will be a further slight delay,' she

informed Lillian Brand and her solicitor. 'DS Rathbone has received an urgent message, which he has to deal with immediately. I expect him back very shortly.'

This assurance was received without comment. An uncomfortable five minutes of silence dragged past during which Lillian, plainly ill at ease, became increasingly restless. Eventually Franklin said, 'Constable Reynolds, as you will no doubt be aware, my client is under considerable stress. In the circumstances, and in the interests of her well-being, I am making a formal request for her to be either charged or released immediately.'

Sukey was spared the necessity of a response by Rathbone's return. He sat down, restarted the tape and said, 'Ms Brand, I have to inform you that there has been a very serious development in the case. In the circumstances I am suspending this interview forthwith, but perhaps you would be kind enough to wait here while I arrange for another officer to explain the situation in more detail.'

'What's happened, Sarge?' Sukey asked as soon as they were back in the CID office.

'What was it the SIO said about not losing another suspect?' Rathbone said, in a tone bordering on despair. The others exchanged glances; each had the same idea, but none had the courage to put it into words. 'You've guessed – a body has been found and it's almost certain it's Hickson's. It seems a drunk broke into a shed on the Woodlands Estate, thinking it was as good a place as any to sleep it off, and nearly tripped over him.'

He picked up the phone, tapped out a number and said, 'Sir, I need to see you urgently . . . thank you, in two minutes.' He put down the handset and snapped, 'Sukey, book a car and stand by till I come back.' As she went to her phone to carry out his instructions she heard him say to the others, 'We'll have to arrange for a family liaison officer to look after Lillian. Penny, take her a cup of tea and stay with her till the FLO arrives, but don't answer any questions – and whatever you do, don't say it's an FLO or Franklin will guess it's something to do with

Hickson,' he added over his shoulder as he hurried from the room.

He returned ten minutes later, grim-faced, and said, 'Right, Sukey, you and I are off to Woodlands.'

'What makes them so sure it's Hickson, Sarge?' said Tim.

'He's wearing green overalls with Woodlands Estate printed on the back. In any case, Collins is a local man and knows him by sight.'

'Any idea how he died, Sarge?'

'Stabbed, by the looks of it. The police pathologist is on his way and we must get there ASAP.' He stopped by his desk to pick up an envelope from his in-tray and scanned the contents. 'Forensics have put in an initial report on Hickson's vehicle,' he said, handing the envelope to Tim. 'You and Penny, go through it and see what you make of it so far. If the body in the shed is Hickson's, then on the face of it someone else dumped his Chelsea tractor and their prints will be all over it. Brand's, I wonder? I'm tempted to say "almost certainly" but this case has more twists and turns than a corkscrew.' He grabbed his jacket and followed Sukey from the room.

'You can imagine what DCI Leach had to say when I told him we'd probably done exactly what he warned us not to do – lose another suspect,' said Rathbone. He buckled on his seat belt while Sukey waited for a gap in the traffic before pulling out of the yard. 'He gave me another roasting for taking the heat off Hickson and for not having guessed Brand was having it off with him. He's right, of course,' he added despairingly, 'he as good as told me I've cocked this case up from the word go.'

'That's not fair, Sarge,' said Sukey. 'We all thought Wendy Downie was the killer at first, and as far as I recall he didn't argue about that.'

'I seem to remember you had your doubts, even before that nutcase got herself topped,' he said morosely. 'One of your famous hunches, Vicky called it.'

'I admit I did wonder whether her outburst was enough to suspect her of being a potential killer, although on the face of it she seemed to have a motive of sorts,' Sukey replied. 'In the event, we were all wrong.'

'In the meantime we'd questioned all the staff at Woodlands.' Rathbone sank lower in his seat and closed his eyes, as if he was thinking aloud. 'As I recall, we weren't entirely satisfied with the explanation Hickson gave of the exchange between him and Maggie that Rosy Brookes over-heard, but he did seem genuinely shocked to learn that Cottrell's death was murder.'

'And when Brand's name was mentioned he had some very disparaging things to say about her,' Sukey reminded him.

'That could have been a red herring. My guess is that from the start of their affair – whenever it was – it was important to both of them to conceal it. In case Cottrell found out, perhaps?'

'Do we go back to the possibility that there was a lesbian attraction between Lillian and Jennifer?' Sukey wondered. 'Or maybe it was only on Jennifer's side, but to keep her sweet – and keep her job – Lillian played along with her while enjoying the chemistry between herself and Giles whenever she got the chance.'

'Could be,' he agreed. 'Anyway, at this point we started to reconsider the cast of suspects and ask ourselves who had the most to gain from Jennifer Cottrell's death. Lillian claimed to have no idea of the terms of her will, and on the face of it she was telling the truth – unless someone in Fraser's office slipped up.'

'And it was then that we started to check on the guests at the dinner parties she'd mentioned as an example of their social life.'

'Right, and when I spoke to the guests at the latest one, and asked them to verify the date, I was suspicious because of the way they were all so sure of it, despite having to answer some quite searching questions.'

'And you were absolutely right, Sarge,' said Sukey.

He opened his eyes, turned his head and gave her a wry smile. 'Thanks for that,' he said quietly. 'I don't expect to receive many compliments when this case is sorted – if it ever is.'

'It will be,' she said, trying to sound confident but privately having serious doubts.

'Well, we've seen Cottrell's editor. What about the other two witnesses – the agent and the publicist? Do they have alibis, I wonder? Mike and Vicky are interviewing the agent in Torquay this morning so we should have their report later on. I told Tim and Penny to reschedule their trip to Oxford to talk to the PR woman so we'll have to wait for theirs. It would be nice, don't you think, if we could eliminate at least one of them?'

'It certainly would, Sarge,' she agreed.

'Of course,' he went on, 'we don't know yet when Hickson died, so they may have to be seen again unless any alibis they produce cover the crucial period. Doc Hanley will give us his best estimate of how long he's been dead, but in these circumstances he can never be a hundred per cent accurate, so alibis will be very hard to prove or disprove.'

They had reached Woodlands. The pathologist's car was already there, away from the numerous police vehicles, and Sukey parked alongside. They were approached by a uniformed officer who said, 'I'm Inspector Jeff Collins. I take it you're DS Rathbone?'

'Correct, sir, and this is DC Reynolds.'

Collins gave a nod in Sukey's direction and then gestured towards the house. 'The only people there seem to be the housekeeper, who's hardly spoken since we told her the reason for our presence – it seems to have sent her into a state of shock – and the daily help, who's in a state of near hysteria. There's a policewoman with them and I imagine you'll want to get statements from them.'

'Later on, sir, thank you,' said Rathbone. 'First we'd like to visit the crime scene.'

'Yes, of course,' said Collins. 'Doc Hanley arrived a few minutes ago and is standing by while the CSIs do their stuff.' He led them across the field nearest to the house but following a different route to the one Wendy Downie – and subsequently her killer – had taken on the day of her and Jennifer Cottrell's murders. On the way he said, 'He's lying with his face partially hidden, but I'm pretty sure it's Giles Hickson.'

Halfway along a gravelled track leading into a group of ash trees they came to a wooden shed. A group of officers were protecting the surrounding area with blue-and-white tape while others were standing by to erect a tent over the path when the crime scene investigators had completed their various tasks. Some of the latter could be seen through the open door of the shed making a detailed record of the body and the floor, while others were doing the same over the ground outside. Dr Hanley, who was observing the scene a short distance away, ambled over to greet the two new arrivals.

'Something tells me this is another twist in the Cottrell saga,' he said, 'but a different MO by the sound of it. Well, we like a little variety, don't we,' he added impishly. 'Personally, I was getting a bit bored with drownings.'

Rathbone gave a dry chuckle, his spirits marginally lifted by this example of gallows humour. 'I don't know about bored,' he said, 'but it is frustrating when our suspects keep getting themselves topped. I'm afraid the SIO doesn't appreciate the joke, though,' he added with a rueful smile.

Hanley smiled sympathetically. 'Ah well, DCI Leach isn't renowned for his sense of fun,' he said.

'That's true . . . but he's a first-rate copper for all that,' said Rathbone in a sudden – and to Sukey somewhat surprising – show of loyalty. 'It looks as if the way's clear for you to see the body,' he added as Inspector Collins approached and beckoned.

'Good show.' Hanley picked up his bag and followed the inspector into the shed. When he returned, he said, 'Can't be very precise at the moment about how long he's been dead. Probably two, three days at the most. He was stabbed a number of times with something with a fairly broad blade, possibly a kitchen knife. When I get him to the morgue I'll be able to tell you which wound actually killed him.' He jerked his sleeve back to check his wristwatch. 'Must get along; I've got another call to answer. Don't get excited; it's not on your patch and you mustn't be greedy!' he added with a macabre chuckle.

The two detectives exchanged wry glances at this further

sally. Rathbone took out his mobile and said, 'Better bring the SIO up to date.' After a brief exchange he snapped off the phone and said, 'Right, before we view the body I want another word with Inspector Collins.'

'It's OK for you to go in now, Sergeant,' said Collins before Rathbone had a chance to speak.

'Thank you, sir, but first I'd like a bit more information about the discovery of the body. This drunk you mentioned; you said he "nearly tripped over him" when he entered the shed. What time of day was this and what did he do next?'

'All we can say at the moment is that it must have been some time during the hours of darkness as it seems he just blundered into the shed – we presume the door was open as there's no apparent sign of a break-in – tripped over something that we assume was Hickson's body, fell down and passed out. When he woke up this morning he'd sobered up sufficiently to stagger into the village with the idea of raising the alarm. It so happens today's the day the mobile station is in Marfield and that's why we were on the scene so quickly.'

'Where is this bloke now, sir?'

'In a café in the village, having coffee and a bacon sarnie. He's still shaken and a bit confused and I've detailed one of my officers to make sure he doesn't wander off. I take it you'll be wanting to question him?'

'Maybe later, after we've seen the women in the house. By the way, does he have blood on his clothes?'

Collins shook his head. 'I haven't seen him myself; like I said, I left him with one of my officers and came straight here. It'll be up to forensics to find out if you think it's significant. Anyway, you go ahead.'

'Thank you, sir.'

Using the stepping boards placed round the entrance, Rathbone and Sukey entered the shed. It was a substantially built structure with wooden walls on a brick base and appeared to have been used principally as storage for the tools and implements used by Hickson for his work on the estate. Like the items in the garage at his home, everything was clean and neatly put away, either against the wall or on shelves. At the far end, below a window, was a work-bench with a vice and various hand tools in a rack above.

Hickson lay in a crumpled heap on the floor, face down in a pool of congealed blood and with both hands beneath him, as if he had fallen forward clutching at a wound in his stomach. Other blows to the back had cut through the fabric of his overalls, on which 'Woodlands Estate' was printed in bright yellow characters. To one side was an over-turned chair on which he had apparently been sitting while in the act of removing his boots when attacked, as one of them lay on the floor and the laces of the other were undone.

At first they studied the body in silence. After a few seconds Sukey gave a start as Rathbone said sharply, 'You won't see much with your eyes shut, woman!'

'Sorry, Sarge,' she said in some embarrassment, 'I was just praying for a bit of help and guidance. You have to admit we could do with some if we're ever going to get to the bottom of this ghastly chain of killings,' she added, seeing his cynical expression.

'You'd do better to rely on your training and experience,' he grunted. 'Right, how d'you think it happened?'

'I'd say his attacker walked in the door and confronted him,' she replied. 'He was taking off his boots so he was probably sitting down. He looked up and saw someone coming at him with a knife. He leapt to his feet to defend himself, but the killer was too quick for him and stabbed him in the stomach. He fell forward on to the floor, clutching at the wound, and to make sure he was dead the killer stabbed him again several times in the back.'

Rathbone nodded. 'That's how I read it,' he agreed. 'What we don't know, of course, is whether the bloke who found him disturbed him in any way. If he was out of his head when he blundered in here, he won't have a clue what happened between passing out and waking up this morning.' There was another short silence while he studied the floor. 'From what we already know of Hickson I guess he swept up at the end of each day,' he commented. 'Now, had he already done it before he was attacked, I wonder? Let's hope not, and that forensics have found some useful

evidence.' He walked back to the door and studied the gravel
scattered on the ground outside. 'Not much to be learned
there by the looks of things, but sometimes they find
evidence barely visible to the naked eye. And no doubt
there will be some on the killer's footwear. How about
praying for some luck in that direction?' he added with a
grin.

'I already have, Sarge,' she said quietly and the grin faded,
to be replaced by a look of grudging respect.

'Well,' he said, 'I think we can tell Collins it's OK for
him to organize a hearse to get him to the morgue. We'll
speak to Mrs Norris and Maggie next, but until we have a
better idea of when Hickson was attacked I doubt if they'll
be much help. And then I suppose we'd better have a quick
word with our only witness before we go back to the station.
I wonder if our two rookies have found anything interesting
in forensics' report on Hickson's car. What's the betting
Lillian Brand's prints will be all over it?'

'Are you saying you think she killed Hickson, Sarge?'

'To be honest, at the moment I hardly know what to
think. If they were lovers, maybe they had a row. Who
knows what passion lies under that cool, controlled exter-
ior? Was Hickson Cottrell's killer, I wonder? If Lillian knew
and had been covering for him, then found out the only
reason he'd been shagging her was for the money she was
going to inherit, she could have got so mad she stuck a
knife in his guts. Or is there some other shadowy figure
lurking in the background that we know nothing about?'

Twenty-Two

PC MacCall, the young policewoman who had been on duty the day Jennifer Cottrell's body was discovered, opened the door in response to their knock.

'They're in the kitchen,' she said in a low voice as she closed the door behind them. 'I've managed to calm Maggie for the moment although she's still pretty shaky. Mrs Norris seems to be functioning more or less normally after the initial shock; she's been making coffee and wondering where Ms Brand's gone and when she'll be back so she can discuss meals with her and so on, but I get the feeling her mind's elsewhere. It's as if she's doing everything mechanically, if you know what I mean.'

'Sounds like a normal reaction to me,' commented Rathbone. 'Three murders in your own backyard is enough to knock anyone sideways. Let's go and see them; I could use a cup of coffee myself,' he added as an afterthought.

When Rathbone and Sukey entered the kitchen they found Mrs Norris and Maggie seated at the table, on which were three half-empty mugs and a plate of biscuits. They both looked up; the housekeeper's face was expressionless but Maggie gave a little cry, leapt to her feet, rushed towards Sukey and flung her arms round her.

'I want to go home to me dad!' she sobbed, her face buried in Sukey's jacket. 'There's a curse on this place and I'll never set foot here again, never, never, never!'

Rathbone turned to PC MacCall. 'Has Mr Pearce been informed?' he asked.

'An officer went to the house, Sarge, but there was no one in,' she said. 'I understand he left a message with a neighbour, asking him to get in touch with us as soon as possible, but there's been no word so far.'

'Have you any idea where he might be, Maggie?' asked Sukey as she gently disengaged from the hysterical girl and led her back to her chair.

'Out on some job, I suppose,' Maggie sniffed, dabbing at her eyes with a tissue that Mrs Norris took from a box on the table and put into her hand. 'He does odd jobs for people in the village.'

'So can you tell us what happened when you arrived this morning? Were the police here or did they come later?'

'There was coppers everywhere . . . lots of 'em . . . an' I was going to turn round an' go home but they wouldn't let me . . . they said to wait in case someone wanted to ask me questions. I don't know nothing . . . I didn't kill no one,' she wailed, once more engulfed in tears.

'What makes you think someone's been killed?' asked Rathbone.

Maggie made a vague gesture in Mrs Norris's direction. 'She said—'

'I rather foolishly told her a body had been discovered on the estate and she immediately went into hysterics,' said the housekeeper, for the first time showing some sign of normality. 'I suppose I should have been a little more tactful, but she naturally wanted to know why the police were here and—' She broke off and stared down at her hands, which were tightly clenched on the table in front of her.

'That's all right, you must have been very shocked yourself,' said Rathbone.

He thought for a moment and then said, 'I think the best thing, Maggie, is for PC MacCall to take you home now and stay with you until your dad comes back. If we want to talk to you we'll come and see you when he's there with you, all right?'

'Oh yes, thank you!' Maggie whispered.

When they had left, Rathbone said, 'Mrs Norris, exactly what were you told when the police arrived?'

'An inspector – I think he said his name was Collins – told me they had received a report of a possible suspicious death somewhere on the estate. You can imagine the effect it had on me . . . it was such a shock, and coming after the other two tragedies . . . I was afraid for a moment that I was going to pass out. I suppose I shouldn't have blurted it out to Maggie like that but I didn't think . . . and now I'm so worried about Miss Brand. I never heard her come in last night; I took her breakfast up as usual but I didn't hear her moving around and when I went up later on she hadn't touched it and she's not in her bedroom or her office.' She looked from Rathbone to Sukey and back again with a question in her eyes that she seemed afraid to put into words.

'If you're worried about Ms Brand's whereabouts, Mrs Norris, I can put your mind at rest straight away,' said Rathbone. 'She's at this moment at police headquarters helping us with our enquiries.'

The housekeeper's mouth fell open and for a moment she appeared too stunned to speak. 'Help . . . helping with enquiries?' she faltered. 'Isn't that what you say when you're questioning a suspect? You don't suppose she—?'

'I'm not supposing anything; I'm here to inform you that we came here as a result of information received and I can assured you that the body found in an outbuilding on this estate is not that of Ms Brand.'

'That's a relief. I know we've never been exactly, well, close, but I'd never wish her any harm.' A sudden thought seemed to strike her. 'Did you say an outbuilding? Do you mean the shed where Giles Hickson keeps his tools and equipment?'

'Are there any other outbuildings within the estate grounds?'

'No . . . not unless you count the garages behind the house.' Receiving no comment from Rathbone, she said, 'Whose body is it? It's not . . . it's not Giles, is it? We haven't seen him for two or three days and I've been wondering—'

'Yes?' Rathbone prompted as she broke off.

'I mean, he disappeared after your people came to see him a second time about Miss Cottrell's death and I thought perhaps—'

'That he'd killed her?' he prompted as she seemed reluctant to go on.

'Well, yes, it did cross my mind, although I couldn't see what motive he could have.'

'Did you discuss your doubts with Ms Brand?' said Sukey.

Mrs Norris made a dismissive gesture. 'Constable, I'm the last person she'd discuss anything with, outside household matters of course. In any case, it occurred to me that if Giles had run away she would probably know where he was, but she certainly wouldn't confide in me.'

'You think she'd be likely to protect him?'

Mrs Norris looked embarrassed and hesitated before replying. 'It may be wicked of me, but yes, I do think that.' She waited a moment before repeating her earlier question. 'Do you know who the dead person is?'

'I'm afraid we can't give you any information that hasn't been officially released.'

'I see. Yes of course – I should have realized—'

'It's a natural question,' said Rathbone. 'Mrs Norris, I'm sure you would have told us, but just for the record, have you during the past few days seen any strange person hanging around in the neighbourhood?' The housekeeper shook her head and he continued, 'Or had any cause to suspect that any intruders have been lurking in the grounds?'

'Absolutely not,' she said firmly. 'The security system here is very efficient and my dog barks if he hears an unfamiliar footstep.'

'I see. Now, I believe Ms Brand will be home shortly and in the meantime you have your dog for company. Where is he, by the way?'

'In my sitting room. He's not allowed in the kitchen except when we go out for our walks.' She indicated the back door, where a dog's leash hung from a hook on the wall, above a pair of shabby flat-heeled shoes.

Rathbone stood up and said, 'Well, thank you for your help, Mrs Norris. We'll leave you now, but we'll almost certainly want to see you again, so please—'

Her mouth crimped in a mirthless smile. 'You're going to say, "don't leave the neighbourhood" aren't you?' she interposed in a harsh voice. 'Where do you suppose I'd go?'

* * *

'A somewhat bitter lady, would you say?' said Rathbone as he and Sukey went back to their car.

'She probably knows by now that Lillian's got the estate and all Cottrell left her in return for all her years of service is a measly annuity,' she pointed out. 'In the circumstances I think I'd feel a bit miffed.'

He shrugged. 'Depends on the size of the annuity. And at least she has a daughter; Lillian's alone in the world.' He settled into his seat and slammed the car door. 'Right, let's go back to the village and have a word with the witness.'

They went into the Copper Kettle Tea Rooms, which appeared to be the only café in the village, but there was no sign among the customers of a man in the company of a police officer. In reply to their enquiry an unsmiling middle-aged waitress in a black dress, a white apron and an old-fashioned white cap with a black velvet bow anchored to her greying hair with metal grips pointed through the window to where the mobile police station was parked in a lay-by a short distance away on the other side of the road. 'Over there,' she said curtly. As they left, an officer, who had obviously been keeping an eye out for them, stepped outside the van and beckoned.

'He's in here, Sarge,' he said as they approached. 'He says his name's Derek Langford and he's given an address in Bradley Stoke. Miss Moon, the lady who runs the tea rooms, asked me to leave once he'd finished his grub, saying the sight of a scruffy individual in the company of a police officer was bad for trade,' he explained with a grin.

'So he's not a tramp?'

'No, Sarge, he was just too drunk to drive home and somehow found his way to Woodlands. He probably fell over a few times as his clothes are in a bit of a mess. He's feeling a bit sheepish as well as shocked, but after two black coffees and something to eat I reckon he's fit to be interviewed.'

'Right,' said Rathbone, 'let's see what he's got to say.'

The man seated on a chair in the specially equipped motor caravan appeared to be in his early twenties; he had untidy fair hair and a gingery bush on his chin, slightly bloodshot blue eyes and an unhealthy pallor that was probably due to a combination of over-indulgence and shock. Rathbone and Sukey sat down on a bench facing him.

'We understand you've had a rather unnerving experience, Mr Langford,' said Rathbone after introducing himself and Sukey. 'Perhaps you can tell us in your own words how you came to be in the groundsman's shed on the Woodlands Estate and what happened between your entering it and waking up this morning.'

Langford was plainly embarrassed. 'The fact is, Sergeant, I was with some friends in the Feathers last night,' he began. 'We were celebrating my birthday . . . and they kept buying me drinks . . . and I suppose I had far too much. When we left I told them I was fine so they all went off home, but I couldn't remember where I'd left my car.'

'Probably just as well,' said Rathbone as Langford broke off to take a sip from a plastic mug of water. 'You could be dead yourself by now or maybe killed someone else.'

'You're quite right, Sergeant. Anyway, I didn't have a clue where I was. I must have started walking . . . I found myself in some woods . . . I think I fell over once or twice – ' he cast a rueful glance down at his muddied trousers and jacket – 'and then I saw this shed in front of me and the door was open so I thought I'd go in and lie down for a while. It was moonlight outside but dark inside and I tripped over something just inside the door and nearly fell over again . . . in fact, I probably did fall over because I don't remember anything else until I woke up and saw—' He put a hand over his mouth and closed his eyes for a moment before continuing. 'It shook me rigid to see the poor chap lying there in all that blood. I went outside and puked and then I screwed up my courage to go back and see if there was anything I could do for him, but when I touched his face it was stone cold and I knew he was dead. I got out my mobile and tried to call the police but I couldn't get a signal so I walked along a gravel path and came to a big house and I heard a dog bark so I hurried into the road and shut the gate in case they let it out. I tried the mobile

again and this time I got through . . . and then I think I passed
out again because I don't remember—'

'That's right, Sarge,' said the officer who had been left
in charge of Langford. 'It must have been nearly ten – it
was while we were on our way here – that we got a message
that someone had discovered a body. It took us a while to
figure out the location but Inspector Collins is a local man
and he put two and two together from what this gentleman
was able to tell us. He was in the road looking pretty groggy
so we brought him here.'

Rathbone nodded. 'I see. Now, Mr Langford, I can understand that the sight of a man lying dead in his own blood
must be pretty unnerving, but I'd be grateful if you'd try
and cast your mind back to the scene for a moment. You
say you went outside and puked and then you went back
to see if there was anything you could do for him.'

Langford nodded. 'That's right.'

'And you touched his hand and found it was stone cold.'

'No, I touched his face. I couldn't see his hands because
they were under his body.'

'Right. Now, having satisfied yourself that the man was
dead by touching his face, did you notice any other details?
Was there anything else on the floor near the body, for
example?'

Langford closed his eyes and thought for a moment. 'There
was a chair behind him and a boot on the floor beside him
– in fact, I think that might have been what I tripped over.
I could only see one of his feet and it had just a sock on it
so I suppose he was sitting in the chair putting his boots on,
or maybe taking them off, when he was attacked.'

'Is that all?'

'It's all I can think of for now. If I think of anything else
I'll let you know.'

'Thank you, Mr Langford. We'll have your statement
printed and one of my officers will bring it for you to sign.
As I think you're still unfit to drive, I'll arrange for you to
be taken home now. And we'd like to take your fingerprints
and also collect the clothes and shoes you're wearing for
forensic examination.'

Langford's jaw dropped. 'You want my fingerprints . . . and my clothes?' he exclaimed, aghast. 'Whatever for? Surely you don't think I—?'

'It's for elimination purposes,' Rathbone explained. 'We'll give you a receipt and let you have them back as soon as possible.'

'And what about my car?'

'Give us the registration number and we'll locate it and have it returned to you when we call for your statement. That's all for now, and thank you very much for your help.'

Twenty-Three

L eaving Langford with the sergeant in charge of the
 mobile station, Rathbone and Sukey returned to headquarters. As soon as they entered the CID office, DC Penny
Osborne hurried over to speak to them.

'Lillian Brand keeps asking to see you, Sarge,' she said.
'The SIO came down to speak to her and her brief after
you left and we understand he told her she could go home
and wait till she heard from us. Mr Franklin advised her to
do that but she insisted on staying till you got back so he
left her with Janine.'

'Janine?'

'The FLO, Sarge. She's still with her; she slipped out
about ten minutes ago to get Lillian a drink of water and
said she still seems badly shaken. All she's been told is that
you and Sukey were called away to investigate a suspicious
death, but she keeps asking Janine if she has any idea of
where the body was found and do we know the identity of
the victim. Janine has a brief idea of the background to the
case, but naturally she hasn't passed any of it on or answered
any questions. Just the same, from remarks Lillian let drop,
Janine believes she's desperately worried about one particular individual and is desperate for you to tell her it's someone
else.'

'What sort of remarks?'

'Things like, "It can't be him" and "Why hasn't he been
in touch?" Janine said that once she covered her eyes and
prayed, "Please don't let it be him!" or words to that effect.'

'She didn't mention a name?'

'No, Sarge.'

'All right,' said Rathbone resignedly, 'I'll see her, but I'm afraid I can't tell her what she wants to hear. This emotional stuff may be just an act, but we'll have to give her the benefit of the doubt for the moment,' he added in a quiet aside to Sukey. He looked utterly drained and she felt a surge of sympathy for him.

'Would you like me to see her, Sarge?' she said. 'If she's genuinely upset she might prefer to talk to another woman anyway, and she knows me.'

He gave her a grateful look. 'Would you? I don't think I'm up to coping with a hysterical woman crying on my shoulder at the moment. And I could do with a strong coffee before I face DCI Leach.'

'I take it you'll want to interview her again once she's calmed down?'

He nodded wearily. 'Yes, but not yet. It looks as if we were right about her and Hickson being an item, so it's more than likely she's the one who left his car in the car park, but we need to study forensics' report first. Just ooze a bit of sympathy, listen to her and observe her re-actions. You're a pretty shrewd judge of when people are lying.'

'Thanks, Sarge,' said Sukey, a little taken aback by the rare compliment, which she was not altogether confident was deserved.

'She'll have to go home for now,' he added, 'but make it clear we'll want to see her again.'

'Will do, Sarge.'

'Thanks. Now I suppose I'll have to face the SIO. Say a prayer for me,' he added as an afterthought, and she sensed that he was not joking.

The first thing Sukey noticed about Lillian was that she was dry-eyed, and secondly that she appeared to be praying, but silently with no movement of her lips. She was seated in her chair with her shoulders slightly hunched, her head bowed and her hands clasped in her lap. Janine was seated beside her with a hand on her arm and when Sukey entered she gave it a little squeeze and said gently, 'Here's DC Reynolds to see you, Lillian.'

It was a second or two before Lillian raised her head. Immediately, she sat bolt upright and clasped her hands together so tightly that the knuckles turned bone white beneath the taut flesh. 'She,' she said in a hoarse whisper, with a nod in Janine's direction, 'says you were called away to investigate a suspicious death. Where did it happen and do you know who . . . ' Her voice died away as if in fear of hearing a reply she dreaded.

'I'm afraid I can't tell you much more than that at the moment,' said Sukey, choosing her words carefully. 'A man's body was found by a drunk who broke into a shed, but it has not yet been officially identified.'

'In a shed? Is it . . . is it the shed at Woodlands?' Lillian gazed at Sukey with fear-stricken eyes. 'It is there, isn't it?' she went on, putting her own interpretation on Sukey's silence. 'Whose body is it?'

'Look, you mustn't jump to conclusions,' said Sukey. 'Our enquiries have only just begun and I can't give you any information that hasn't been officially released.'

'But you know, you've been there, you've seen the body?' The words tumbled out in a rush. 'Did you recognize him?'

'I'm really sorry I can't help you,' Sukey said. 'You are obviously greatly distressed,' she went on gently. 'We believe you are afraid the victim may be someone you know. Is that the case?'

It was several seconds before Lillian spoke; when she did there was a firmer edge to her voice, as if she had made a supreme effort to control herself.

'I thought perhaps . . . if the shed where the body was found is the one in the grounds of Woodlands—'

'You know the location of this shed?'

'Of course I do; it's where Giles . . . that is, it's where tools and equipment are stored. I never go there myself,' Lillian added hastily, 'but I was thinking . . . it might be someone who lives nearby—'

'Do you have anyone in mind?'

'Well, there are several houses in the neighbourhood . . . and people sometimes walk their dogs in the field . . . they're not supposed to, but they do . . . Hickson orders them off if he catches them. And then there's Bill Pearce.'

'Pearce? You mean Maggie's father? Does he use the shed?'

'He might do, when he's helping out with some job on the estate. Of course, if it's him you wouldn't . . . I mean, I don't suppose you know him by sight.'

'Do you?' The question was out before Sukey could prevent it and she felt sure that Rathbone would not have approved of her putting it. She reminded herself that she was not conducting an interview; just the same, Lillian's reaction was significant. She appeared startled and put her hand to her mouth for a moment before replying.

'No, of course not,' she said hurriedly. 'I think I told you, I've never set eyes on him. Perhaps Maggie . . . oh poor girl, if it is her father—' She assumed an expression of concern that Sukey sensed was false. Feeling that she had done what was required of her, she decided it was time to end the discussion.

'Look, Lillian,' she said, 'you've been under considerable stress and I suggest you go home and get some rest. Janine will look after you as long as you need her, and you'll be informed as soon as more information is released. It will of course be necessary for us to proceed with the interview that had to be cut short earlier, so we'll be in touch again very soon, possibly later today. Do you understand?'

Lillian nodded. 'Yes, I'll do that,' she said resignedly. 'You've been very considerate; thank you.'

Sukey stood up. 'Then I'll leave you for now.' She returned to the office and Rathbone reappeared shortly afterwards, looking slightly more relaxed. 'How was it?' she asked.

He gave a faint smile. 'It could have been worse. I think on reflection DCI Leach has recognized that we're up against a pretty cunning villain. He's told us to have some lunch, write up our reports and see him again after the others come back.'

'Mike and Vicky are already on their way back, Sarge, and should be here by two. Tim and Penny made some notes on forensics' initial report on Hickson's vehicle and put them in your in-tray before leaving for Oxford. Their appointment's for two o'clock so they won't be back till five at the earliest. Are we supposed to wait for them?'

'Call Tim on his mobile and tell him to ring in as soon as he's finished the interview,' said Rathbone. 'Did you manage to get rid of Brand, by the way?'

'Yes, Sarge. I'd like to have a word with you about that later.'

He nodded. 'OK, let's have a look at that report.'

The report raised more questions than it answered. Hickson's prints were, naturally, found in many places on the interior and the bodywork of the vehicle. Lillian Brand's prints were found on both sides of the passenger door handle, the seat-belt clip and parts of the console, indicating that their suspicions about her relationship with Hickson were at least partially justified. The next point in the report, however, raised a different question.

'It says here,' Rathbone remarked, 'that prints on the steering wheel and the gear shift are badly smudged in places although Hickson's are partially or completely detectable in others. Likewise on the driver's door handle and the rear-view mirror. What does that tell us?'

'Not a lot,' said Sukey, 'except that the person who drove it to where they left it probably wore gloves, but didn't see the need to wipe round anywhere else so long as they didn't leave any prints of their own. She – assuming it was Lillian, which seems likely – knowing the vehicle belonged to Hickson anyway, and obviously aware that we knew as well, would have realized there was no point in trying to disguise the fact. I see they've taken samples of dirt from the footwell and fluff from the upholstery for examination,' she added.

'I suppose we'll have to wait until next week at the earliest for the more detailed results,' said Rathbone gloomily. He put the report back in his in-tray and stood up. 'Right, I'm hungry. Let's go and grab some lunch.'

By the time they went back to the office Vicky and Mike had returned from their interview with Jennifer Cottrell's agent in Torquay. 'His jaw dropped when we asked him where he was the day her body was found,' said Vicky. 'He was most emphatic that it never occurred to him that he might be a suspect and said killing Jennifer would be like killing the goose that laid the golden eggs. He does have what appears to be a cast-iron alibi as he was in London for a couple of days talking to some of his other authors. He insisted on getting his secretary to give us a copy of his itinerary, together with times, phone numbers and so on.'

'Hm, I'm always a bit suspicious when a witness is over-eager to be helpful,' said Rathbone. 'In this case, the guy can probably be eliminated, although you'd better check his alibi for the sake of form. What did he have to say about giving a false date for the party?'

'Much the same as the others,' said Mike, 'in other words, it was to protect Jennifer's name. We had the impression that he was a bit miffed when he was told her editor had let the cat out of the bag.'

'You think he'd have stuck to it?'

'Probably. He seemed genuinely upset, not just by her death, but also by what he called her mental breakdown. He went on at some length about how tragic it was that such a brilliant, creative mind could disintegrate so suddenly, claimed to be gobsmacked by her accusations and assured us he had always been meticulous in accounting to her for all her royalties.'

'I get the impression you didn't exactly take to this character?' said Rathbone.

Vicky and Mike exchanged glances before Vicky said, 'Not really, Sarge. We have the feeling that he was as much concerned about possible financial loss as about Jennifer's death, and he seemed uneasy about her threat to include all her "wild assertions", as he called them, in a book she was going to place elsewhere.'

'Well, we haven't so far found any evidence to support her claim,' said Rathbone. He glanced at the clock on the wall. 'Right, we'd better get on and write our respective reports. Sukey, you print out Langford's statement ready for him to sign. As soon as we hear from Tim and Penny I'll let DCI Leach know.'

Shortly before four o'clock, Tim called in to say they

had just finished interviewing Jennifer Cottrell's publicist, with results very similar to those reported by Vicky and Mike. Rathbone was on the point of calling DCI Leach when a messenger arrived with a sealed transparent bag and a note from Dr Hanley, which read, 'Herewith the contents of Hickson's pockets. Have sent the clothing to forensics, but thought you should have these right away. PS Will do the PM on Monday.'

'Well, there's something to look forward to,' said Rathbone, without a flicker of expression. 'Now this lot might tell us a thing or two,' he went on as he turned the package in his hands. 'Ignition keys and . . . aha, a mobile phone! We couldn't find his mobile account in the house, remember? We thought he must have destroyed it. Well, someone did and I'm sure we all have a shrewd idea who that was. What else now? A separate bunch of keys,' he jiggled the package about for a moment then gave a grunt of satisfaction, 'with a small one that probably fits the padlock on the shed door. He'd have unlocked it when he returned after finishing the day's work and then put the keys back in his pocket with the intention of locking up when he left. His killer was either in too much of a hurry – or too squeamish – to search for that stuff and just did a bunk after finishing him off.'

'Leaving the place unlocked for Langford to blunder in and discover the body,' said Sukey.

'Right. And as the car keys were still in his pocket, there must be a second set somewhere. Now, I wonder where that's kept?' He gave a grim smile of satisfaction. 'One thing's for sure, it doesn't take a genius to figure out who'd know where to find it.'

DCI Leach's reaction to the summary Rathbone gave him of their progress to date was unequivocal. 'It looks pretty certain now that Brand is our killer,' he said. 'That woman must be as hard as nails. I've spent the past couple of hours reading the complete file and with hindsight we should have nicked her before now. We were on the scene too late to save Downie but if we'd been a bit more on the ball we could have saved Hickson.' It was significant, Sukey noted mentally, that he included himself in the catalogue of failure. 'All right, Greg,' he went on, 'pull her in again to resume the interview that was interrupted, but remember she was in for questioning about Hickson's disappearance, not his murder. It's up to you to judge the right moment to tell her we've found his body.'

'Right, sir.'

'She'll want her brief, of course – and don't forget to remind her she's still under caution.' Sukey glanced at Rathbone and saw his jaw tighten, but Leach showed no sign of having noticed. 'You can take it in turns to grill her but make sure she has her statutory rest periods,' he continued. 'She's not going to be a pushover and from all accounts Franklin knows his stuff so whatever you do, don't put a foot wrong. Have a team go over her quarters at Woodlands with a toothcomb, take away footwear and clothing for forensics to examine, and see if you can find the second set of car keys. Meanwhile, have Hickson's mobile checked for recent calls and texts – you know the drill. And don't forget to check up on the alibis of the witnesses who were interviewed today. Any news of his next of kin, by the way?'

Before Rathbone could reply there was a knock at the door and a uniformed officer entered with a message for Rathbone. He scanned it and said, 'It's the answer to your question, sir. Roger Hickson has just flown down from Scotland; he was met at the airport by one of our officers and taken straight to the morgue. He's identified the dead man as his brother Giles Hickson.'

'At least that's something concrete we can give to the press,' said Leach. 'There's been some pretty wild specu-lation going on for the past few days. Right, you all know what you have to do. Have a nice weekend, everyone!'

Twenty-Four

It was nearly half-past five when Tim and Penny returned to join the other four members of the Woodlands team, who were drinking coffee and reflecting on their meeting with DCI Leach. Reading from her notes, Sukey ran through the list of instructions he had given them but without mentioning the more caustic comments, as Vicky was quick to point out.

'Sukey's left out the nasty little digs,' she informed them. She was obviously still smarting under the criticism. 'The SIO is not best pleased with us; he thinks we should have had Lillian Brand banged up days ago.'

'He was the one who told her she could go home,' said Tim.

'Presumably because we didn't have enough evidence to charge her,' said Penny.

'Apparently that's because we haven't been doing our job,' said Vicky.

'At least he acknowledged, in a roundabout sort of way, that maybe he should have had his own eye a bit more closely on the ball,' Mike pointed out.

'That didn't stop him treating us as if we were rookies on our first case,' said Sukey, aware that she spoke more in Rathbone's defence than her own. 'As if any of us would have needed reminding that Lillian is "still under caution" and that we "mustn't put a foot wrong".'

Tim and Penny exchanged glances. 'Just as well we missed the meeting, then,' Tim said flippantly. 'Seriously, though,' he added, 'does he really expect us to get down to all this right away, Sarge? I mean . . . it's getting on for six and it's Saturday tomorrow.'

'So we give Brand the entire weekend to prepare for the resumption of the interview and make sure there's no evidence lying about?' said Rathbone scathingly.

'But Janine will be with her, Sarge,' Penny pleaded.

Rathbone gave a snort of contempt. 'Get real, Penny! Janine's not a detective, she's not even a police officer, she's there as a nursemaid to make sure the poor vulnerable witness gets the comfort and support she's entitled to. I could do with a bit of comfort and support myself at the moment,' he added, with some feeling. The phone on his desk rang; he grabbed it and barked, 'Yes, what is it? Who? Yes, put her through.' He mouthed, 'FLO,' while waiting for the connection. 'DS Rathbone here. Is there a problem?' He listened for several moments in silence, his expression showing increasing signs of frustration. Eventually he said curtly, 'All right, Janine, thank you. What's the name of her GP?' He reached for a notepad and jotted down some details. 'Right. Now I've got something to tell you. We're just about to release a statement to the press that the dead man has been officially identified as Giles Hickson. I'll get some advice from Dr Brymer about how and when we should break it to her, so don't say anything till you hear from me.' He slammed the phone down on its cradle. 'Shit!' he exclaimed through clenched teeth.

'What now, Sarge?' said Vicky.

'That bloody woman's worked a flanker – she's managed to get a doctor to say she's suffering from stress and needs complete rest for at least three days. It seems her acting skills are even better than we thought.'

'It could be genuine, Sarge,' said Sukey. 'Even for an innocent person, the events of the past couple of weeks would have been pretty traumatic. If Lillian's guilty—'

'What d'you mean, "*if* she's guilty"?' Rathbone interrupted. 'Even the SIO's convinced—'

'You said yourself we have to give her the benefit of the doubt, Sarge.'

'All right, point taken,' he grunted.

'So let's just say,' Sukey went on, '*assuming* she's guilty, she's going to have to watch herself every minute to make sure she doesn't slip up. That would put a strain on the strongest person.'

'I suppose so,' he agreed reluctantly. 'At least Janine's had some nursing training so she can watch out for any sign of malingering. She'll need backup, though. I'll get Inspector Collins to detail a couple of his officers to keep a round-the-clock eye on Brand until she's fit to be brought back for questioning again. And meanwhile I have to talk to her doctor. You lot, go and do something useful . . . write out your reports . . . Sukey, finish Langford's statement and print it off . . . and someone check Hickson's mobile.' He waved them away and picked up the phone.

They scattered obediently while surreptitiously keeping their ears cocked. They heard him have a short and mostly one-sided conversation with Dr Brymer before hanging up. He picked up the phone again and spoke briefly to DCI Leach, hung up again and hurried from the room. He returned a few minutes later to say, 'Well, that's that – no chance of talking to Brand till the medic says so. He's given her a prescription for a sedative that Mrs Norris is collecting from the pharmacy and he's going to call and see her again on Monday. I've informed the SIO and he simply shrugged and said we have to go along with that.'

'Did the doctor give any advice about telling Lillian that it's Hickson's body found in the shed, Sarge?' asked Vicky.

'He said to try and keep it from her until the medication has had time to work. It'll be on the TV and radio news, of course, and in the papers if she reads them, so she's bound to find out before long. OK, here's the programme. Those of you who interviewed witnesses today start checking alibis first thing Monday – no point in trying to contact business people over the weekend. I'll pass the doctor's advice on to Janine. Sukey, on your way home you can call on Langford and get him to sign his statement.'

In less fraught situations Sukey might have ventured to point out that to call at Langford's address on her way home meant a considerable detour, but in the circumstances she prudently said, 'Will do, Sarge.'

'Any joy from the mobile?'

'Yes, Sarge,' said Vicky. 'The personal directory contains several numbers; one is the kitchen number at Woodlands and most of the others look like businesses but there's one – a mobile number – listed as simply "Lily", presumably his pet name for Lillian. There's also one listed as Bentley. Could that be Bentley Thorne, the solicitor he made an appointment with, I wonder?'

'Could well be.' For the first time that afternoon, something like optimism dawned in Rathbone's expression. 'Maybe he can help us. It's worth checking anyway. What else?'

'He made frequent calls to Lily, the latest on Tuesday afternoon, followed shortly after by one to the kitchen. We know Mrs Norris is responsible for placing orders for supplies so it was probably about stuff for the estate. The last call was to Bentley, presumably asking to see him.'

'That supports our theory that he was killed as he was preparing to go home after finishing work on Tuesday,' said Rathbone. 'His killer probably waited until late that night to take the car to the place where it was found.' He frowned and gnawed his lower lip. 'The next question is,' he added, avoiding Sukey's eye as he continued, 'how did she get back to Woodlands unobserved? Taxi? Surely the dog would have heard it and barked, and possibly woken Mrs Norris. Of course, the taxi driver could have dropped her off down the road and I suppose the dog would have recognized her footsteps.' He made notes as he spoke, finishing by saying, 'Plenty there for us to work on. I'll ring Thorne on Monday and ask him exactly what Hickson said when he rang to make the appointment. He didn't give much away when he rang to say Hickson hadn't shown, but that was probably professional ethics. Now his potential client's been topped he might be a bit more forthcoming.' He closed his notebook and put it in his pocket. 'Work out your strategy over the weekend and I'll do the same. Make sure your mobiles are switched on in case I need to contact you. And be ready to get stuck in first thing Monday morning.'

Rush-hour traffic was at its height by the time they left the station and it took Sukey well over half an hour to reach

Langford's house. He signed his statement without comment, but then delayed her by several minutes with anxious enquiries about the clothes that had been taken for forensic examination. It was almost seven thirty by the time she reached home; she plodded wearily up the stairs, dumped her bag and jacket on the sitting-room floor, poured a glass of wine, sank into a chair and contemplated without enthusiasm the supermarket fish pie awaiting her in the refrigerator. As she sipped the wine and nibbled a few nuts she gradually relaxed. At least, she thought, Lillian's collapse – real or contrived – meant that the weekend with Fergus would not be disrupted. She spent a few pleasant minutes turning over in her mind possible activities or outings they might share during their time together. She was about to go into the kitchen to put the pie in the oven when her phone rang. Fergus was on the line.

'Hi, Mum,' he said, 'this is just to let you know I've borrowed a car so there's no need for you to go to the bus station in the morning.'

'Well, that's nice to know,' she said. 'I can do with a lie-in.'

'Have you had a heavy week?'

'You could say that.'

'And lost another suspect,' he added wickedly. 'Don't waffle on about "not officially identified" – it was announced on the seven o'clock news. Your lot really are careless – you can't say I didn't warn you.'

'You and the SIO,' she said ruefully.

'Never mind, I believe you have another. "Helping with enquiries", so the announcer said.'

'Yes, well, that's getting complicated as well.'

'I can't wait to hear the details. See you tomorrow!' He cut the connection before she had time to make her usual protest about not being able to talk about the case. He had his own way of worming information from her, usually by reference to some case he had discussed with a lecturer in psychology who had a particular interest in the criminal mind. She had to admit there had been occasions when he had shrewdly put a finger on something the professionals

– Rathbone and Leach included – had failed to spot. It was with a lighter heart that she prepared her meal and ate it while watching a quiz show on the television before going to bed and sleeping peacefully until the following morning.

Fergus was in his usual ebullient spirits when he arrived, bringing the customary bag of laundry. While Sukey stuffed the assortment of shirts, socks and underwear into the washing machine he tucked with gusto into hot croissants and regaled her with the latest chat from the campus.

'Any ideas about what you'd like to do while you're here?' she asked as she sat down with him, helped herself to a croissant and poured out the coffee.

'I thought perhaps a drive into the countryside,' he said with a casual air that immediately aroused her suspicions.

She cocked an eyebrow. 'Any particular destination?'

'Not too far afield,' he said. 'Marfield sounds an interesting village.'

'Now why doesn't that surprise me?' said his mother with a sigh. 'Before we go any further, if you're thinking we might go on to Woodlands and have a snoop round the scene of the crime, forget it. There's still a police presence there and if I'm spotted taking my son on a sightseeing trip I shudder to think what DS Rathbone, let alone the SIO, would say. I'd probably be taken off the case and sent back to uniformed to do traffic duty.'

'I suppose that would be a pity,' Fergus chuckled. 'Well, we can just as easily talk about the case here.'

'I thought I told you—' she began.

'Oh, come on, Mum, the papers have been buzzing with it ever since Jennifer Cottrell was killed. Everyone knows Wendy Downie was a suspect because she was a fruitcake who imagined herself in love with one of Cottrell's characters; when she got herself topped the media cast around for another suspect and there's been loads of unconfirmed rumours that the killer could be a member of Cottrell's own household. And now one of her employees has been added to the list of corpses and everyone's wondering who's going to be next. Is the person who is "helping with enquiries" the current suspect or the next victim?'

'Next victim?' Sukey paused with a piece of croissant halfway to her mouth. 'Are you suggesting Lil—?' It was too late to bite back the name and her son's eyes sparkled in triumph.

'So it is Lillian Brand, the PA,' he said gleefully. 'I thought it might be.'

'How in the world do you know her job, let alone her name? Apart from naming the victims once they were identified, we haven't spoken to the press and we asked everyone at Woodlands not to speak to them either.'

'Easy. I logged on to Jennifer's website. Until her death she – or most likely Lillian – wrote a weekly blog with chatty and mostly trivial details about her work, her booksigning and lecture tours, her idyllic life in the country, her devoted staff . . . blah blah blah. Add to the odd morsel you've let drop it wasn't difficult to build up a picture of her household. Now Hickson's met his comeuppance, Lillian is obviously the next on the list of suspects . . . and we know what happens to your suspects, don't we?'

Twenty-Five

To Sukey's relief, there was no word from Rathbone or Janine on Saturday, which meant she was free to enjoy the day with Fergus. She stood firmly by her refusal to take him to Marfield; instead they enjoyed a brisk walk in the grounds of Blaise Castle during the afternoon and ate their evening meal on trays while watching an old James Bond movie on the television. On Sunday, to Sukey's surprise and pleasure, Fergus expressed a desire to go to church so together they went to morning service at a little church she occasionally attended a short distance from her home. Afterwards they walked into the city and had a pub lunch before returning to the flat. Sukey was concerned that her twenty-year-old son would not have to drive an unfamiliar car late at night, and despite his protests at being treated like a learner when he had had a licence for a full year, she insisted that he leave, complete with clean laundry and a bag full of provisions, soon after tea.

Half an hour later her mobile rang. Rathbone was on the line. 'I realize you're off duty,' he said, 'but I've been going over my notes and you said you wanted a word about your last conversation with Lillian Brand.'

'That's right, Sarge.' She reached for her own notes. 'Several things: one, she gave up trying to get me to reveal the identity of the victim and instead tried to trick me into telling her where the body was found. All I said was that a drunk had blundered into a shed and she immediately wanted to know if it was the one on the Woodlands Estate where Hickson kept his tools and equipment. She referred to him at first as "Giles" and then changed her tack and hastily went out of her way to say that she knew the whereabouts of that particular shed – which of course is to be expected, seeing her job is to know all about the estate – but she never went there herself.'

'I don't suppose she made a habit of it,' said Rathbone. 'It isn't an ideal place for a bit of nooky and we know she visited him at home, but there's no doubt Hickson was killed where we found him so she went at least once. We must check all her footwear. What else?'

'She mentioned local people walking their dogs on the estate and said if Hickson caught them he saw them off . . . and then she went on to wonder if the victim might be Bill Pearce. She pretended to be very concerned about Pearce as he sometimes went into the shed if he was doing a job on the estate. Without any prompting on my part she said, "I don't suppose you know him by sight," and without thinking I said, "Do you?" I know I shouldn't have questioned her,' Sukey hurried on, 'but she was so anxious to talk and it just slipped out. As it happens, I'm glad it did because she hastily backed off and was at great pains to assure me she'd never set eyes on him.'

'And you didn't believe that either?'

'No, Sarge. And she went on to pretend to be very concerned on Maggie's behalf.'

'I see.' There was a pause before Rathbone spoke again. 'I'm sure you realize that we can't use any of this as evidence – or refer to anything she said then – when we question her again. Her brief would come down on us like a ton of bricks if he thought we'd taken advantage of his absence to worm more information out of her.'

'Yes, Sarge; I realized that at the time, but I thought you should know.'

'Yes, well, let's hope she doesn't drop us in it next time she talks to her brief. What did you deduce from her demeanour generally?'

'She's obviously on a knife-edge, and her desperate pleas for information could mean one of two things: either her fear that Hickson's the murder victim is genuine, in which case she isn't the killer, or that it's part of the role she's playing to avert suspicion that she killed him herself. We're agreed she's a pretty accomplished actress and we know she's capable of lying through her teeth. Presumably she's heard or read reports by now that Hickson is dead; it'll be interesting to know how she reacted to the news and what state she's in now.'

'Janine is pretty certain she hasn't,' said Rathbone. 'The drug the doctor prescribed seems to have induced a kind of lassitude; she spends most of her time either asleep or staring out of the window.'

'That could be part of the act,' Sukey suggested.

'You may well be right,' he said. 'Do I take it that you are now a hundred per cent convinced that Lillian's the killer, then?'

'Let's say ninety-nine per cent, Sarge.'

'So what's the one per cent about?'

'It may sound silly, but . . . it's just that we've already lost two suspects and—'

'You're not seriously suggesting there's some knife-wielding maniac out there and Brand is the next name on his death list?'

'I know it sounds bizarre, and there's so much circumstantial evidence against her, but—'

'I'd forget the "buts" if I were you,' said Rathbone firmly. 'We'll regard this conversation as an off-the-record chat.'

'If you say so, Sarge,' she said meekly, and the line went dead.

An hour later the phone rang again. This time Vicky was the caller. 'Hi, Sukey, how's your weekend been?'

'Fine, thanks. Fergus tried to get me to show him round Marfield but needless to say I didn't. We had a good time, though . . . plenty to talk about.'

'I'll bet he pumped you over the Woodlands murders.' Sukey had regaled her colleague more than once with details of her son's interest in their cases. 'What advice did he give you this time?'

'He reminded me of our record at losing suspects and hinted we should keep a protective eye on Lillian.'

'No kidding! I can't believe you told him she's our prime suspect, so how did he find out?'

'He checked Jennifer Cottrell's blog and put two and two together.'

'Bright lad, your Fergus,' said Vicky. 'Anything else?'

'I had a call from DS Rathbone an hour or so ago. He wanted to check on my meeting with Lillian after we got back from Woodlands on Friday.' Sukey gave her friend a brief résumé of the conversation.

'I hope you didn't mention your son's advice!' said Vicky with a chuckle.

'I did, actually . . . that is, I didn't say the idea came from Gus but I did mention our record of losing suspects.'

'What was his reaction?'

'He told me to forget it – and also that the conversation was strictly between the two of us, so—'

'Don't worry, your secret is safe with me! By the way, we're both due for some leave. Once we've got this case wound up, why don't you and I go off on a trip together?'

'That's not a bad idea,' said Sukey. 'Have you anywhere particular in mind?'

'Not at the moment. Somewhere interesting.'

'What sort of interesting?'

'Somewhere with historic buildings and art galleries and things,' said Vicky vaguely.

'What about Chris? Wouldn't he object?'

'He's only interested in cars and food.' Vicky's partner was a chef at one of Bristol's leading hotels and a fan of motor racing. 'Of course, if I suggested going to watch the Grand Prix he'd jump at it – especially if I offered to pay for the tickets – but he's not exactly a culture vulture.'

'Well, it's a nice idea,' said Sukey. 'Let's talk about it some more. See you tomorrow!'

When the team reported for duty the following morning they were informed by Rathbone that Dr Brymer would be calling on Lillian during the day and would let him know if and when she was fit to be interviewed.

'With luck, we should be allowed to see her tomorrow,' he said. 'Strictly speaking I should lead the interview, but Doctor B. hinted that in what he called her "fragile state" she might be less intimidated by women detectives. She's obviously playing the sympathy card for all she's worth,' he added sourly, 'but he's been reasonably helpful to us so far and the SIO says we have to play along with him. Sukey and Vicky, as soon as he gives us the all-clear you can set up the interview; in the meantime you can all take the opportunity to catch up with some paperwork.'

'Will you be here if we need to check anything with you, Sarge?' said Mike.

'Is that a roundabout way of asking how I'll be passing the time?' said Rathbone dryly. 'For your information, I'll be checking with Bentley Thorne, the solicitor, to see if Hickson said anything that could be helpful when he made the appointment. After that I'll be looking at the details of Hickson's bank account and then I'll be off to the morgue to witness the PM on Hickson. Any more questions?'

At three o'clock Rathbone reappeared, having left two hours earlier to witness the post-mortem on Hickson's body. Without a word to anyone he made for the drinks machine and poured a strong black coffee. When he had drunk it he tossed the plastic cup into a bin and said, 'Right, everyone, here's the latest. Hickson suffered multiple stab wounds; the one to his stomach was probably the first and was certainly the one that killed him. The others were to the back and were probably inflicted to make sure he was dead. The size and depth of the wounds is consistent with the weapon being a large kitchen knife – probably one of a set, and pretty sharp, judging by the state of the wounds. Doc Hanley can't be precise about the time of death, but the state of the body and the blood is consistent with our estimate.'

'So Lillian would have known he'd be there at about that time,' said Mike, 'or maybe she called him on his mobile saying she wanted to see him.'

'It would have been dark by then,' said Vicky doubtfully.

'She could have taken a torch, but in any case, after living there for so long she must know her way there blindfold,' Mike pointed out.

'She was taking a risk – supposing Mrs Norris spotted her?'

'Mrs Norris was probably in the kitchen . . . or maybe having a cup of tea in her sitting room, but in any case she would have had the curtains drawn.'

'What about the security lights? They would have come on – didn't Mrs N. say she always set the system after dark?' said Sukey.

'That's something you and Vicky can check when you go to question Lillian,' said Rathbone. 'The next thing is, Hickson's bank statement shows a number of fairly substantial payments that have been traced back to Lillian's account. And finally, I had a word with Bentley Thorne and he was quite helpful. Apparently Hickson said he was being questioned about a suspicious death and he was worried because on an earlier occasion he'd given false information to the police. He didn't give any more details, but I think we can make some interesting deductions.'

'Maybe he knew – because Lillian had told him – that the cover-up about the date of the dinner party was phoney,' suggested Penny. 'He decided to come clean, told her what he was going to do and that's why she decided to kill him.'

Rathbone gave an indulgent smile. 'You'll have to do better than that, Penny,' he said. 'Remember, Lillian herself admitted the cover-up. No, I think he'd seen something more incriminating than that.' He broke off as the phone rang. 'Yes? Oh, Dr Brymer, thank you for calling. Yes . . . of course . . . thank you very much. Goodbye.

'Lillian will be fit to be questioned tomorrow morning,' he informed the team, 'but she's asked for the interview to take place at her home because she finds the atmosphere in the station intimidating. Now, is that a clever ploy, I wonder?' He thought for a moment. 'OK, we'll go along with her for now, but just in case it's some sort of try-on I'll come along as well and be ready to take over if you think she's up to it.'

Twenty-Six

Lillian Brand was seated at her desk with her solicitor at her side. She was pale and drawn but appeared composed. She watched calmly as Sukey and Vicky set up the portable tape recorder and said quietly, 'I understand,' when reminded that this was a resumption of an earlier interview and that she was still under caution.

'Ms Brand,' Sukey began, 'the last time we spoke you pleaded with me to reveal the name of the man whose body was found in the tool shed on this estate, but I was prevented from doing so by rules governing police procedure. You had already given the impression that you were particularly concerned because you feared it would be someone known to you. Who was that person?'

Lillian cast a nervous glance at Franklin, who nodded. 'I was afraid it was Giles Hickson,' she said in a low but clear voice.

'And you now know that it was in fact Giles Hickson?'

'Yes.'

'Ms Brand, I'm going to ask you a very personal question,' said Vicky. 'What was your relationship with Giles Hickson?'

Lillian raised her head and looked first at Vicky and then at Sukey with something of her former air of defiance. 'We were lovers,' she said.

'Did Jennifer Cottrell know?'

The question appeared to take Lillian by surprise. She opened her mouth, shut it again and looked at Franklin – who seemed equally taken aback – before saying in a shaky voice, 'I don't know . . . thinking back, I suppose she may have done, but she never said anything . . . I mean, we were very discreet because she . . . I mean we—'

'If she had known, she might have been jealous, mightn't she?' said Sukey. Lillian remained silent. 'Because she was a lesbian, and attracted to you?'

A slow flush crept over Lillian's pallid features. 'Yes,' she whispered.

'Was the attraction mutual?'

For a moment Lillian appeared to have difficulty in replying. 'I . . . this may sound ridiculous but I was in my thirties and I'd never had a satisfactory relationship with a man. She made me believe that was because I was . . . like her. I was never really sure, and when I met Giles I—' She was plainly close to tears and Sukey waited a moment before continuing.

'So she was attracted to you from the start and used every inducement to make you stay with her, even though you never really wanted to leave London, including making you her heir.'

'I didn't know that,' Lillian protested. 'She never told me until—' She broke off and clapped a hand over her mouth. 'I mean, I didn't realize . . . she'd had too much to drink one night and she got maudlin and told me how much she loved me and—' She broke off, pulled a face and took a hasty gulp of water from the glass at her elbow.

'Please, go on,' said Vicky after a long pause.

'Next day she apologized and told me to forget everything she said . . . made out it was just something she'd been turning over in her mind but hadn't actually done.'

'When was this?'

'Not long after we came to Woodlands.'

'Round about the time you met Giles Hickson?'

'Well, yes, I suppose so.'

'And there was an immediate attraction between you?'

'Not right away. In fact, we crossed swords on more than one occasion and then one day . . . Jennifer was off giving one of her talks . . . and he came up to my office with a question about some estate matter and we . . . well, it just happened.'

'And you didn't tell Jennifer?'

'Absolutely not. We both knew our jobs would be on the

line if she found out. I was happy in my work, I was genuinely
fond of her and most of the time I enjoyed her company. I
found her attentions distasteful, but she wasn't all that
demanding, she just enjoyed exchanging caresses. She liked
to see me in mannish clothes . . . trousers rather than skirts
. . . and she wouldn't let me wear perfume. And she was quite
possessive – Giles and I had to be very careful—'

'Naturally,' said Sukey. Despite her belief that she was
questioning a murderess, the sheer misery in the woman's
voice and expression struck a chord of sympathy. 'Now,'
she went on in a more gentle tone, 'I'd like to go back to
the day in November when Jennifer invited you and some
of her business colleagues to lunch. She surprised you all
with a sudden outburst, accusing each of you in turn of
cheating her in some way and effectively dismissing you.
After her death, you put out what you later admitted was
false information about the date of that lunch, claiming that
it was to protect Jennifer's reputation. Have you anything
to add to that?'

'No, because it's true.'

'Ms Brand, I put it to you that your real motive was to
conceal the fact that you were Jennifer Cottrell's heir and
were afraid she had found out about your affair with Hickson
and intended to disinherit you?'

'I wasn't the only one to be affected,' Lillian protested.
'She accused all of us . . . it never occurred to me . . . I
genuinely thought she'd had a brainstorm.'

'But just the same, you told Hickson what had happened
and the story you'd told the police.'

'Yes.'

Sukey and Vicky exchanged brief glances before Vicky
said, 'Jennifer Cottrell's death was very convenient for you,
wasn't it?'

Lillian winced and put a hand to her face as though she
had been slapped. Her mouth quivered and she struggled
for control. 'That's a dreadful thing to say,' she protested.
'You can't be suggesting that I—'

'The news of Jennifer's outburst must have come as a blow
to Hickson as well,' Vicky continued relentlessly. 'He knew

of your "prospects", shall we call them, and as his own were largely tied up with yours, perhaps you were afraid he—'

'Stop!' Lillian pleaded. 'Giles and I . . . we were in love!' Tears filled her eyes and slowly overflowed. 'I just can't believe he'd—' Her voice died away and she covered her face with her hands. Her shoulders heaved.

'Can't believe he'd do what?' said Sukey. 'Dump you if the money supply was cut off? I suggest it suddenly dawned on you – perhaps from something he said – that it was the money, and not you, that was the attraction. You'd killed Jennifer to stop her changing her will, and then you realized—'

'No! No! No!' The words came in one continuous scream until it seemed there could be no air left in her lungs. She drew shuddering gasps of breath and began moaning like a wounded animal.

Franklin intervened. 'I request a short break to allow my client time to compose herself,' he said.

'Granted.' Sukey checked her watch. 'Interview suspended at ten fifteen,' she said and stopped the tape. 'I'll pop down to the kitchen and ask Mrs Norris to make some coffee, OK?' she added to Vicky, who nodded and whispered, 'Is this a good time to call in the DS?'

'Definitely,' she whispered back.

When Sukey entered the kitchen, Rathbone was sitting at the table with a mug of coffee and a plate with a half-eaten slice of fruitcake in front of him. After asking Mrs Norris to make strong black coffee for Lillian she said in a low voice, 'Could I have a word, Sarge?'

'Sure.' He followed her from the room and closed the door. 'How's it going?'

'She's beginning to crack, Sarge. She's emotional but doesn't show any sign of being "fragile" in the medical sense.' She gave him a summary of the interview so far.

'She kept her end up until you put it to her that after killing Cottrell she somehow realized Hickson was only interested in the money and staged a breakdown to give herself time to think?' he suggested.

'That's how it seems to Vicky and me, although up to then I seriously wondered whether after all she was telling the truth.'

'Right. Give me a moment to finish my coffee and then we'll take Lillian's up to her. On second thoughts,' he added, 'we'd better stick to two people questioning her at one time or her brief will probably start muttering about harassment of a vulnerable witness. You can stay here and talk to Mrs Norris, but be ready to join us if I call you.'

Mrs Norris was unusually communicative. She put down the knife she was using to chop onions. 'I'm just making a drop of soup for lunch,' she explained as she picked up the coffee pot and filled two mugs. Somewhat to Sukey's surprise she put both mugs on the table and then sat down opposite her. There was a strange expression in her eyes as she leaned forward and said in a confidential whisper, 'Are you going to arrest her?'

'I'm sorry, I can't discuss the case with you,' said Sukey. She stood up. 'Perhaps I'd better go back upstairs.'

'No, please stay. It's all been so upsetting – I need someone to talk to.'

A little reluctantly, Sukey sat down again. 'Isn't Maggie here?' she asked. 'I know she said she wouldn't come any more, but you must still need some help.'

'Oh yes, she's agreed to come so long as the police are here. It's obvious you think Ms Brand did it or they wouldn't be staying, would they? We, Maggie and I, reckon they planned it together . . . first Ms Cottrell's murder so they could have all the money . . . and then she found out it was only her money he was after so she did him in as well.' The housekeeper leaned forward on the last words; something about her expression made Sukey vaguely uneasy. Then she sat back in her chair and said, 'I'm sorry; I shouldn't have said that. Please forgive me.'

'Mrs Norris,' said Sukey, 'you have made some very serious allegations, which I shall have to report to my superiors. They will almost certainly want to take a statement from you.'

'Oh no, I don't want that . . . I was only repeating what Maggie and I were saying. But she is going to be charged, isn't she?' The woman was breathing heavily; she seemed

at the same time tense and expectant. Sukey felt an urge
to change the subject. Her eyes travelled to the door to
the garden, where Piper's lead hung from its hook and the
down-at-heel shoes were in their usual place. On an
impulse she walked over and picked them up.

'What are you doing with those?' Mrs Norris demanded.

'You know of course where Hickson's body was found?'
said Sukey casually.

'In his shed, of course. Everyone knows that.'

'Have you ever been there?'

'Of course not. What reason would I have had?'

'I just wondered.' Sukey turned the shoes over and
pretended to examine the soles. 'Just the same, I'm afraid
I have to take these away for examination. For elimination
purposes,' she went on, aware that her heart was beginning
to race. 'We think that whoever killed Hickson must have
traces of gravel from the path leading to the shed on their
shoes. But of course, if you've never been to the shed—'

A piercing scream from behind made her swing round.
Maggie was standing in the doorway, her eyes wide with
horror. Sukey had barely a split second to realize the cause
before the knife aimed at her throat made its deadly downwards thrust. She made a frantic grab at the hand holding
the weapon, but her attacker dodged and and lunged at her
again. 'Maggie! Help me, for God's sake!' Sukey yelled,
but the girl seemed paralysed with fear and simply continued
screaming. Sukey held the shoes in front of her in a desperate
attempt to shield herself from the next blow, but she was
off balance; for one terrifying moment she felt herself
lurching into the path of the knife, but recovered and made
a second grab. This time her fingers grasped the raised arm
but failed to take hold and the knife began another down-
ward thrust. Desperately, she threw herself out of its path,
just as Maggie was pushed roughly aside and DS Rathbone,
with Vicky behind him, came charging across the room.
Elsie Norris struggled, swore, kicked and spat at the detectives. Her strength was astonishing; it took the combined
efforts of all three to subdue her.

Epilogue

'Be thankful Maggie has a good pair of lungs,' said Vicky. 'That banshee wail would have wakened the dead. I'd no idea the Sarge could move so fast,' she added with a chuckle.

'Thank the Lord he did,' said Sukey with feeling. 'I wouldn't be here now if he'd arrived a couple of moments later.'

'That knife – I wonder if it was the one she used to kill Hickson,' said Vicky. 'It might even be the one missing from Wendy Downie's kitchen.'

'I guess we'll know in due course,' said Sukey. 'Just imagine harbouring a grievance like that for all those years,' she went on reflectively. 'It must have been like a cancer gnawing away at the poor creature.'

Vicky nodded. 'Jennifer Cottrell was a possessive, manipulative woman,' she said with feeling. 'I'm tempted to say she had it coming to her . . . but not at the expense of two more deaths and three ruined lives.'

Sukey nodded. 'I've just been thinking back to the time you persuaded me to go with you to hear her give that talk at the library,' she said. 'You were a passionate fan of her books, but after you heard her speak you took against her.'

'That's right, I did,' Vicky agreed. 'Just the same, it was a shock to learn that there was someone who liked her even less!'

'She was determined to keep Elsie Norris in her employ, but she didn't want a child in her house so she made what on the face of it was very generous provision for her. It was an offer that Elsie simply couldn't refuse. Then, when she moved to Woodlands, she threatened to withdraw all the support she'd been giving little Kate if the mother refused to go with her.'

'It must have caused her a great deal of heartache,' Vicky agreed. 'While they were in London she was able to see Kate quite regularly, but once she was at Woodlands the contact must have been very difficult to maintain.'

'She managed it, though, with the help of the foster parents.' Sukey gave a sad shake of the head. 'They'll be devastated when they learn what their devotion led to.'

'That the girl they had come to regard almost as their own daughter should have aided and abetted a murderess—'

'By moving Hickson's car and then sneaking into his house to arrange a few details like removing his toilet things and his mobile-phone account to make it look as if he'd done a runner—'

'And planting the bottle of perfume her mother had pinched from Lillian's dressing table,' Vicky finished as Sukey paused for breath.

'How did Kate get into Stony Cottage, I wonder?' said Sukey. 'There was no sign of a break-in.'

'According to Pearce, the house was once part of the estate. The previous owner assigned it to Hickson's father, and when he died Giles inherited. There must have been a spare set of keys lying around that Cottrell took charge of and somehow Elsie knew about it.'

'I guess so.' Sukey laid down her fork with a sigh of appreciation. 'Vicky, this chicken is to die for!'

'Yes, my boy knows his stuff,' said Vicky proudly.

The two were in the flat Vicky shared with Chris and enjoying a meal that he had prepared for them before leaving for work. Vicky took their plates to the kitchen and returned with the dessert. 'I wonder,' she said as she sat down and picked up her spoon, 'whether we'll ever know the whole story.'

'My guess is that Elsie's resentment against Cottrell began even before the move to Woodlands,' said Sukey. 'It's obvious she was jealous of Lillian from the start, and once she cottoned on to the relationship that was developing between them, she felt disgust as well as jealousy. It's obvious she did a lot of snooping around.'

'And eavesdropping, probably.'

'That, and using Maggie as a kind of spy. The girl's pretty simple, but we know she overheard that phone conversation Lillian had the day before Cottrell was killed because she told Hickson about it, probably without realizing how things were between them.'

'Yes,' agreed Vicky, 'and she may have picked up other titbits from time to time and passed them on to Elsie. One of them may even have overheard a tipsy Cottrell telling her beloved that she was to inherit her fortune. And if Elsie overheard her outburst at the lunch party it must have come to her in a flash that she had a golden opportunity to kill the woman who had used her child as a bargaining counter and at the same time throw suspicion on someone she'd nursed a grudge against for years. But why kill Hickson, I wonder? Surely not just to cause Lillian even more grief?'

'It's more likely he saw her hurrying back to the house after she'd caught and killed poor Wendy Downie,' said Sukey. 'Maybe he didn't think anything of it at the time – or maybe . . . supposing he mentioned it and she asked him not to say anything to us because . . . oh, I don't know, because she wasn't supposed to be out walking the dog at that particular time or some other excuse. When he felt he was coming under suspicion he became worried about withholding information from us, so he decided to tell her he was going to call his brief and come clean. She was obviously desperate to stop that happening so she had to kill him.'

'And when she thought you might be on to her, she tried to kill you,' said Vicky. 'She must have been totally unhinged by then. I wonder what they'll do with her? And what about Kate? They can't pretend she's unfit to plead, surely.'

'It'll be a long time before we get answers to all our questions,' said Sukey, 'and even longer before it comes to court.' She gave a deep sigh. 'It's one of the saddest cases I've heard of for a long time. What will become of Lillian now, I wonder? Alone in that rambling old house . . . ' She thought for a moment while savouring a spoonful of strawberry trifle. 'At least she's not hard up, and even if Jennifer did flip her lid at the lunch party, she was presumably of sound mind ten years ago when she made her will. Perhaps she'll go to Oz and visit her sister.'

'Well, there's nothing more we can do for any of them,' said Vicky philosophically, 'so in the meantime, why don't we put the dishes in the dishwasher and then have a browse through some of those travel brochures I've been collecting?'